MATING CLAIRE

Sea Island Wolves 1

Jenny Penn

EROTIC ROMANCE

Siren Publishing, Inc.
www.SirenPublishing.com

A SIREN PUBLISHING BOOK
IMPRINT: Erotic Romance

MATING CLAIRE
Sea Island Wolves 1
Copyright © 2008 by Jenny Penn

ISBN-10: 1-60601-340-8
ISBN-13: 978-1-60601-340-3

First Printing: November 2008

Cover design by Jinger Heaston
All cover art and logo copyright © 2008 by Siren Publishing, Inc.

Printed in the U.S.A.

PUBLISHER
Siren Publishing, Inc.
www.SirenPublishing.com

DEDICATION

To my mother for her support in all things and all ways, and my father for giving me the strength to pursue my dreams.

MATING CLAIRE
Sea Island Wolves 1

Jenny Penn
Copyright © 2008

Chapter 1

Monday

11:47 AM…11:49 AM…11:50 AM.

Claire Hallowell glared at the clock, having half a mind to take her heels off and throw them at the offending timekeeper.

Was the Chief ever going to show up?

She slammed the file drawer closed and stalked back to her desk. She had worked so hard to make sure his welcome back would go smoothly. At seven sharp, she had arrived and made a fresh pot of coffee. All the papers and files he needed to review were neatly stacked in order of priority and waiting on her desk.

After a weeklong vacation, she had expected him to arrive early, anxious to catch up on work. As the minutes had expanded to hours, her annoyance had grown to exasperation. Exasperation had bloomed into amazement. Now, she was outright mad.

The police chief was supposed to set the example all his officers would follow. No wonder his crew was so laid back. While they enjoyed going out on patrol or answering distress calls, they were all lax about the paperwork and follow-ups.

That affected her job. In her one week working there, she already had several minor skirmishes with some of the officers about getting reports done in time. None of them had taken offense at her abrasive attitude. Just the opposite, they appeared to delight in prodding her temper, finding some twisted form of amusement in it.

She had not let it bother her. There were more important things to worry about—like her case. This assignment was turning out to be a champ. Missing girls nobody could prove were dead, visions of a demonic serial killer and town full of werewolves, this was not the kind of investigation they'd trained her for in the FBI.

Not that the FBI would touch this case. They certainly wouldn't have assigned her a ghost for a partner. Technically the Masters of Cerberus hadn't assign Kate to her.

Then again, Kate was not technically dead either. She had just lost her body or it had been stolen from her. Kate didn't know exactly how she had lost her physical form.

Not being a true ghost, Kate was not trapped into haunting a single location or person. She could travel to wherever she wanted. For reasons that were only known to the contrary apparition, she chose to annoy Claire.

Everything about her current assignment irritated Claire. The only thing that had gone her way was getting the job as the chief's assistant.

Of all the undercover assignments she'd done over the years, playing Dorothy Walker was the easiest. Being Dorothy, Claire could be the uptight, anal-retentive person she really was. All she had to remember was to respond to the name Dorothy.

"Hey, Derek! How'd the fishing go?"

11:56 AM.

Claire rolled her eyes as she listened the officers out in the small lobby greet their boss. About damn time the man showed up, not that she understood why he had bothered. In a half hour, it would be lunchtime.

Her phone rang, interrupting her silent criticism.

"Chief Jacob's office. How may I help you?" Claire pulled the message pad across her desk.

"I've got some news for you."

The sound of Mike's grim tone brought a scowl to Claire's face. If their organization were more formal, he would probably carry the title Director of the Southeastern District. As it was, his title was simply "Boss."

"What's up boss?" Claire flicked the pen in her hand away as she tilted her chair back on two legs.

"It's bad."

"You never call for any other reason."

She tried to make light of his comment, but her stomach muscles quivered with nerves. She had been waiting for this, expecting it for the past several days. When she stumbled into a pile, she normally ended up neck-deep in the manure. As it was, she was only up to her ass. She was due two more feet of crap.

"Agakiar was released yesterday afternoon."

That was not two feet. It was a full-scale drowning.

"Shit!"

Claire lost her balance at that startling news, barely managing to stop from toppling backward. As the legs of the chair slammed down, she flew forward into the pile of papers on her desk. The neatly organized stacks fell into a chaotic mess on the floor with a plop.

"Damn it!"

"You alright?"

"No. It took me two hours to organize all those reports. I stayed late last night to get it all done. Not that the jerk cares, showing up five hours late! What kind of example is that to set? I tell you these small town badges have it too easy. It's no wonder they aren't even aware there's a killer running loose in their town!"

"Uh, Claire."

"Great. This is just great. So now what?" Claire slid to the floor. Attacking the files allowed her to vent some of the aggression prowling through her body.

"About?"

"About Agakiar."

"Now nothing." Mike's voice remained calm.

"What do you mean nothing?"

"I mean nothing."

"You can't do nothing!"

"What would you have us do? We can't make the state's case for them. The only option is to eliminate him and that can't be done without endangering you."

"So he just walks away?"

"We're going to monitor him. Don't worry, Claire, he's not going to get away with anything we can stop."

"So who are you going to send down here to replace me?" Claire cradled the phone between her shoulder and chin so she could restack the papers into a neat pile.

"Nobody. You're staying on the Wilsonville case."

"You can't leave me here in boondocks of South Carolina. I have a right to be in on whatever you've got planned for Agakiar."

"Sorry, kiddo, but that's too dangerous."

"Dangerous? How much more danger can I be in? I'm already branded."

"You could be in hell."

"And who says Wilsonville isn't hell?"

"Claire—"

"Don't play dad, Mike. It's not your role."

"It's my job to keep you safe."

"Bullshit. You know my newfound psychic ability comes from that damned demon's brand. Every time I use my new gift, it strengthens Agakiar connection to me. If you were really worried, you wouldn't have me on any case."

"You're making a really good argument for why I should lock you up in a safe house and let you rot, Claire."

"I thought that's why you sent me to this no-where town."

"No, I sent you there to find a serial killer. You should be glad I'm not pulling you completely out of the field."

"Gee, I'm overjoyed."

"We're not arguing about this. You focus on your case and leave Agakiar to us. Got that?"

"Guess I don't have a choice."

"You keep me posted and your guard up."

"Whatever."

She did not bother to place the phone back on the hook, but dropped it on the floor so she could crawl further under the desk. It took a moment to round up all the scattered pages. As she checked to make sure she had collected everything, the flicker of white caught her attention.

A piece of paper was trapped between the back of the desk drawer. It was not one of her papers, but it annoyed her nonetheless. Everything had a proper place and sticking out of a drawer was not it.

Tugging on it did not get the paper to budge. Narrowing her eyes, she yanked hard and the page ripped in half. The sudden loss of tension sent Claire falling back into the side of the desk.

She banged her head into the underside of the table. It was not her day, Claire grumbled as she rubbed the sore spot on the top her head. Slapping the scrap of paper on top of her files, she crawl back out from under the desk.

A pair of black boots crossed in the doorway drew her attention and her scowl. They were standard issue for the officers. She was not in the mood for any teasing. Sitting back on her heels, she looked up to give the man a set-down.

The words froze on her lips as the piercing blue gaze of the stranger trapped her eyes. He was large and heavily muscled. The charcoal gray shirt was pulled taut over a solid wall of steel.

His black slacks rode a little low on his hips, held down by the heavy gun belt. It added to the air of danger he exuded, emphasizing the narrowness of his hips and the thickness of his thighs.

Handsome was too pretty a word for his features. They were rough, rugged and inspired a primal thrill in her. His dark hair was a little long, falling around his ears and framing those amazing eyes.

Claire could sense the wolf prowling, stalking her, through those eyes. He was leaning against the doorframe. His stance was deceptively relaxed, but Claire wasn't buying into that lie.

She could feel the tension coiling in him as he studied her like a hunter sizing up the prey he was about to take down. Not with violence, though, but with barely restrained sexuality.

Her heart began to race as instinct whispered she should flee. Claire ground her teeth together, her hands curling into fists as she watched him sniff the air, scenting her arousal.

Her body's response to his blatantly sexual look riled her already inflamed temper. Narrowing her eyes on him, she rose to her feet. Carefully she set the stack of files on her desk and replaced the receiver.

"Can I help you?"

"I'm Chief Jacob." The man nodded his head slightly. "You must be Dorothy."

"Very perceptive." Claire was unable to keep the sarcastic edge out of her tone.

"So you're my new assistant."

The smooth southern drawl dripped like honey down Claire's spine and pooled warmly between her legs. Claire clamped her thighs together in a futile effort to hide his effect on her.

She looked at Derek Jacob, keeping her eyes off his face and away from those captivating eyes. The problem with that tactic was it meant she had to look at the rest of him. His hard, toned muscles were no less mouthwatering, no less mesmerizing.

Her mouth went dry as she watched the bulge in his gray slacks grow impossibly larger. Quickly she looked away, feeling her panties dampen in response.

The bastard sniffed the air again and her eyes shot back to his face. The edges of his lips kicked up in a satisfied smile and Claire knew exactly what she was dealing with. A werewolf.

Her eyes narrowed to dangerous slits as his gaze traveled downward, stopping and staying on her breast. Despite her annoyance with the jerk, she felt her breasts tighten. Her nipples hardened, straining against the flimsy silk blouse.

The phone rang just then, jarring her out of her growing anger.

"Chief Jacob's office. How may I help you?"

Claire saw Derek snicker as her tone changed, becoming pleasant, almost cheerful. It was a farce. One she pulled off with ease as she listened to a breathless woman asking if the chief was in.

"Yes. May I ask who's calling?" Claire had to stop herself from rolling her eyes. With the Chief back, she was probably going to get a lot of these calls. No doubt the man had a whole harem of women who loved hard-bodied men in uniform.

"Never mind." The line went dead before Claire could respond.

"Well, Assistant Dorothy." His joking use of her title had Claire's teeth grinding. "You ready to catch me up?"

"Of course, Chief Jacob." Claire managed not to snarl. Just barely, but she managed. Gathering his schedule, the files he needed to review, and papers needing his signature, she turned.

"After you." Derek gestured to the open door of his office.

Lucky girl. That man is sizzling.

Kate's hungry voice echoed through Claire's mind. Claire saw the ghost materialize for just a moment before fading back into the air. The apparition's habit of popping in and out always irritated Claire.

"Something wrong?" For the first time the chief sounded serious, almost alarmed as he looked around the room.

Yeah, he has too many clothes on.

"No."

Tell him to get naked.

"Nothing." Claire's words were sharper than necessary. This time though her annoyance was not directed at the chief.

Trying to ignore Kate, she focused on Derek. That was a mistake. Trapped in the small office with him not more than a foot away had a disastrous effect on her equilibrium. As sexy as he was at a distance, he was outright gorgeous close up.

The small scars on his forehead and chin, the bump from a break on his nose, the laugh lines around his mouth, every little flaw added to his appeal. Derek Keller was the living personification of the sexy bad-boy.

A walking wet dream, that's for damn sure.

Women don't have wet dreams, Claire mentally retorted, exasperated with the ghost.

The hell they can't.

I never had one.

I'm having one right now.

You don't have a body!

That's not stopping me.

"You alright?"

Claire took a deep breath, trying to clear her head. It didn't help. She stepped back, trying to put some distance between them.

It was a futile effort, one the chief took notice of with a raised eyebrow. His infernal smug smile reappeared. Arrogant wolf, he was probably used to women responding this way to him.

"Are you sure you're alright?"

"I'm fine," Claire muttered.

"A little hot maybe?" The humor in his tone was evident. "You look a little flushed?"

"No."

"Hmm." He considered her for a moment. "You're breathing a little fast. You got asthma?"

"I said I was fine."

"No need to be snippy." Derek shrugged.

"Snippy?"

"I was just being polite."

Polite was not the word for what the man was being, but Claire held her opinion back behind clenched teeth.

"Are you ready to work?"

"By all means." Derek nodded to a chair as he moved around his desk. "Have a seat and let's get to it."

* * * *

Derek was having trouble concentrating on what Dorothy was saying as she went over his schedule for the week. Unable to take his eyes off her, he completely ignored the slips of missed phone calls, reports, and whatever else as she went through the stacks of paper she had piled on his desk.

None of that mattered. All that mattered right now was Dorothy and the amazing effect she was having on him. Never before had he been so instantly, so totally aroused by a woman.

Short, curvy with wavy honey hair, and swirling hazel eyes, she was perfect. After years of waiting, here was finally the woman who evoked all his primal instincts. His mate, the perfect woman for him, was finally within his reach.

When he had walked into the office and seen her on her knees, waving that plump ass in the air while she crawled under her desk, he had been tempted to walk right up behind her, slide that prim skirt up to her waist and give her the ride of a lifetime. Once they knew each other better, he would not restrain those kinds of urges.

Once he had her completely under his thrall, she would be his to use whenever, however, he wanted. His cock pulsed with the idea, quickly conjuring up all sorts of images.

After a minute, he realized she was not speaking anymore, but looking at him expectantly. Shaking his head, he tried to clear all the fantasies running through his mind.

"Pardon me?" He fought the urge to drag her across the desk, shove her prim black skirt out of the way, rip off her panties and bury his face between her soft thighs. He would make a feast of her.

"Are you paying attention to me?"

"Of course, sweetheart. You're the sole focus of my attention."

"I'm not your sweetheart." Dorothy leveled a finger at him. "And keep your eyes right here," she pointed to her flashing ones, "and off my chest."

"I'm still concerned about your breathing, doll." Derek intentionally dropped his eyes back to her straining nipples. "You still appear a little short of breath."

"The only thing I'm short of is patience."

"There's no need to get upset. I'm just worried about your condition." Derek lowered his voice to a husky draw, knowing its effect on her. "Perhaps there is something I can do to help you…relax."

Her eyes were darkening to chocolate and he knew he shouldn't tease her, but he couldn't help himself. The guys had already made it clear she was a paperwork Nazi, a stickler for rules and procedure. A real tight ass.

His cock jerked at that. He liked tight asses. Especially nice plush ones designed to cushion a man while he…

"Chief Jacob!" Her fist hit the desk with a small thump.

"Sorry, sweetheart," he said unapologetically.

"I am not your sweetheart and I demand you behave in a professional manner!"

"Professional?" Derek blinked in innocent confusion. "Have I been anything but?"

"No." Dorothy's control was obviously slipping.

"No? What have I done that's unprofessional?"

"I don't know." She mocked his blank expression. "Perhaps, it's the fact you are lewdly staring at my breasts. I'd say that was crass and completely inappropriate!"

"Oh, I see. Like when you looked me over in the doorway and were trying to decide whether you could handle the ride I'd give you?"

At his words, her ears went hot. He could swear he saw smoke come out her cute little nose as it flared. The pencil in Dorothy's hand snapped. Derek's smile widened.

"I'd rather ride a porcupine naked."

Derek broke out in full laughter. As much fire as she was showing now, he could imagine what kind of wildcat she would be in bed. Hell, he would probably have to tire her down to the bed just to keep from being bucked off when he fucked her.

"A porcupine, huh?" Derek rubbed his chin. "Hell, darling if you enjoy the feel of bristles between your thighs, I'll grow out my beard for you."

"How very professional of you. Tell me Chief, have you ever heard of sexual harassment."

"It's not harassment if the woman enjoys the attention."

"Of all the arrogant, backward ass, chauvinistic things to say! You're a cop, for God sakes." She jumped out of her chair and leveled an accusing finger at him. "You should know better!"

Without a backward glance, she stormed out of the office. That went well, Derek snorted to himself as he stood. He should probably apologize and try to make it sound sincere.

Dorothy was doing a good job of ignoring him as she slammed her desk drawers. Before Derek could think of something to say, the bell over the lobby door chimed. Derek looked up and groaned. He did not need this and he was going to have to handle it quickly.

* * * *

Claire looked up at the blonde woman entering the station. She was dressed to be noticed. The short-sleeved sundress flattered her tall, lean frame and displayed her large, perfect breasts. With her big blue eyes and lip-gloss, she looked like a Barbie doll.

"Derek! You're home!"

Derek had moved quickly to intercept his beautiful admirer as the blonde launched herself into his arms. That figured. The bastard probably had lots of centerfold wannabes stored somewhere.

I want to join.

Shut up, Kate.

Oh, I should have said you want to join.

Go away.

Disgusted and, for some horrifying reason jealous, Claire turned away as the woman planted a deep kiss on the chief's mouth. She tried to ignore the spectacle they were making as she gathered the mail.

It was lunchtime and, after she stopped by the post office, she had a half hour free from this insanity. The only thing stopping her was the chief and his woman. She was not about to go into the lobby until they left. Hopefully, they would do that soon.

Fiddling with a pen, she waited, looking for something to do. She saw the scrap of paper she had dislodged from the back of the desk drawer.

She studied the image of a young girl that looked frighteningly familiar. Long, light brown hair, big hazel eyes, about sixteen. The girl could have been a twin for the other twenty-six girls whose pictures were plastered on Claire's wall. Finding those girls' murderer was the whole reason she was in this small southern town.

With no evidence, the cases would never be picked up by law enforcement. All Claire had was her own visions and that really wasn't much, but it was enough to convince the brains at Masters of Cerberus to send her here.

Or so they claimed. They'd probably known Agakiar was getting out and had shipped her here to get her out of the way. Agakiar was smooth and slick and, for some unexplainable reason, completely focused on her.

There was no telling what it was that had drawn the demon's attention to her. He'd said it was because of the purity and the strength of her spirit, but Claire knew she was far from pure and weaker than a rotted tree limb in a hurricane, just waiting for the wind to snap her free.

Never trust a demon. They never spoke the truth. Whatever attracted Agakiar to her was his secret to keep. The only thing Claire knew was that he enjoyed the suffering of humans, enjoyed torturing and tormenting them before he took their last breath.

Agakiar was not alone. Lucifer had many legions in his army and, thanks to Agakiar's brand, she had eyes that could now see into their darkest desires. She couldn't stop them, couldn't eliminate the threat they presented. All she could hope for was to save their victim.

Claire looked back down at the scrap of paper. There was nothing much on it, just a name, the small picture and a general description.

Kathleen Harper, welcome to my case.

Chapter 2

Tuesday

Derek rolled over and hit the off button on his alarm clock. Five minutes later, he was dressed and stretching for his morning run. He preferred to run in his fur and did so at every opportunity. Still, he enjoyed his two-legged morning jogs.

They helped him clear his mind and get him ready for the day ahead. This morning he needed that refresher. He was still suffering from the effects of the vivid, erotic dreams that had awakened him through the night. Cold showers and masturbating had not helped his hard, aching dick. Only wearing himself out on the object of his desire would cure him.

It was a shame Dorothy was a human. If she had been part of a pack, he could claim her and she would know better than to resist her mate. Hell, she would be honored. Any bitch would be if her Alpha chose her as mate.

As it was, her being a human complicated the issue. Not only because he had to sweet-talk his way into her bed, but then he had to convince her to go furry. Derek could imagine what his serious, sharp-tongued, little assistant would have to say to that. She would probably suggest he check himself into a mental institution.

That was the reason he had left work early yesterday to go seek Kristin's advice. His twin had been a big help once she'd finished laughing and teasing him. Though he had sought her out so she could tell him what to do, Kristen had spent most the time telling him what not to do.

His sister had warned him that to move too fast or seduce Dorothy too quickly would just make her think he was looking for a quick and easy fuck. Patience was needed. Patience was not an attribute mating males were known for. The instinct was to capture and hold.

Kristin had suggested he romance Dorothy, but not in his normal way. It was not the time to take her to the Lost Soul for some beers and a spin on the dance floor as a prelude for going back to his place and taking a spin in bed.

Even if Dorothy were not his mate, he would know she was too classy for the Lost Soul. He already had a plan that was sure to work. He would enact it this afternoon.

Marie, the owner of Biscuit's, was going to have a picnic basket ready for him by early afternoon. Then he would have Dorothy accompany him to his meeting with the park services coordinator. That should last into the early evening. It should not be too hard to con the sexy Dorothy into a romantic picnic dinner.

Derek grinned at the idea. Soon he would know all about what Dorothy liked and did not like. He would use that knowledge to seduce his way into her bed and her heart. It would not be long before she was begging him to bite her.

Duke, his golden retriever, was waiting patiently by the front door. As Derek approached, the dog spit his tennis ball out onto the floor. It made a disgusting spat when it hit the well-oiled wood.

Derek didn't bother with a leash. He opened the door and Duke bounded down the stairs. Derek was quick to follow, taking a deep breath and savoring the fresh morning air.

Instantly, the blood drained from his head to his dick as he recognized the sweet smell of his mate. Dorothy's scent drew him across the street to where it was stronger. Like a man in a trance, he followed the tantalizing odor as he made his usual warm up jog to the park.

The trail led him down the beautiful tailored jogging path and he picked up speed. Two minutes later, he saw her up ahead. She looked good from behind, her little jogging shorts swaying over her bouncing rear quickly mesmerized him.

She had a perfect ass. A little big by most standards, it would be the perfect handhold for when he drove himself deep into her warm, wet, clinging cunt from behind. The idea solidified into an image so erotic it had his hands reaching out to touch.

The instant his fingers bit into her soft flesh she reacted. Swinging around, her elbow caught him in the neck. The painful blow stopped the flow of oxygen to his lungs and he stumbled backward gasping for breath.

Duke responded immediately to the attack, lunging forward to knock Dorothy down to the ground. She hit the asphalt hard and Duke made sure she stayed put. He pinned her down with his weight, snarling and growling at the woman who dared to harm his master.

"Get this dog off me!"

Dorothy tried to shove the large beast back, but the dog's increasing growls stilled her motions.

"Duke," Derek's voice was strained with the need for air, "sit, boy."

The dog sat down on top of Dorothy.

"That wasn't what I meant!" Dorothy whispered furiously over the dog's snout at him.

Derek was bent over at the waist, trying to catch his breath. He patted his leg and called the dog. Duke reluctantly came to his side, allowing Dorothy to sit up.

"What the hell do you think you're doing?"

"I could ask you the same." Derek winced as he felt his neck.

"Me?" Dorothy scrambled up. "Me? I'm not the jackass sneaking up behind unsuspecting women and groping them."

"Not women. Woman," Derek corrected.

Dorothy clenched her hands into tight fists and Derek could smell the barely suppressed violence in her taut body. Things weren't going well and he had a suspicion he was digging a bigger hole for himself.

Damn, she looked cute when she was mad.

"You," Dorothy leveled a finger at him, "are the most annoying man I have ever met! You are lewd, crude, and lacking in any decency."

She began to advance on him step by step as she leveled one accusation after another. Derek wisely took a step back. Duke followed, though the dog continued to growl.

"I have never met anybody so insulting in my life. You treat me as if I'm some second-class stripper at the local nudie bar looking for a tip. I've only got one thing to say to you, Chief Jacob. I QUIT!"

Her roared resignation stunned him and, for a moment, he just stared in amazement. Okay, so things were a lot worse than he had imagined. If she quit, it would be much harder for him to seduce her.

Dorothy was not waiting for his response. She had already turned and began to storm off. Derek quickly moved to stop her. Catching her arm, he swung her back around to face him.

"Hey, wait a minute."

"Don't touch me!" Dorothy spat, yanking her arm free of his hold.

"Okay." Derek held up his hands. "Okay, but just give me a minute."

"Why should I?"

"Because," he took a deep breath and prepared to do something he rarely did, "I'm sorry."

"And you have a bridge to sell me, too, right?"

"I mean it." Derek tried for sincerity and not the desperation lurking just beneath. "You're right. I've been a complete ass. That's no reason for you to quit, though."

"It's not?"

"No, it's a good job with good hours and I can be a very lenient boss."

"So, I've noticed." Dorothy sneered. "I hate to break this to you, but your work ethic is a mark against you as far as I'm concerned."

"My work ethic?" Derek blinked, taken aback.

"You come in at noon after a week's vacation, hang around just long enough to irritate me and make a spectacle of yourself with your little blonde friend and then you disappear for the rest of the day. I'd say that redefines lenient."

"I happened to have pressing engagements yesterday afternoon. I wasn't off—"

"Tickling your toy?" Dorothy offered.

"I wasn't out with Carolyn."

"So it was a different woman. From what I hear, you have them stacked a mile high." There was more than just condescension in her tone. Derek grinned.

"What the hell are you smiling about?" She did not wait for his answer. "See, it's that attitude that I can't live with."

"You're quitting because I smile too much?"

"Because it's a smug, patronizing smile."

"I'll try not to smile then." Derek forced a frown. "Is that better?"

"No! Jesus, you are—"

"I know and I'm sorry," Derek interrupted her before she could launch back through the list of his faults, "but I wasn't out tickling any woman yesterday afternoon. I was on an important mission."

"Mission? What are you, a secret agent?"

"I was with my sister. We had to discuss an important family matter." Dorothy's smirk said she clearly did not believe him. "How the hell did we get on this conversation?"

"You were bragging about your lack of a work ethic."

"That's not what I said." Derek was beginning to feel frustrated. "I'll be the toughest boss you ever had, if it's what you want. Whatever it takes to make you happy."

"What would make me happy? Try never seeing you again."

"Well, that I can't do."

"I can. I quit. See how easy it is."

"That's not a solution." Derek felt like pulling his hair out.

"It's not? Sounds like one to me."

"Look, Dorothy. If you quit, you'll have to get another job. I'll have to get another assistant. That will take time and effort on both our parts. Why go through all that? Wouldn't it just be easier to work through our differences?"

"We don't have differences to work through. This isn't you like 'your coffee strong and I like it weak, that you want the radio on country and I like rock and roll'. You're an asshole. That is a permanent personality deficit."

"That's just the thing. I'm not an asshole." At her snort, he sighed. "I admit I have been behaving like one but that's in the past."

"Oh, really? So you were intentionally being an ass?"

"No, I didn't mean it like that." Damn it, the woman had a way of twisting everything he said.

"No? What? Is it like a split personality thing? I could buy that. It's obvious you have some form of mental problem. Though I would've said it was just a complete lack of maturity and—"

"I know. Decency," Derek finished for her. "I get it, but I can be different."

"If you want to be."

"Right."

"Okay, so tell me why you haven't been."

"What?" Derek blinked, thrown by her request.

"Tell me why you haven't been decent and I might, just might, not quit."

Derek hesitated, trying to think of a lie that would work well. He needed something here that would help his case. Nothing came to mind.

"I want the truth," Dorothy prodded as if sensing his internal struggle.

"The truth. Okay." Derek took a deep breath. The truth it was. It was not like he had anything else to lose.

"I want you."

"What?" Dorothy's mouth fell open with her shock. That didn't last long. "Never mind. I don't know why I bothered talking to you."

With that stony declaration, Dorothy swung away and stomped off again.

"Damn it, wait!" This time when Derek grabbed her arm, he held on tight. He knew he was sinking, but if she didn't stay put, he wouldn't have a chance to stop drowning.

"Let me go!"

"Just listen to me."

"Listen to what? Lies?"

"I'm not lying! Damn it! You are making this unnecessarily hard."

"I've no reason to make it easy."

"I grant you that, but just give me a moment. One moment without interruptions and when I'm done if you feel the need to hurl insults at me, I'll let you."

"And if I want to leave, will you let me do that?"

"Fine." Derek forced the words out from between clenched teeth.

"You've got one minute."

"Thank you." Derek let go of her arm and she immediately crossed them over her chest. "Okay, I admit my behavior yesterday was… ungallant."

Dorothy snorted at that, but otherwise remained as silent as she had promised.

"I am attracted to you." More than she could possibly understand. "I admit I gave in to the urge to goad you. It was juvenile of me, and I apologize. It won't happen again."

"I'm not attracted to you."

That was a lie. The sexy Miss Dorothy was attracted to him. He knew it. Even as she argued, he could smell the sweet odor of her desire.

"I understand that." Derek smiled slightly. "I accept it."

"Good. So are we done here?"

"Are you going to show up for work?" At her hesitation, Derek spoke up quickly. "How about we do like a probation thing? You give me the rest of this week to prove I'm a decent, hard-working guy. If I can't, then you quit."

"I can quit whenever I want."

"Come on. Just give me one more chance." Derek could sense she was weakening. "Please."

* * * *

"Fine." Claire caved, not pleased with her decision.

Derek obviously was, from the grin that put two damn dimples on display. The man was too appealing by far. It should be illegal for him to run dressed as he was. It was indecent.

He was wearing a pair of baggy shorts, worn sneakers and his chest was temptingly bare. The display of golden skin rippling over hard muscles was enough to give any woman heart palpitations.

The patch of curly, black hair that started between his pecs narrowed toward his hips, drawing her eyes downward to where his erection was making itself obvious against the thin fabric of his shorts. Claire swallowed hard and quickly dropped her eyes lower.

He had powerful looking legs. Heavily muscled thighs assured a woman he could spend hours pumping into her, driving her from one orgasm to the next. Claire blushed at her thoughts.

Without another word, she turned and jogged away. It was futile to hope he would just leave. Without a comment, he fell into step beside her.

Claire picked up her speed, slowly increasing it, testing him. He did not break a sweat because of the faster pace. The fact he easily kept up with her annoyed her even more. She became more reckless in her need to win, losing focus on her pacing.

By the time they had made the three-mile trek around the park, her lungs were oxygen starved and she was panting almost as much as

Duke was. Her body was not up to this strenuous a work out. Since being kicked out of the FBI, she had put on some extra pounds and put off exorcising. Over the past week she'd taken up jogging again, trying to rebuild her stamina.

That obviously wasn't something Derek needed to work on. His breathing was still smooth and even. So much for trying to outrun a werewolf.

He stayed beside her as she left the park causing her to break down and talk to him.

"You're not going to follow me all the way home, are you?"

"It's not safe for a woman to be out alone this early in the morning."

"I can take care of myself."

"I don't doubt you think you can," Derek agreed in an arrogant tone that grated on her nerves.

"Whatever," Claire muttered before going back to ignoring him.

Though she was already worn out, she didn't let up on the speed until she reached her driveway. As she cut up over the yard, she stumbled. Claire would have hit the ground if Derek had not moved quickly, grabbing her by the arm to steady her.

"You alright?" There was a hint of laughter in his tone, making Claire growl out her answer.

"Fine. Thank you."

"What's that?"

He was pointing at her lower back where her shirt had risen when she had stumbled. With a jerk, she yanked her shirt back down.

"Nothing."

"It looked like a brand." He didn't sound happy. The hint of anger in his tone confused Claire. Why did he care if she was branded?

"It's none of your concern."

Not waiting for him to ask another question, she turned and headed toward the front door of her rental.

"You live here?"

Claire ignored Derek and his question. After stepping into the rental, she turned to close the door. She paused as she saw him cross the street and cut up the yard of the opposite house. She stood clenching and unclenching her fist as she watched him unlock the door.

I guess our neighbor's back. Kate sounded hungry.

"He's a jerk." Claire slammed the door.

That sounds like a short summation, compared to the whipping you gave him in the park.

"Must you always lurk about, eavesdropping on my life?"

Not like I have much else to do.

"You could go look for your body."

It was not right for her to take her anger out on Kate and she knew it. She just couldn't stop herself right now. She was miserable, and anybody who got in her way was going to suffer the consequences.

The man got under your skin quickly.

Ignoring Kate's comment, she stepped through the ghost, knowing how much it irritated Kate when people did that. Kate shimmered before blinking out of sight only to reappear in the bathroom after Claire had slammed the door.

"Get out." Claire reached through Kate to turn on the water.

The cold water comes from the other tap. Kate advised her.

"I don't need a cold shower."

Oh, you took enough last night, huh?

"Don't start with me Kate." Claire began ripping her clothes off.

I could hear you moaning all the way down the hall.

"Be glad you're already dead," Claire snarled before stepping into the shower and yanking the curtain closed.

Leave it to Kate to bring up the subject Claire most wanted to avoid. As much as she tried, she couldn't get the dreams out of her head. God, what she had let Derek do to her in them. Claire scrubbed harder, trying to remove his phantom touch from her skin.

It was no use. The only thing she could do was keep her defenses up. Dreams or no dreams, they were not going to become reality. The best way to assure that didn't happen was to live up to her threat by quitting her job.

If Derek were the only consideration, she would have done just that. But Derek wasn't the real issue here. A demon and a killer were lurking out there. As long as they were hunting down innocent, teenaged girls, Claire was going to get past her personal problems and solve the case.

Working in the police station gave her access to her most likely suspects. She certainly wasn't keeping the job because of the Chief's desperate pleas or his laughable lies about being attracted to her. No, her decision had nothing to do with him.

Just keep telling yourself that.

Shut up, Kate!

Chapter 3

The sun still reigned high in the sky as it approached six in the evening. Claire blinked against the glare as she looked out over the lagoon bordering Wilsonville's largest park.

Her clothes felt sticky, her body icky. Through the heat, humidity and bloodsucking bugs, she had dutifully followed Derek around the park taking notes. The Chief, focused on figuring out how to control and patrol the crowds that would gather for an upcoming festival, couldn't be bothered to think, walk and write at the same time.

Claire was hot, tired and annoyed. The only positive thing about this entire journey was that Derek hadn't been a complete jerk. He had been considerate enough to stop by her house so she could change into shorts and sneakers for the coming hike.

Though his professionalism had slipped some when she had come back out. His dog had been in the bed of the truck and Claire was concerned about the hairy beast's safety.

"Is the dog going to be alright back there?" She turned to frown at the mutt as she slid into her seat. The retriever had two paws up on the edge of the truck and was sniffing the air.

"Who? Duke?" Derek glanced back at the hound. "He'll be fine."

"Duke?" Claire remembered Derek calling the dog that earlier. The connection had not hit her then. "You named him after the dog in the baked bean commercials?"

"Hey," Derek shot her a warning look. "I like those baked beans."

"Talk about a lack of creativity."

"Oh?" He raised an eyebrow at her. "What would you have named him?"

"I don't know. It depends on his personality."

"Excuse me?"

"Well you can't just name an animal without knowing them. The name reflects the inner spirit of the animal." Claire scowled as he began to chuckle. She should never have bothered to talk to him. "Never mind."

"He's a dog. He likes his ears scratched, his belly rubbed, a bone now and again. He loves to chase balls, and occasionally he licks himself. That's Duke's inner spirit."

"I see you two have a lot in common."

"I like to have more than my belly rubbed, thank you very much," Derek responded seriously.

"That's nice," Claire said crisply.

"And I like women to do the lick—"

"Thank you!" Claire drowned out his dry tone. "That's enough."

"Hey you started it."

"And I'm ending it."

"Would you prefer I show you what I like to have licked?" Derek asked innocently enough.

Instinctively Claire's eyes dropped to the bulge pressing against his black, uniform trousers. It looked huge, appeared to grow even larger before her eyes.

"Should I take that look as a yes?" Derek's tone had dropped to a seductive drawl. Claire swallowed and quickly looked away.

She had not said another word to him until they were at the park. Claire knew she should call him on the return of his provocative comments, but he had been right about one thing. She had started it. That would teach her to talk to him.

Duke whined, drawing her attention. He had picked up a hefty limb and had been carrying it around during their hike. The treasure now lay on the ground in front of her feet.

There was a hopeful gleam in the dog's big brown eyes as he glanced from her to the stick. He backed away, his tail wagging so hard his body shook. Claire would have to be completely dumb not to know what Duke wanted and completely cold hearted to turn him down.

"Okay. I'll throw it."

Claire threw the stick with all her strength. With unadulterated enjoyment, the dog chased his limb. Less than a minute later, he dropped the stick at her feet and backed up for another round. Claire tossed it several times before deciding to see if the dog liked water.

Claire beamed the limb into the lagoon. A small, stone seawall kept the water at bay. Without hesitation, the dog leaped off the wall and into the water to hunt down his stick. Undisturbed by the change in the game, Duke returned to drop the stick at her feet again.

He appeared to enjoy getting wet. Claire moved closer to the water's edge so she could get the stick further out into the lagoon. Swimming eagerly after his stick, Duke appeared to be having the time of his life.

"Duke, no!" Derek's voice broke through the late afternoon serenity. "Damn it!"

Claire grinned. Finally the jerk was annoyed. Duke, on the other hand, appeared completely unconcerned about his master's recent command. Claire was equally unconcerned and, without hesitation, she launched the stick back into the lagoon.

"Damn it, Dorothy!"

"Damn it, Dorothy." Claire snickered in high-pitched, whiny voice as she mocked Derek under her breath.

Duke dropped his stick at her feet again. She lifted it, raising it behind her head to heave it back into the water. A strong hand closed over her wrist, halting her throw.

Instinct took over and before Claire could think about it, she turned and put her shoulder into his middle. A second later Derek went sailing over her to cannonball into the lagoon. Fortunately it was not shallow near the edge, and he sank beneath the water.

Claire stared at him, horrified by what she had done. She had too many years of training, was too on edge because of Agakiar, and she just didn't like the chief. None of those excuses sounded as if they would work as he bobbed, cussing, in the water.

Duke jumped off the edge of the wall to join his master in an early evening dip. In the process, the dog sent a second wave of water right into his Derek's face. Impatiently, Derek shoved his hair from his eyes and pushed Duke out of his way.

Those crystal blue eyes honed in on her with laser precision. The predatory intent in them was unmistakable. The moment he began to move toward the lagoon's edge, Claire turned and fled.

She knew it was futile, but still she ran as fast as she could and almost made it to his truck before two arms snaked around her. A second later they tightened down with the strength of steel bars. Her feet left the ground as she found herself being hefted easily over a heavily muscled shoulder.

"Put me down now!"

She kicked and jerked, not surprised her struggle had little effect. Instead of liberating herself from the humiliating position, she flailed about like an errant child. The big, wet golden retriever yapping at Derek's heels completed the image.

"In a moment, sunshine," Derek assured her in a cheery voice.

It was the complimentary pat on her ass that had her pounding her fist into his back. He gave no reaction to the blows. The fact the hits probably didn't even bruise him fueled her anger.

"Listen to me you two-watt, inbred, hick from hell. If you don't put me…ahhhh!"

Claire's threat ended in a shriek as she went airborne. She remembered at the last second to close her mouth before the cool water of the lagoon closed in around her. She surfaced sputtering and ready to skin the jerk alive.

Her mouth opened to do just that, but no sound came out. Derek was removing his shirt. It was impossible not to admire the way the sun reflected off the droplets of water that ran down his chest, highlighting the muscles that rippled with his movements.

A second later she got a face full of water as he jumped in. A third wave hit her as Duke joined them in the lake. Both dog and man were grinning at her.

With his body safely under the murky water, Claire found her anger returning. So what if she had dunked him in the lake? It had been an accident.

"I quit!" Claire spat as she began to make her way back to the edge.

"Hey that's not fair. If you didn't want to play, you shouldn't have issued an invitation."

"It was an accident." Claire hefted herself up onto the wall.

"That's one hell of a move to be an accident," Derek commented. He didn't appear in any hurry to get out of the water. "You're lucky I didn't crack my head on the wall."

"It probably would have helped your mental capacity."

Her shirt was sticking to her like a second skin. Claire pulled the cotton away and began to wring the water out. Her hands stilled when she noticed Derek was staring at her. He was smiling that arrogant male smile again.

Claire had little doubt what he was staring at either. Her nipples had hardened at the sight of his chest. Thanks to her dip, her shirt did little to hide that fact. She crossed her arms over her breast.

"Don't stare."

"Why not? You did." Derek grin got bigger as her eyes narrowed on him.

"I did not!" It was a lie, but she still managed to sound indignant.

"You were watching every drop of water rolling down my chest and wishing you could lick it off me. That, by the way, is one of the places I do like to be licked."

"I think you have heatstroke," Claire snarled. "You're hallucinating."

"Don't bother to deny it." Derek ignored her outrage. "Why do you think I took my shirt off?"

"What?"

"You can't help it, no woman can. You women pretend you're above ogling, but you're not."

"You…I…." Claire's mind was blanked by outrage. "That is…."

"I know, I know. I'm lewd, disgusting, without decency."

"You forgot juvenile."

"You're not much better yourself, are you Dorothy?"

"Excuse me?"

"Why do you bother with the act?" Derek heaved himself up and over the short retaining wall. "You got a little hidden pervert in you. Just admit it."

"I am not a pervert."

"You're still staring at my chest." Derek's chest puffed out. "Go on and lick it, honey. I don't mind."

Claire growled. Before he could defend himself, she stepped up and shoved him back into the lake. Quick as a snake his hand latched on to her arm for support.

There was no way she could hold up that much weight. Her knee hit the edge of the wall as she was dragged back into the cool water.

When she surfaced this time, he was way too close. Barely an inch separated them. Claire's knee throbbed, the salt water stinging her scraped skin.

"You hurt my knee."

"You pushed me into the water *again*."

"At least you're not bleeding."

"Are you bleeding?"

His grin vanished in an instant, replaced by a look of true concern. Claire wasn't buying it. Nor did she believe he was innocently bobbing toward her. Quickly she paddled backward and away from him.

"Like you care."

"You want me to kiss it and make it better, baby?" Derek offered in a smooth voice that matched his slow, easy motion as he crowded her against the seawall.

"Try it and just see if you make it out of this lagoon in one piece."

"A challenge." Derek had her neatly pinned in without enough room to scramble out of the water. "I never back down from one."

Instantly, the steel bands he called arms wrapped around her and pressed her tightly against him. Her hands came up to push him away. That was a mistake. His chest was so warm and hard. He felt as good as he looked.

Pinned against his hot, corded length, her mind faltered and her body melted. A faint voice in her head told her to struggle, but it was too late. Engulfed in his warmth, Claire felt drugged by his raw masculine scent.

His mouth settled on hers in a warm invitation she didn't have the will to resist. When he nipped her bottom lip in silent demand, her mouth slid open. Instantly his tongue invaded, drugging her with his taste. With a small sound, she moved closer, desperate to deepen the kiss.

Warm, hard lips moved against her softer ones, tasting, exploring until she was dizzy with desire. His questing tongue devoured her, stroking into her sleek, moist interior in rhythm with the hard, thick cock pushing against her soft, round stomach.

The late afternoon heat slipped away, replaced by a more ravenous fever. There was no subtle adjusting, no slight movements as they tried to fit together. Their bodies blended perfectly, as if they were longtime lovers.

Claire wound her arms around him, needing his solid weight as an anchor in a world spinning away. His arms, so strong and thick, lifted her up against him. The lean line of his hips pressed into her legs, forcing her thighs apart and making a place for his cock to press into her creaming cunt.

He rubbed against her, thrusting his hips in a primal rhythm that had her hips moving in beat. His big hands roughly gripped her ass, angling her so his mouthwatering erection could grind harder into her welcoming heat.

Tumbling headfirst into the sexual abyss, Claire gave in to her hunger and wound her legs around his waist, increasing the pressure of his cock against her pussy. Each rotation of his hips pulled the soft fabric of her panties across her clit, making the sensitive nub throb in demand for more.

It felt so good, but it was not nearly enough. She wanted him skin to skin, to feel him buried deep within her, pounding into her soft, wet flesh. Her pussy ached with the need to be filled. The piercing sensation was almost unbearable.

Claire tore her mouth free, gasping for breath. Her heaving chest forced her hardened nipples to drag against his thick torso. Lighting bolts of pleasure shot out from her breast, sending sparks of pure, addictive fire through her body.

Again and again she rubbed her breasts against him, silently begging him to touch her tender flesh. He didn't deny her, sliding his hands under her shirt. Her breath caught in her throat as his work-callused fingers rasped against the smooth skin of her sides.

She whimpered as his hands slipped upward so softly the caress almost tickled. Her whimper turned to a gasp as he cupped her swollen globes, making her back arch, offering her aching flesh for more of his touch.

As his thumbs flicked over the sensitive tips, he licked and nipped a heated path from her jaw to her ear. Sharp teeth bit down on her soft lobe and sent a striking bolt of pain through her.

The sensation blurred to pleasure as his fingers closed over her nipples. He pulled and rolled the hardened nubs, tormenting her until she caught her lower lip between her teeth and fought to hold back the cries of pleasure that threatened to erupt from the depths of her very soul.

"So responsive," Derek growled, the vibrations echoing down her body.

One hand slid down over the quivering muscles of her stomach and toward the sodden waistband of her shorts. Claire could not hold back her moan of protest when he eased back, separating their bodies.

The moan turned into a cry of desperate need as his hands slipped beneath the elastic band of her panties. His finger found her swollen clit and began to toy with the sensitive nub. Around and around, tighter and tighter, he rubbed her nipple and clit in rhythm.

"Your pussy is soft, wet, weeping for me. I want to taste you, Dorothy. I want to taste what is mine, to bury my head between your soft thighs and devour your sweet flesh." His voice was low, deep, filled with the promise of the forbidden, erotic secrets and ecstatic pleasures.

"I'll show no mercy, driving you from one orgasm to another until I've had my fill. You'll be weak and sweaty when I'm done." Derek slid two fingers into her clinging cunt.

"You'll beg and plead you can take no more, but you will." Claire arched her hips, allowing his invading fingers to slip further into her tight sheath.

"I'm going to bury my hard, thick dick deep inside your tight, little pussy. I'm going to stretch you to capacity, 'til you scream my name." He slid a third finger into her, widening her until he stretched her small opening to the point of painful pleasure.

"And still I'll feed you more until you're so packed full of cock you won't know where you end and I begin. I'm going to savor that moment. Savor feeling all you muscles clamping down on me, trembling around my hard flesh."

He began to pump his fingers into her, fast and hard. His thumb followed, picking up speed as he twirled her clit. Claire's nails bit into his shoulder as lightning shocks of ecstasy began to rip through her body.

"Then I'm going to fuck you. Hard and fast, slow and deep, I'm going to turn and bend you anyway I want. You're going to love it, every minute, every thrust. You're going to sob out your pleasure. When I'm done with you, you will never think to deny me. You're mine."

Pleasure detonated throughout her body as the tension broke. She jerked and bucked as waves of ecstasy ripped through her.

* * * *

Derek shuddered with barely suppressed need as he held Claire through her orgasm. The warm gush of her pleasure filled his hands, teasing him. And her scent! Jesus, all he could think was of spreading her thighs here and now and lapping at her like the wolf he was.

He would perch her up on the wall and bury his face in her pussy to do just as he promised. He would devour her. Lick through her slick folds, taste her creaming slit with long, hungry licks. He would fuck into her with deep, greedy strokes of his tongue until he felt her inner muscles clench and she flooded him with waves of sweet arousal.

He wanted to eat her alive. Bite by bite. The beast within him was stirring, demanding its due. The wolf wanted his mate. Wanted to sink his fangs into her as he bent her over and drove himself into her warm, wet, welcoming home.

His dick throbbed against the painful confines of his wet jeans like an angry dictator demanding release as images from the beast materialized in his mind. Dorothy on her knees, legs spread wide, showing him the sweet, pink folds of her pussy. He would take a quick taste before he fucked his full length deep into her, claiming what was his.

He would take her with the ferocity of the beast, having no mercy as she pleaded and begged for more. Her screams of pleasure would be music to the wolf's ears and he would ride her long and hard, drawing out the sounds until his body exploded.

He needed her. Now. Needed to be buried all the way in her, feeling her tight sheath clamping down on him as he drove himself into her with ruthless, savagery.

With single intent, he forced her legs down, away from him. Instead of fighting to break his hold, Dorothy fought to maintain it. Derek would have enjoyed the moment of sweet success if his body were not painfully demanding he fuck, now.

As it was, he growled and forced her away, intending to remove her shorts as fast as possible.

Chapter 4

Duke, seeing his opening, butted in. Jealous his master had found a new playmate, the dog widened the small gap between the would-be lovers until he had successfully separated Derek from Claire.

Derek growled, trying to shove the dog out of the way, but Duke was not to be denied. Barking excitedly, the dog swam happily around his master, blocking Derek's every attempt to get near Claire.

"Damn dog," Derek snarled. "I should take you back to the pound."

Personally, Claire would have rewarded him with a metal of honor, if she could just get over her shock. One kiss from the jerk and she had been offering her body up to him, rubbing against him, allowing him to touch her any way he wanted. It was mortifying.

If he ever tried that stunt again, she would have to take immediate and drastic measures. She would have to punched him in the gut, knee him in the groin, bite his adventurous tongue — anything but kiss him back.

Hell, whom was she kidding? Her pussy was throbbing, her hands shaking, her body on fire with need. Not only had she melted under the persuasive touch of the jerk, she had turned aggressor in their heated embrace, demanding satisfaction.

"What's wrong?" He did not sound so much annoyed as amused now. "Cat got your tongue?"

That arrogant male smile made her snap. Without warning, she reached out and twisted his nipple.

"Ow!" He hollered, his hand coming up to rub his wounded flesh. "What the hell did you do that for?"

"Returning the favor." Claire gave him a cold, brittle smile before lifting herself back out of the water.

"Yeah, but you liked it when I did it," Derek whined, as he followed her to the seawall.

"I must have heatstroke," Claire shot back before stomping off toward the truck.

* * * *

"Women!" Derek turned to Duke, who joined him on the grass. "Just be glad you're fixed, dog."

Duke's response was a vigorous shake.

Derek could tell Dorothy was gearing up for a serious snit. She didn't like him. It irritated her that she lusted after him. Just like a woman, always mixing up liking somebody with sex. As if the two had to go together, Derek snorted.

No doubt, she was silently listing all the reasons she would not have sex with him. Despite whatever Dorothy was telling herself, she was his and he would have her. As far as he was concerned, there was no reason for delay.

If it had not been for Duke, he would be sheathing himself in her warm, wet body right now. Forget the fact they were in a public park and anybody could come up on them. Forget Kristin's advice about moving slowly. Forget any damn rational consideration.

His dick hurt and he was going to do something about that. There was no way in hell he was going to let her escape. With that thought in mind, Derek immediately decided his next attack.

First, he had to get her somewhere private. The truck was private enough, especially if they were lying down. Derek grinned to himself and picked up his speed.

She was waiting by the truck, arms crossed over her breast, no doubt in an attempt to hide her taut little nipples from his gaze. Derek went to the crossover toolbox in the bed and snapped it open. The first thing he saw was the picnic basket.

Forget that, he knew what he wanted to eat and it was not a sandwich. After a moment of rifling, he found what he was looking for.

Dorothy caught the flannel shirt he tossed her. Defiantly, refusing to speak to him, she shot him a questioning look.

"Put it on before you catch a cold," Derek instructed.

"It'll just get wet."

"Not if you take off your wet shirt." Derek's tone was just as condescending.

"In your dreams." Claire launched the shirt back at him. Derek caught it and added a pair of jeans to the pile before slinging it back to her.

"There is a bathroom right up there for your changing privacy." Derek worked to keep his tone mater-of-fact.

"These will never fit." Claire stared at the jeans.

"A belt," Derek tossed her a length of rope, "should help with that."

* * * *

Claire's mood hadn't improved by the time she got back to the truck. The dry clothes swallowed her, engulfing her already inflamed senses in Derek's smell, and irritating her by keeping her body in a semi-aroused state.

She had to hold the jeans to keep them from falling around her ankles. The rope belt had been of little use. There was too much fabric, and, bunched as tight as she could make it with the rope, the jeans had still slipped down.

To top off her list of complaints, she had a splinter from the wooden stall door.

Duke appeared happy, lying in the back of the truck. The dog looked up, thumping his tail at her approach. Claire ignored him.

Even if he were her savior, he was also her downfall. If she had not started playing fetch with him, nothing would ever have happened. She would be home — warm, safe and protected — working on her case.

Instead, she was cold, wet and horny. Worse, she was about to climb into a small cab with a man who irritated her as much as he aroused her. Damn the man. Did he have to look so refreshed, relax and so damn sexy, sitting in the front seat?

Claire slammed the truck door. It was a juvenile thing to do. Not too bright either, as the action put pressure on the splinter. Claire grimaced slightly over the stinging pain.

"What was that?" Derek frowned at her, attuned to her slightest expression.

"What was what?" Claire repeated guardedly, as she dropped the pile of wet clothes on the floorboard.

"That expression. Is your knee really bothering you?"

"I don't know what you're talking about." Claire refused to look at him.

"Bull."

"Whatever."

"We're not going anywhere until you tell me what is bothering you."

"Bothering me?" Claire turned narrowed eyes on him. "Do you want an alphabetical list?"

"Paining you," Derek corrected himself. "I can tell something hurt you a moment ago."

"It's nothing."

"Dorothy."

"Fine. I got a splinter from that stupid bathroom door. Happy now?" Claire snapped. "Can you just take me home?"

"We should get the splinter out. You don't want it to get infected." Derek slid a little closer on the seat.

"I can get it out when I get home."

"Why wait?" Derek reached across the seat. Claire sucked in her breath and flattened herself against the seat, careful not to let him touch her. "I can get it out for you right now."

"With that?" Claire looked stunned as he pulled a long hunting knife out of the glove box. "You'll cut my finger off."

"Don't worry. I got a first aid kit in the back. I can sew it back on."

"Ha. Ha. Very funny."

"Where is the splinter?"

"Like I trust you with a knife."

Derek made no comment, just held out his hand, waiting for her to give him her injured hand. Claire didn't move.

For over a minute, they sat silently. Claire glared at him while Derek patiently waited for her to get the message. Finally, Claire folded. With an extravagant sigh, she slapped her hand in his.

"It's there," she pointed to the spot, "on my ring finger."

He closed his large hand over her much smaller one and pulled it up so he could get a better look. Claire was dragged closer to him in the process.

For a moment, she sat tensely, trying to get her rioting emotions under control. Being so close to him, with her body still humming from their recent tryst, worsened the pleasant sensations coursing through her.

After a moment, when he turned the knife on her, Claire gave in to another worry. Concerned he might actually cut her finger off with the machete he called a knife, Claire leaned in close to watch him work. Inadvertently she blocked his view, and he yanked her hand higher.

Claire squeezed her eyes closed when she felt the knifepoint dig into her flesh. A moment later, the sensation disappeared. She held her breath waiting for it to come again.

"You can stop grimacing, it's out." Derek's dry comment caused her eyes to pop open. Claire snatched her hand back to inspect it. Sure enough, the splinter was gone.

"Thanks," Claire muttered begrudgingly.

"How about a reward?" Derek's suggestive tone wasn't lost on Claire. "Perhaps a little kiss?"

"Don't even—"

The man could teach a snake a thing about speed. In the blink of an eye, he had her pinned against him, his arms so tight around her she could barely breathe. Her traitorous body soaked up the hard heat of his muscles as they bit into her softer flesh.

In a vain attempt for freedom, Claire shoved against the solid wall of his chest. The hard muscles burned her fingertips, enticing her to touch, caress. Nearly blinding need swirled, panicking her and she bit into his lower lip.

Claire tasted the copper wash of blood as she felt his growl of excitement. It echoed through her already trembling body, sending spasms of pleasure, sweet and thick, flowing through her. His kiss turned forceful, demanding, as he sealed their mouths together.

A lightning flash of pleasure shot down to her toes, as his tongue invaded her mouth, searching for hers. His taste mingled with his scent, drugging her body and weakening her resolve. There was no fighting the surge of hunger rushing through her blood.

Claire offered no resistance as he pushed her down, covering her soft body with his heated one. Instinctively, she wrapped her legs around his narrow hips, soaking up the outline of the erection cradled between her thighs. She could feel the pulse of his cock as it pushed against the denim.

His lips moved over hers, his tongue stroking into her mouth with ravenous mimicry of the thrust of his hips against her pelvis. The maddening motion drove an echoing throb through her clit, as she helplessly ground herself against him

Need rose from her pussy as it begged for the feel of his long, hard shaft thrusting deep into her. She wanted him to fill her, branding her forever so she would never be cold or empty again.

He laved her flushed cheeks with small licks and kisses as he moved down over her neck and across her collarbone. Distantly she heard the small pops as the buttons on her shirt when flying. The sound was lost in the roar of her blood rushing through her veins, as his big hands splayed against her ribs, brushing the undersides of her breasts.

"You took off your bra." The gravelly comment thrilled Claire.

She could feel the tremble in his muscles. He exhaled a long, ragged breath that betrayed how touching her deeply affected him. The telling sign seduced her more than anything else could.

He wanted her, with the same desperation filling her. It was a powerful aphrodisiac to know this man, this sexy bad-boy, was trembling because of her.

She whimpered in protest as his head lifted, his eyes dark and stormy with lust. Claire felt her breath catch at the hungry look in his eyes. She felt her breast swell, her nipples harden, responding to his look.

The whimper turned into a groan, as his thumbs traced the outline of her nipples. Sensation exploded through her, surprising her with their intensity. She arched helplessly against his caressing hands, begging for more of his touch.

His thumbs rubbed over her nipples again, and her clit twisted with a sensation so sharp it was painful. He rolled and pulled on her distended nipples until she arched her back, bringing them closer to his face as an offering to his lips.

With unexpected tenderness, he leaned down and rubbed his cheek against the tops of her breasts, his hands lifting and pushing them closer so he could nuzzle her soft flesh. She arched in sensual reflex, seeking to increase the drugging feel of his rough, hot skin against her softness.

With agonizing slowness, his tongue came out to taste her, deliciously circling the tip of her breast. She moaned her pleasure. Her hands wound through his hair to press him harder against her, begging for a more.

He was not going to be rushed. Gently, without haste, he nuzzled her soft flesh, kissing the curves, licking and learning the shape of her. When Claire was certain she could not stand another moment, he began sucking her with slow, firm pressure.

Cupping the back of his head, she held him to her breast, writhing against the seat as he toyed with her nipple. The graze of his teeth, the stroke of his velvety tongue, each touch exploded fireballs through her body. The heat pooled in her cunt until it spasmed, overflowing with musky cream.

He turned his attention to her other breast, and the air chilled the wet tip, making it pucker even more. The sensation was a sharp, tingling pain. Claire moaned in protest, soothed only when his hand came up to cover and heat her abandoned nipple.

As he fondled one nipple and tormented the other with his talented mouth, his free hand slid down to her waist sending sparks of electricity through her. With tantalizing deliberation, his fingers paused to rub her belly, teasing her stomach muscles into tremors she felt down to her aching pussy.

* * * *

Derek's cock felt like a length of hot, living steel, driving him almost beyond control with the primal beat of lust pounding through his body. With every wave, his painfully tight flesh whispered demands.

Fuck. Claim. Mate. Now.

Perspiration poured from his body, as he fought the need to move faster. He wanted to pound into her, fill her, mark her as his forever. First, he wanted to hear her scream her satisfaction, scream his name, and beg him for more.

With an impatient motion, he shoved the jeans, with her sodden panties, down her legs. The material easily slid away, falling to the floorboard. The sweet scent of her arousal filled the steamy air.

The smell beckoned him, drugged him, as he slipped his fingers into the soft, wet folds of her pussy. She moaned, her hips jerking up toward his caress as his finger rubbed against her clit and began a slow circular motion that mimicked the slide of his tongue around her nipple.

She was hot, wet, ready and he nearly exploded in his jeans just from touching her. Silken muscles tightened as he plunged two thick fingers into her tight, clenching core. The muscles of her cunt tightened with biting force on his questing finger, driving Derek nearly mad with the need to replace his hands with his driving cock.

Ignoring her moans of protest, Derek lifted his head from her breast. Wanting to imprint the image of her open, wet with her desire, Derek stared down at her, not missing any detail of her delicious sex.

His body tightened at the sight of glistening female cream on her silken curls. The small lips pouted, parted, revealing her swollen clit, the tiny entrance to her tight sheath. His cock jerked, demanding release.

Unable to resist one taste, just one, he lowered his head to her pussy, his hand abandoning her breast for his jeans. With his other, he spread her pussy lips wide, examining the sweet heaven he was about to lay claim to.

Bending his head, he flicked his tongue out to taste the thick cream coating her sensitive lips. He licked one side then the other, making her moan and buck beneath him as he slipped past her clit, carefully avoiding the sensitive nub.

"My mate, hot, wet, hungry for me," Derek growled a second before plunging his tongue into her passage, making her cry out. "Mine, all mine."

Derek lifted one leg over his shoulder, opening her further for his conquering mouth. He showed no mercy as he fucked his tongue into her spasming cunt, licking upward to tease and flick her clit occasionally. Her other leg fell off the seat as her lower back lifted, offering him whatever he wanted.

Derek grasped his erection, stroking himself in an attempt to prolong the exquisite agony. He was not ready to give up his delicious treat, but his cock was making adamant demands. It wanted to be inside her, pounding into her, and his dick wanted that now.

The tenuous control he had maintained so far snapped. Promising himself he would dedicate hours later to tasting that sweet cunt that now belonged to him, he lifted himself up. Sliding his hands beneath the soft globes of her ass, he angled her toward his cock, placing the head against her opening.

He clenched his teeth against the pressure tightening his balls, fighting the exquisite agony of holding back, as he slowly forged into her hot, wet passage. Her muscles rippled, convulsing as he fed her his full length.

Her sweet pussy ate every inch, the slick walls hugging his inflamed flesh, pulling on him, begging for more until there was no more to give her. Seated fully inside her, he held himself still, savoring her tight hold, enjoying the feel of pleasure bubbling from his balls and up his spine.

It had never been like this. Now it would never be any other way. She was his mate, the woman who fit him perfectly, completed him.

Dorothy's eyes were squeezed closed, her mouth open as she panted, her features composed in the most beautiful expression of desire he had ever seen. Derek leaned down to trail butterfly kisses over the flushed cheeks, the motion settled him deeper into her, bringing a moan to her lips.

"Open your eyes, baby. I want to see them as I make you mine," Derek murmured again her heated flesh.

Dorothy's eyes slid slowly open, blinking up at him in dazed confusion. They were almost completely green now, the same color as when she argued with him. Gone were the sharp edges, the sparks of fire, instead they were hazy, molten with desire.

"You're mine now, sweetheart, and I'll never let you go."

Before she could respond, he pulled back, driving forward a second later, thrusting deep. He did not have the strength or sanity for a slow, delicate fuck.

His fingers bit into her curved flesh, holding her still as he slammed into her. Long, hard, and fast, he felt the beast's demands rising in him. His howl bounced through the truck interior as he felt her tighten around him, her cries slicing through him and touching him to his soul.

"Derek?" The radio on the dash crackled to life. *"Derek you there?"*

Chapter 5

The sound of the officer's voice was an arctic blast, cooling the temperature in the truck cab several degrees. Derek felt Dorothy stiffen beneath him. He could not stop now.

Despite the interruption, his body screamed with the need for release. Unable to control himself, his hips thrust forward seating himself deep within her, driving reality back out of Dorothy's eyes and dragging a moan from her lips.

"Derek?" Troy's voice demanded from the radio.

Not stopping as he pounded into her warm, honeyed folds, Derek almost yanked the radio completely off the dash as he picked up the handset.

"What," Derek snarled into the communicator, "do you want?"

* * * *

Dimly, at a distance, Claire heard Derek talking between the static omissions from the radio. She could not grasp what was being said, could not control the moans escalating to screams as reality retreated.

The world outside no longer existed. There was only Derek, driving his hot, hard, cock into her over and over again. His strokes were fast, savage and they elicited a primal, animalistic response in her.

Of their own volition, her legs wrapped around his pounding hips. Her fingers biting into the inflexible muscles of his arms, as she held on to him. She had no control over her body as it bucked upward, meeting his thrusts.

Every thrust penetrated deeper into her cunt, caressing sensitive tissues that had never been touched. She could feel his cock swelling in side of her, growing harder, thicker, longer. Derek snarled, a sound that belonged to the wolf within, and slammed into her even harder.

It felt so good, so right. His savagery was just what she craved. It had been so long since she had sex, too long. It had never been like this. She would never have dreamed it could be like this.

"Oh God!" The words were ripped from her soul. "Fuck! Yes!"

He gave it to her harder, faster until the liquid sounds of his cock pillaging her wet depths was all Claire could hear. The truck shook with the force of his thrusts. Claire slid along the seat with each stroke, her head banging into the door.

Claire fought the final battle against her orgasm, unwilling to let the pleasure of the moment end. She felt his teeth rake over her shoulder, biting down into the sensitive skin of her neck and her whole world shattered. White-hot streaks of ecstasy scorched her insides as she splintered into a thousand fragments.

She was barely aware of Derek reaching his peak a second later. He roared as hot jets of semen spilled into her womb. For an eternal moment, they stayed caught in the splendor of a completion so perfect neither had anything to compare it to.

Claire groaned as Derek fell on top of her, his heavier weight crushing her. Her muscles felt as if they had been turned to pudding, unable to fulfill their function. For long minutes neither moved, both panting for breath as the world slowly solidified around them.

Claire slowly opened her eyes. The first thing she saw was the blurred image of Duke looking through the fogged glass. She stared back at the doe-eyed dog as the ramifications hit her.

God, what had she just done?

* * * *

Derek bit back a curse as he felt Dorothy tense beneath him. The pleasantries were over and she was obviously already regretting what had happened. It was his bad luck he didn't have enough time to convince her to let it happen again.

He could take her back to his place, overwhelm her resistance with a few passionate kisses and some heavy petting, and then spend the rest of the night in bed, exhausting her with the best sex she had ever had. By morning she wouldn't have the strength left for regret.

But no, he had to go catch an armed robber. Never before had he regretted having to walk away from a woman because duty called as much as he did right now. He didn't have an option though.

There had been an armed robbery outside the town limits. The assailant had fled home to Wilsonville's less than savory side, and been tracked there by the Collin's County Sheriff Department. Outside his jurisdiction, Sheriff McBane had requested Derek's help.

McBane would not be pleased Derek was late as it was. As a fellow wolf, alpha of his own pack, the sheriff would easily scent what had delayed Derek. Not only did Derek have McBane's censure to look forward to, but the teasing of his own deputies as well.

Troy got quite an earful during their radio conversation. He was probably under the mistaken impression the woman was Carolyn. Travis and Troy would be delighted at the idea Derek had worsened his chances with the lovely Dorothy.

Derek would enjoy correcting them. The men beneath him could not challenge his interest in Dorothy. So, they had hoped she would reject him. Soon they would know it was a false hope.

"Get the hell off me!"

Derek cringed. He had forgotten about the naked, and now irate, woman lying beneath him. Grimacing from the pain of having to leave the warmth of her body, he slowly sat up. Dorothy apparently didn't suffer from the same problem.

She shot up, hastily yanking on the oversized jeans he'd given her. The row of buttons apparently took too long to work and she settled for wrenching the two halves of her shirt together.

Derek righted his own clothing more gingery, wincing in discomfort at having to tuck his still engorged cock back behind the confinement of his zipper. He caught Dorothy's disgusted look and knew even as her mouth opened, what was coming.

"You are the most reprehensible, vile, loathsome man I have ever met!" Dorothy spat. "I quit!"

"Dorothy—"

"Don't Dorothy me!" She roared. "You are a single-minded slut. God knows what kind of diseases you're carrying."

"Diseases. I don't have—"

"I swear if you gave me anything that itches, grows lumps, discolors any part of my body, can kill me or put me on medicine for the rest of my life, I will hunt you down and cut off your—"

"Don't even joke about that!" Derek's temper flared. He snatched at the finger she was waving in front of his face, making her jerk her hand back and bang her elbow into the truck door.

"I'm not joking!"

"The only thing I gave you, woman, is the best orgasm you've ever had!"

"Ha! I could get a better orgasm drinking beer, watching porn and using a vibrator operating on half its battery power!"

"Oh, you—"

The shrill ring of a cell phone cut off Derek's words and intentions to prove her wrong. It was his and he could well imagine who was calling. Without looking at the number blinking on the screen, he snapped the phone open.

"Not now, McBane!"

"Then when, baby?"

It was Carolyn. Derek sighed and reached back to rub his neck. His bad luck just turned worse.

"Not now," Derek snapped. He dared not say her name or else Dorothy's opinion of him would drop lower than it already was. "I'll talk to you later."

"You hang up the phone Derek and you'll regret it," Carolyn warned.

She sounded angry and he knew the source. Their long-running, on- again, off-again relationship had never been serious. At least not for him and no matter how much he explained that to Carolyn, she just yessed him and went on acting like she owned him.

It was ridiculous, because she knew he would mate one day. She knew it wasn't going to be her. If sex hadn't been so hot, he'd never put up with all of Carolyn's drama.

"Listen, I'm in the middle of something. I'm going to have to call you back."

"Don't worry about me," Dorothy spoke loudly. "You can go on and talk to your centerfold wannabe, I'll re-button my shirt!"

Derek cringed. Despite his attempt, Dorothy had guessed who, or at least what, was on the other end of the phone. Figured. It was probably thanks to her low opinion of him.

"Who the hell was that?" Carolyn shrieked.

"Nobody." It was an instinctive answer and the minute the word hit the air Derek knew he'd screwed up big time.

"Don't lie to me," Carolyn snapped.

"I didn't mean that," Derek stated, looking at Dorothy, whose eyes were flashing with the devil's own fire. He tried quickly to undo his mistake, even though he knew it was hopeless.

"No," she sneered. "You meant nobody of consequence."

"I'm talking to you Derek!"

"It just came out—"

His desperate explanation was cut off by the sound of another phone ringing. This time it was Dorothy's. Shooting him a dirty look, she turned her shoulder to him and answered. Derek took advantage of the break to deal with Carolyn.

"Carolyn—"

"Don't Carolyn me! You have some explaining to do!"

"I don't have time, Caro. I have an armed robber to—"

"An armed robber? Let me guess, the female, shirtless kind, right?"

"I can explain—"

"I don't want to hear it. You throw me out of the police station yesterday, say you're too tired to have me over last night, and now I catch you with some cheap whore!"

"She's not a whore!" Derek shot back. "She's..."

No, that wasn't a good idea. If Carolyn knew who Dorothy was, what she meant to him, all hell would break loose. Dorothy would receive the sharp end of Carolyn's temper. His position with Dorothy was precarious enough as it was. He didn't think their relationship could handle Carolyn's revenge at this point.

"She's what?" Carolyn demanded.

* * * *

"What?" Claire snapped into the phone.

"Well, well, well, sexy. It's been awhile." A familiar voice purred on the end of the phone. The sound of it sent turned her blood to ice.

"Agakiar." Claire felt all the hurt and anger churning insider her morph into a much more dangerous rage.

"Been thinking about me?" The man chuckled, sending cold shivers straight down Claire's spine.

"Wishing you were in hell." Claire took a deep breath and struggled for control of her emotions.

"Probably hoping you could send me there." Agakiar was not the least bit put off by her comment. Just the opposite, the man sounded downright thrilled with the venom in her tone.

"With as much pain as possible."

"My dear, such words turn me on or did you forget that I enjoy pain?"

"What do you want Agakiar?" Claire growled.

"Just to say hello," Agakiar purred. "It's been a long time, beautiful. I've been so bored locked in that stupid prison, nobody to play with."

"Really? You miss me? Well why don't you come down for a visit? I'm sure we could devise some way to entertain ourselves."

"You tempt me, my love." Agakiar sighed. "But you have so much valuable work to do. I wouldn't want to interfere."

"What do you know about my work?"

"My sweet Claire, don't you know? Every time you use my gift I can sense it." His voice dropped to a husky drawl. "Oh, I can feel it all, the pain and fear those girls suffered. What a delicious treat to get when I was locked behind bars with those who were already weak.

"Ah, Claire. They were so easy. Not like you. Such spunk, such drive, you are going to be a true treat to turn."

"Never." Before she could continue, the line went dead.

Claire closed her phone slowly. She felt strangely empty. It was a welcome sensation. It was far better than the humiliation and pain Derek had inflicted on her, safer than the rage that Agakiar inspired in her.

All her life, Claire had valued her ability to control her emotions. She did not scream, or cry, or even laugh too loud. Nothing had ever threatened to undo the skills she had honed to perfection, nothing until Agakiar.

Three years back, she had met Agakiar and everything had gone to hell. She had been a decorated FBI agent when she had been handed an undercover assignment to help break up a ring of sex-slave traffickers.

Claire had gone into the assignment with her eyes closed. Not believing in demons, she had been happy in her narrow view of reality. Agakiar had taken advantage of that ignorance.

The demon had wooed her, drugged her and then marked her with his brand. She had easily fallen into his trap, but it was not going to happen again. Not with Agakiar — and not with Derek.

"Dorothy, I—"

"Whatever," Claire cut him off, not interested in anything Derek had to say. "Just take me home."

* * * *

Derek could sense her withdraw. Silently, he cursed his own stupidity as he started the truck. Kristin had been right. Dorothy was pissed. She thought he had used her for sex. In one rash moment, he had allowed desire to rule his body, and confirmed all the prejudices Dorothy held against him. He knew he had blundered, but he could not regret it, and would not have done differently.

The moment he had slid into her tight, clinging pussy he knew he had found heaven. Never before had a climax so drained him, leaving him wanting to curl up and take a nap with his woman held securely in his arms.

That was new. Derek was not a cuddler. He gave any woman coming to his bed the best time she'd ever had between the sheets, but when it was over, she left. He had never even let Carolyn spend the night, and she was as close as he had ever gotten to a long-term relationship.

With Dorothy, it was all different. Even now, he wanted to wrap his arms around her and assure her everything was all right. He wanted to tell her he wanted more than just sex. He wanted to feel her breath against his chest, to run his hands through her hair and rub her back while she snuggled into him.

Jesus, he even wanted to talk to her. Talk to her? Now that was weird.

Now wasn't the time. Dorothy wasn't in the mood to listen to anything he had to say. She needed some time. He would give her the night. Tomorrow he would feel her out, and if she looked as if she was withdrawing or, heaven forbid, really quitting her job again, he would take matters into his own hands.

* * * *

Claire slammed the front door so hard the wall shook. Kate appeared, a smug look on her pert features.

"Don't!" Claire warned her, tossing her the pile of her wet clothes on the floor. "Not one word, Kate."

Kate held up her hands in defeat and slowly disappeared.

Good. Claire was not in the mood for any snide comments or imaginative quips. All she wanted to do was bathe away the memory of Derek's touch. If such a thing were possible, with her cunt still vibrating with aftershocks. The ride home had been tense and silent. Derek had finally shown some common sense and left her alone.

It would have been one thing if he had forced her. Then at least, she would not have to claim any responsibility for what happened. Instead, she had to deal with the fact she had wanted him.

Desired him with an intensity that frightened her, because it was not just physical. Oh, God. She had to get out of this town. Far from Derek before she did something stupid — again.

She wasn't going to let it happen. She was going to remain calm and focus on her case. Ten minutes later, dry and dressed in fresh clothes, she marched into the second bedroom where she had set up her makeshift office. She paused as she always did, moved by the wall of victims.

They hung there, all twenty-six missing person posters. Honey brown hair, hazel eyes, youthful faces, they looked back at her from neat little rows. There was a small bag tacked to each poster, personal effects of the departed girls.

Claire used them to get her visions. The visions were a side effect of Agakiar's brand. Because the source of her gift came from a demon, her ability was very specific. While she needed a piece of a victim's personal possessions, she didn't see through their eyes. She saw through the eyes of the killer, but only killers who were tainted by demons.

Claire threw those thoughts off. Sitting down at the little desk, she flipped open her laptop. Taking a deep breath, she focused on the only hunch she had. It would hopefully lead to break in her case and way out of this town.

Four hours later she sat back and smiled.

Good news? Claire turned around to find Kate floating in the middle of the room.

"I got it."

Got what?

"Janice and Dean Howard ran a foster home on a farm outside of town. All the kids were taken away back in the late 1940s. There aren't a lot of details, because the file is so old, but it appears it was an abusive home."

That's it?

"That's a lot given the age of the file. Besides it's the only foster home shut down in these parts, at the right time."

And why are you looking at foster homes again?

"I'm looking for a house worthy of a demon. You know as well as I do, demons like to haunt places that have pain bled into them."

So, you just automatically think of old foster homes. You're cynical, you know that?

"I need to check the place out." Claire tapped the end of her pin against her chin, ignoring Kate's criticism.

"Tomorrow I'm going to the library. Of course, I quit my job so I can probably do both."

Don't you think you're being a little quick on the quitting?

"Quick? I've been there over a week. Now, I've got to spend tomorrow and the following day shuffling papers when there are actual leads to follow up."

That's not why you're quitting.

"It doesn't matter why." Claire was growing annoyed with Kate. Leave it the nosey ghost to ruin her good mood. "All that matters is the job no longer benefits my case."

And what if those leads require you to access police files?

Claire did not respond to that taunt.

Chapter 6

Wednesday

As Claire shoved open the door to Biscuit's, she was greeted by the smell of fried foods and noisy conversations. The small diner was packed with the morning rush of locals come to gorge themselves on eggs, bacon, grits, and, of course, Biscuit's legendary biscuits.

This was the first rush. Later the tourists would waken and wander in. Claire had not eaten breakfast at the diner before, but had watched the crowds pour in and out from the station house across the square.

Having left her car at the station house yesterday afternoon, she knew Derek would be expecting to give her a lift to work. The arrogant jerk would dismiss her resignation as feminine pique, easily gotten around by his double dimples and southern accent. Oh, how she would love to have stood her ground on that one and given it to him.

Problem was Kate was right. She might need access to the police files. That was why she had gotten the job in the first place. She was not going to let the conceited police chief bully her, or seduce her, out of her clothing, either.

She was not quitting. She had to placate her own need for revenge by ditching him this morning. She had skipped her run, opting instead to walk the five-mile trek to the town square. Her reward for outthinking her opponent was breakfast.

She found an empty stool at the counter and slid in. Surveying the menu her stomach grumbled, aroused not only by the words but the smell of the diner. A haggard-looking waitress ran a wet rag over the linoleum counter before slapping down a glass of ice water and utensils rolled in a napkin.

"Ready to order?"

"Yes. I'll have the bacon and cheese omelet and hash browns with onions."

"Butter, honey, or gravy with your biscuits?"

"Butter."

"To drink?"

"Water is fine thank you."

The older woman did not respond but turned to the window. She yelled Claire's order back to the kitchen in a southern accent so thick she sounded as if she were speaking a foreign language. For several minutes, Claire watched as waitresses scurried about in a frantic pace, listened to the conversations going on around her, and felt herself shrinking.

She hated eating out alone. It was boring and she tended to eat her food to fast. She should have brought a book to read. Better yet, the book she was writing to work on. Chewing her bottom lip, she thought of the manuscript sitting at home waiting for her to read and correct it. This would be her second attempt, the first already with an agent trying to get it published.

The muted ring of her cell phone broke Claire's thoughts away from her fantasy. Fishing it out of her purse, she groaned when she saw Max's name flashing on the screen. She debated not answering, but finally opened the phone.

"Hey Max." Claire tried to sound happy to hear from him.

"Don't 'hey Max' me," Max retorted with unusual anger. "What are you doing?"

"I was about to get something to eat," Claire explained with false cheer.

"Don't, Claire. I want to know what Wall said to you."

"How do you know I talked to Wall?"

"We're tracking him, how else?"

"If you're tapping his phone, then you know what he said to me." Claire's response was just as curt.

"We're not tapping his phone. We're just...you know."

She knew. They couldn't get a warrant to tap his phone so they were monitoring the records. They probably didn't have authorization for that, either.

"We didn't talk about much."

"You shouldn't be talking to him at all. Do you know how that looks?"

"Do I care?"

"You should. Perst hit the ceiling, he wants to bring you back for questioning."

"He can question me all he wants. I don't know anything."

"It doesn't look that way and you know it," Max barked. "You are one of only five people he's been in contact with since he was freed."

"So? I can't stop him from calling me."

"How does he know your number?"

"How the hell should I know?"

"Claire."

"Max."

"I'm worried about you." Max sounded defeated, tired and old.

"I'm not your responsibility anymore."

"I know." Max tone softened. "I really am sorry about how things went down."

"It's not your fault." Claire had been saying that for so long now it lacked in sincerity.

"I should have backed up your story."

"And lost your job too? I didn't want you to do that." Claire looked up as the waitress slid two plates of food before her. "Thanks."

"Thanks? For what?"

"I was talking to the waitress. I told you I was getting something to eat."

"Please tell me what you and Wall talked about?"

"Is that the agent asking?"

"Does it matter?"

"He just wanted me to know he was free and missing me." Claire gave in. If she did not answer Max's questions, she would never get to eat her breakfast.

"That's it?"

"That's it."

"Claire."

"The conversation went downhill from there. I might have threatened him a little. Not that he cared."

"Threatened him?"

"Yeah." Claire sighed. "I might have told him to drop by for a visit, but not in a welcoming way."

"Why did you do that? You know how dangerous he is."

"It just slipped out." Claire did not need this. She could only be thankful it was Max and not Mike. If Mike found out what she had said to Agakiar, he would probably lock her into a safe house with a twenty-four hour guard.

"Where are you?"

"I'm in a small town in South Carolina, Wilsonville."

"I'm coming down there."

"Why?"

"Because you're going to get yourself killed."

"Well, that would certainly make it easier for the agency, wouldn't it?" Claire continued before he could respond to that zinger. "Since I've been so forthright, why don't you tell me what happened to Janet?"

"It looks like suicide, complete with a note. She took a headfirst dive off the roof of her apartment complex. And before you ask, we've done the handwriting analysis and it is her."

"So your star witness is dead and your case died with her," Claire commented.

"I know Wall's hand is in this."

Claire could see him in her mind. He was pushing up his glasses and rubbing his nose. Max always did that when he was frustrated.

"Can you prove it?" Claire knew the answer to that.

"No," Max admitted after a moment.

"Then you're screwed. You're going to have to find another rope to hang him with."

"Claire?"

"What?"

"I miss you." His voice went soft.

"Max—"

"I know." He cut her off. "I know. You have every right to hate me. What I did was wrong."

"Stop beating yourself up. What you did, anybody would have done."

"Not you," Max stated solemnly. "I hope you can forgive me."

"Already forgiven." But not forgotten.

"It's alright." Max did not sound relieved. "You don't have to say that just because I want to hear it. I know I have to prove to you that I can be trusted again. I'm going to do that. Just give me the chance."

"Max—"

"Shit. I have to go," Max cut her off. "See you soon sweetheart."

"Max, wait." The line went dead.

Claire growled and snapped her phone closed with unnecessary force. She would have to call him back tonight and make sure he did not show up in Wilsonville. She did not need Max riling up Derek or Derek riling up Max.

She was sure Derek's interest in her would disappear now that he had had her. After all, not even five minutes after they had finished screwing he told the bimbo on the phone she was a 'nobody'. Still, there was no telling what the arrogant, macho jerk would do when he saw a rival enter the field.

Claire unwrapped her napkin. Pushing her food around her plate, she took a tentative bite. Stimulated by the delicious offering, her hunger returned and Claire began attacking the plate with vigor.

She had demolished her omelet and over half the hash browns when she sensed a presence beside her. Turning she found herself eye-to-neck with Derek's long, lean blonde friend. Swallowing hard, her eyes drifted up to a set of striking blue eyes assessing her with cold distain.

"You're Dorothy, right?" The woman regally demanded.

"And you are?"

"Carolyn, Derek's fiancée," the woman said with such haughtiness Claire felt the hair on the back of her neck rising.

"Nice ring." Claire looked down to the woman's empty finger.

"It will be. It'll be beautiful once the jeweler is done. Derek insisted on a custom design."

"A special ring for a special woman, huh?"

Claire did not believe a word of what the woman was saying. Derek was a slut. One of those permanent bachelors who chased after college girls in bikinis well into his seventies and whose greatest fantasy was to visit the Playboy Mansion. Definitely not the marrying kind.

"I see you understand."

"More than you want me to."

"Pardon me?"

"You have to leave?" Claire asked sweetly, intentionally misunderstanding the other woman. "What a shame. It was nice to meet you and I'll remember to congratulate Derek when I see him."

"You stay away from him," Carolyn growled.

"Kind of hard considering I'm his personal assistant," Claire responded airily. "After all, it is my job to see to any and all his needs."

"Listen here you pudgy little—"

"Ouch." Claire grabbed her chest with a dramatic flair. "That's an arrow to my heart. Now, if you'll excuse me, I have to eat my biscuits."

Carolyn's mouth opened and closed for a minute. Obviously, she did not know how to respond. Claire paid her no mind as she began to butter up her cooling biscuits. After a moment, Carolyn turned and stormed off. Claire rolled her eyes before biting into the biscuit.

"Damn this is good," Claire said to nobody in particular.

"Thanks," the waitress responded, drawing Claire's attention up to her. "You're new in town."

"Yeah, been here for just a few weeks."

"You work over at the police station." The waitress did not return her smile.

"You seem to know a lot about me?"

"It's a small town. Word travels fast."

"I'm surprised anybody would be talking about me."

"I'm going to give you some advice." The waitress leaned in close. "Don't piss Carolyn off, she can make your life here hell."

"Thanks, I'll remember that," Claire said calmly.

"But you're not listening, right?" The waitress picked up on what Claire had left unsaid.

"I can handle myself."

The waitress grunted, her eyes flickering over Claire's shoulder. In an instant her demeanor changed, she straightened with a smile. Claire turned to see what or who had brightened the dreary woman's continence.

With a groan, she turned back to her plate as Derek approached.

"Morning Chief." The waitress quickly wiped down his spot as he took the empty seat to Claire's right. Instead of water, she poured a cup of coffee and slid it across the counter at him.

"Morning, May," Derek greeted the waitress with true enthusiasm. "The usual?"

"That'll do me." Derek waited as May dithered off to call in his order before turning his attention to Claire.

"No 'good morning' for the boss?"

"We're not at work yet," Claire muttered. She could feel the heat in her cheeks and hated herself for it.

"Does that mean you'll be more accommodating when we are?" Derek drawled.

"I prefer professional," Claire snapped back.

"I wanted to apologize about yesterday." Derek actually sounded sincere. Not that Claire was buying it.

"Aren't you supposed to be apologizing to your fiancé?"

"My what?" Derek leaned back, the shock obvious in his voice. Just as Claire would have bet, Carolyn had lied.

"You know, that blonde Amazon you're engaged to."

"Carolyn," he growled her name with suppressed anger.

"I'm impressed you remember her name." Claire nodded. "I hear that you're buying her an amazing, one-of-kind ring. Hope it doesn't land you in the poor house."

"Lies, all lies, Dorothy."

"That's what they all say."

"Damn it, Dorothy. You can't possibly believe her. Do you?"

"What does it matter what I believe?" Claire refused to look at him. "I'm a nobody, remember?"

"I didn't mean that."

"Whatever."

"It just slipped out. It was an instinctive response, you know. Like when somebody asks you how you are doing and you automatically say fine even if it's not the truth."

"The fact you've been in that situation enough times to have an instinctive response says a lot about your character."

"Damn it, Dorothy! Why do you always twist everything I say?"

"Why do you always say such stupid things?"

"You're not going to make this easy are you?"

"Actually, I will. Let's just drop it."

"Drop it?"

"Forget it ever happened. It was an inconsequential and insignificant event that does not deserve further conversation."

"Are you referring to my comment or the sex?" Derek asked cautiously.

"Both." Claire gave him a tight smile. "Forget it. I already have."

"Dorothy—"

"Forget it."

"Fine. If that's the way you want to play it."

A plate of food slid in front of him. May delivered his plate with a smile and a speed she had not treated Claire to. The waitress chatted with Derek for a moment while Claire polished off the last of her biscuits.

"That was slick of you slip out this morning," Derek commented casually though there was no denying the amused edge to his tone.

"There was nothing slick about it. I left my car in the square yesterday."

May appeared to pick up her plate.

"Anything else, miss?" The waitress's tone was politer now that Derek was sitting beside her.

"I'm fine," Claire assured her.

May ripped off a ticket and was just putting it on the counter when she looked over at Derek. Claire felt the sudden tension. Before May could respond, Claire slapped her hand down on the bill. For a moment, the woman tugged on it, and then gave up. Casting an apologetic glance at Derek, she scurried off.

"Let me get that for you." Derek's offer sounded more like a demand.

"No thank you." Claire slid the ticket away from him, making it impossible for him to grab it without making a scene.

"Come on, Dorothy. Let me buy you breakfast."

"You know," Claire turned to him, "I might, just might, agree to that if I believed for a moment, you were actually going to pay."

"What are you accusing me of?"

"Please." Claire fished out her wallet. Intentionally keeping it angled so he could not see Claire Hollowell on her Georgia driver's license.

"Please what?" Derek tried to sound indignant and failed miserably.

"We both know you're not going to be paying for anything you get here."

"Why do you make that sound as if it's a crime?"

"Because, technically, it is." Claire slapped ten dollars down on top of her bill. Without waiting for him to respond, she hopped up. "I'll see you at the office."

Claire hurried out of the diner and across the square to the police station. If she thought she would find refuge in the professional environment of the workplace, she was sadly mistaken. The minute she entered the conversation died and all three officers looked at her with obvious amusement.

"Morning, Dorothy," they sang out in unison.

Claire faltered for a moment, feeling everything that was going unsaid. Taking a deep breath, ignoring the heat she could feel blossoming in her cheeks for the second time that morning, she marched forward.

"Good morning."

Head held high, she went toward the break room and a much needed cup of coffee. She could hear the murmurs pick up as she disappeared down the hall. It was the laughter though that had her grinding her teeth.

* * * *

Derek nodded to his officers, paying them little attention as he made his way through the lobby. His focus was on the voluptuous beauty hiding in the office. She was shrewder than he had given her credit for.

She had snuck out of the house, catching him off guard. He had stood at her door knocking for almost ten minutes before he had given up. Finding her at the diner had completely shocked him. Hearing Carolyn had already made a move on Dorothy had not.

He was pleased she hadn't believed Carolyn's lies, but he didn't think it was out of growing respect for him. Just the opposite, Derek would bet. Her impression had sunk so low she thought him incapable of a serious relationship.

There was no way to talk her out of that opinion. Only time, and his actions, would prove he was very serious about her. That's why he had dropped the discussion about yesterday's unfortunate incident.

He wasn't going to let her forget what had come before. He had promised to give her the night and, as he'd suspected, she had decided to try to build a barrier between them. She was going to pretend the other day never happened, that their relationship was merely professional.

He was not going to let her get away with that. If she needed another demonstration, then he would gladly give her one. With that in mind, he made his way into the office. She barely glanced up from the computer where she was inputting last night reports into the database.

"Dorothy." He kept his tone polite, giving no indication of his true intent. "You ready to go over my schedule."

"Of course, Chief." She turned and pulled out a planner and some papers.

He stood back, allowing her to enter his office first. She settled down into one of the chairs, her back ramrod straight. As composed as she was, he could smell the faint trace of her arousal.

Derek closed the office door. The blinds were already down. When he flicked the lock, her head snapped around. Derek did not bother to disguise the feral look of hunger in his gaze. It had her jumping out of her seat. The papers in her lap fell to the floor with a plop. She stepped back quickly, even as the scent of her arousal grew stronger.

"What do you think you're doing?" She demanded, unable to disguise the frantic note to her voice.

"You said you would give me a proper 'good morning' when we got to work." Derek advanced steadily on her.

"Did I? Well, good morning. Now can we get to work?"

"Sugar, we're a lot more welcoming than that in the South."

"Derek, damn it, stop! We're not doing this again."

"Why not? We both enjoyed it."

"This is not the place for this kind of thing." Dorothy had circled his desk, putting it between them.

"I wouldn't have thought so either, but it was your suggestion, honey. And I must, say I'm kind of surprised at you, Dorothy."

Derek was enjoying himself. Dorothy was aroused and flustered, and so damn sexy, he was not sure he could keep this game up for much longer.

"This wasn't my suggestion."

"You were the one who said at the diner you would—"

"I know what I said," Dorothy snapped. "And you know what I meant! Now stop this foolishness and behave as a police chief should!"

"You're right." Derek nodded. "This is foolish."

Dorothy shrieked as he cleared the desk. Grabbing her by the waist, he held her tightly to him.

"Now, this is more like it."

"Derek. If you don't unhand me now..." Dorothy ground out between clench teeth.

"Do you really think I'm going to stop?" He could see she understood what he was saying perfectly. "Now then, about my greeting..."

Chapter 7

Jerking her head away, she clenched her jaw tight in blatant defiance. He could see the expectation of a deep, devouring kiss in her wary eyes.

"Your skin is so soft."

As he spoke, he brushed his cheek gently against hers. Placing feather-light kisses along her brow and down the sides of her temple, he breathed deeply. Her unique scent stirred the beast within, warning him there was only so long it would be constrained.

"So sweet."

Derek tasted his way down her chin and along the graceful line of her neck. She sighed, her eyes closing as her tension began to ebb. Her head rolled back, her neck arching, offering the sensitive flesh up for more of the tiny love bites.

Dorothy sighed as she slowly melted into him. The feel of her surrender increased the intensity of his own desire, driving more blood to his already engorged cock. His dick demanded freedom, wanting to be buried deep in her. The beast echoed that demand, but Derek fought back.

Even as she succumbed to his sensual lures, she was still skittish. To push too fast now would only make her withdraw. Despite the beast's desires, he needed to gentle his mate into submission.

Slowly he slid his hands down her arms, enjoying the feel of her soft skin under his palms. Working his way back up, he curled her arms around his neck. Her hands fisted together, tightening and pulling him in closer.

He obeyed the silent command, fitting their bodies together with sensual precision. Long lashes lifted revealing illustrious hazel eyes. Their beauty transfixed him, the color shifting between green, to honey, to gold, never still.

He lowered his head, pausing to whisper against her lips.

"You are so beautiful. I've never wanted a woman the way I want you."

He felt her shiver as his breath teased her lips. They trembled, parting in invitation. Her trembles turned into shudders as he softly, repeatedly, brushed his lips over hers. The tip of his tongue slid out to outline their full shape before his teeth nipped into her lower lip.

Dorothy moaned, pressing her mouth more firmly against his. That was what Derek had been waiting for. His fingers slid into her hair, holding her still as he fitted his mouth firmly to hers.

Electric charges lit up his nervous system as she surprised him, becoming the aggressor. Her tongue stroked into his mouth, swirling around, devouring him as if starved for his taste. The tight control he had been exerting over his dominant side snapped, and he crushed her to him, taking control of the kiss.

He could feel her heart pounding against his chest, matching the driving beat of his own. His nostrils flared, smelling the moisture pooling between her thighs . She was ready for him.

That knowledge elevated his need to take what was his. He wanted her naked, bent over the desk, screaming with pleasure as he fucked her.

He yanked at her shirt, stepping back long enough to pull it over her head. It tangled around her wrists, and he twisted the soft cotton, binding her with it. Dorothy whimpered as he used the shirt to force her back to arch. The motion thrust her chest out, making an offering of her breasts.

He cupped her breast, enjoying the way her nipples strained against the white cotton bra. A second later, with a quick flick of his wrist, there was nothing obstructing his view of the beautiful pink buds. She writhed against him, fighting to be free of the shirt as he began to rub her nipples in alternating circles.

The wolf inside growled his displeasure at her lack of submission. He bit down on her nipple, flicking the trapped nub with his tongue until she lost her ability to fight. Nibbling and licking, he tormented one breast, then the other, as his hands made quick work of her skirt and panties.

Dorothy offered him no resistance, whimpering and panting under his administrations. Forcing her legs wider with his thighs, his hand tunneled through the damp, dark curls coving her mound.

The thick cream of her desire spilled into his hand as he parted the swollen folds of her sex. Dorothy groaned into his mouth, her hips flexing in silent demand. Derek pushed first one, then a second, thick finger into her tight, little cunt.

She bit down on his lip, sucking it into her mouth as he stroked into her, arousing her to a fevered pitch. She was hot and wet, soaking with her arousal. Derek could hold back no longer. With rough, impatience he flipped her over.

* * * *

Claire could feel Derek moving behind her. The pop of a button coming undone was followed by muttered curses. She could hear him working on the zipper and chimed in, moaning at the loss of his touch.

All logical thought had ceased, leaving in its place naked need. Only the feel of him pounding deep inside her would quench the fires of lust raging through her blood. She needed release. A release only he could give her.

A calloused hand smoothed over the rounded curves of her bottom, following the crease until he was again caressing her molten core. Thick thighs pushed against hers, forcing them wider.

Claire yielded, groaning as she felt his cock sliding between her legs. Teasing her, he did it again, allowing the bulbous head to rub against her clit. The scalding friction had her hips rotating. Grinding herself against his cock, she whimpered, begging for more.

"I'm going to fuck you now, Dorothy," he rasped against her ear, pulling back until the tip of his cock brushed against her opening. "Tell me what you want."

"Please, Derek," Claire cried, jerking back to try and force him into her.

He fed her just an inch, letting the rounded knob of his dick slip past the tight ring of muscles at the entrance to her cunt. Her greedy internal muscles sucked at him, trying to pull him in deeper. Claire heard him groan, felt the perspiration on his forehead as his head dropped to her shoulder.

His hand slid down her hip and settled over her clit. Slowly, he began to tease the sensitive nub, making her writhe and moan incoherently with need. Those slick fingers withdrew, sliding over her butt to delve between the cheeks. He circled her anus, causing her to gasp, and her muscles tensed with erotic fear.

"Tell me what you want."

"You," Claire strangled on the words, trying to catch her breath. "Please, I need you."

That was all he needed to hear. His cock rammed all the way into her at the same time he pushed one blunt, wet finger into her anus. Without pause, he began to violently pound into her, riding her with a ferocity that had her keening and moaning.

She lost all control of her body. He was filling her, slamming so deep inside her she could feel his shaft butting into her cervix. The thickness beating into her body became her reality, the repetitive slap of his balls against her swollen flesh her heart beat.

As he increased his speed, pistoning into her faster and faster, her body wound tighter and tighter until everything snapped. Claire screamed, clawing at the shirt still wrapped around her hands.

Still he did not stop. She could feel her muscles spasming around his hardness, clamping down and intensifying her climax while her body milked the orgasm out of his. The room filled with his shout, her name, as he fucked her like the animal he was, riding his climax to the final crash.

* * * *

Derek had given up on catching his breath. It required too much effort. If he were to die, now was the perfect moment to go. As he left the world his final smells would be the sweet perfume of his satisfied mate, the feel of her sexy, sweaty body beneath him, the sounds of her gentle sobs as she perished with him from the inferno of desire that consumed them.

Death though was not on the agenda for the day. His heart began to slow and his mind started to function once more. His cock was still semi-hard, more than willing to do a repeat performance if he could just get the rest of his muscles to function. The idea was good and he would have followed through on it if he had not felt Dorothy slowly tensing beneath him.

With a sigh of regret, he pulled back out of her and shifted so he was no longer crushing her beneath his weight. Dorothy did not move but for the bunching of her muscles. With gentle fingers, he massaged his way down her neck and over her spine, working the stiffness out of them.

"You okay?" He finally asked.

"Okay?" Dorothy gave a muffled snort. "No. Not even close."

"I didn't hurt you, did I?"

He had lost it there for a moment, fucking her with the passionate frenzy of the wolf claiming his mate. It was the second time that had happened. One of these days he was going to make love to her with the slow and easy seduction of the man and not the rabid lust of the beast.

"Dorothy?" He prodded when she did not respond.

"No, you didn't hurt me."

Dorothy rolled backward and off the desk. For a moment, she swayed on unsteady legs. With angry, jerky movements, she tried to get her shirt unsnarled from around her wrist. Derek watched her, wanting to offer to help but knowing he would be rebuffed.

Despite all her talk about decency and professionalism, Dorothy was a passionate, volatile woman. She appeared to be a contradiction. All the order and control she exerted in the office, compared to the exuberance that showed itself when they were arguing or making love.

She had her shirt back on and was bending to reach for her skirt when he reached for her again. God, what an ass. Derek's lecherous mind immediately began to imagine all the things a man could do to an ass like that.

Unconsciously, he reached out to caress the smooth, rounded bottom. Dorothy must have caught his motion because she turned quickly and smacked his hand. She yanked her skirt up, giving him a hard look.

"Don't even think about it. You've gotten your hello and then some."

Derek growled, the sound of the wolf warning its mate not to defy him. Dorothy growled back. The sound of a true bitch oddly comforted and amused Derek. It helped him see reason. She was right, now was not the time.

Now it was time for them to come to an understanding. That meant talking. Derek stood and began straightening his clothes. Dorothy skirted around the desk and bent to retrieve the papers she had dropped on the floor when he had first entered the room.

"Here is your schedule for today."

She slapped them down on his desk and was obviously about to make a hasty exit. Derek grabbed her wrist, stopping her from leaving. Her eyes narrowed on him in warning.

"I think we need to talk, Dorothy."

"Don't call me that," she snapped with barely suppressed venom.

"Why not?" Derek scowled, confused by her anger. "It's your name."

Her mouth opened and closed as if she were not sure what to say. His eyes narrowed slightly, sensing a change in her tension.

"Call me Miss Walker. Perhaps it will help you remember we have a professional relationship and nothing more."

She tried to sound waspish, angered, but he heard the tenure of uncertainty. There was a faint scent mixing into air. Deception. The hairs on the back of his next began to rise. Something was not right.

"No, that's not it," Derek whispered to himself. "You're hiding something from me."

"Hiding something?" Derek realized he had spoken out loud at her indignant question. Despite her tone, he could smell her nervous fear. "What? Are you afraid my boyfriend is going to call? Don't worry, you're lower than a nobody."

"What is it, Dorothy?" He pressed, refusing to respond to her antagonistic remarks.

"What is what, Derek?"

"I want to know what you're hiding."

"I'm not hiding anything."

"You are."

"Oh, really?" She raised an eyebrow at that. "How do you know that?"

Well, damn. She had him cornered with that question. Now was not a good time to explain he was a werewolf or what it entailed.

"I just can," Derek growled. "I'm a cop. I have certain instincts."

"Oh, you're a human lie detector. Is that it?"

"Something like that."

"Well, I suggest you get your antenna fixed, Chief Jacob." Dorothy yanked her wrist free. "Because I'm not hiding anything. Now I have work to do."

With that she stormed out of the office, slamming the door so hard the wall shook. Derek checked the impulse to go after her. Dorothy would dig her heels in if he confronted her directly. There would be no getting answers out of her when she was mad and defensive.

He would need a different approach

Chapter 8

You know donuts don't constitute a well-balanced dinner, don't you?

"Go away, Kate," Claire muttered before biting into another powdered donut. She had already consumed two and was contemplating eating all six.

So, are you going to tell me why you're so upset?

"Nope." Claire reached for her fourth donut.

You're brooding over what happened in the police chief's office, aren't you?

"No." Claire scowled. "This has nothing to do with that irrelevant event."

Irrelevant? Do you think by constantly denying what is going on between you and the chief you can somehow make it go away?

"There is nothing going on. It was just a stupid mistake."

Claire did not want to think about that subject anymore. It had been a long, tiring day of tolerating the officers knowing looks and the arrogant smirks. The small hand on the clock had plodded along on its path, frustrating Claire's desire to see the day done. The moment the clock had clicked on five, she had flown out the door.

Hoping to find an escape from thoughts of Derek, she had sought sanctuary in the one place that had always brought her peace. The library. As a child, it had been the one safe place she'd gone to hide from the world.

She had always done her homework before losing herself in the rows of books. An avid reader, she had found escape within the books. Each was a doorway to another life, to being a different person.

Come on, Claire, you need talk about it. Sitting here, looking at the faces of the dead, and gorging yourself on donuts isn't going to help.

"Life sucks and donuts are my friend, now leave me alone," Claire retorted.

The hottest man in town can't keep his hands off you. Are you sure it's life that is sucking?

Claire did not respond to that taunting question but finished her fourth donut. She was just reaching for the fifth when the box went flying across the room. Kate — that no good, bossy ghost — was always interfering in her life.

"Just leave me alone," Claire shouted at the apparition. "I don't need or want your help."

You need a smack in the head. If I had an arm, I'd give it to you! Why don't you just stop pouting about what happened in the office today and be thankful you enjoyed the experience?

"This has nothing to do with that!"

Oh, please. I've been haunting you for how long now?

"Two frickin' years. You'd think you'd get the message by now and move on."

See, I know you. When you get upset, you stuff yourself with junk food.

"So what? I can eat whatever I want. What the hell are you picking on me for?"

Because you're the only person who can see me.

Claire closed her eyes. "There. Now leave me alone."

Ha, ha. You're just so funny.

"You're still here?" Claire asked pointedly.

Yes and I'm not going anywhere. I'll only become more annoying.

"God knows that's the truth," Claire muttered, opening her eyes.

Kate did annoying better than anybody else, even Derek Jacob. With his weird sense of humor, he found amusement in insults, making it difficult to upset him. Apparently, it was a family trait.

Claire had run into his sister, Kristin, at the library. Not that she realized it at the time. When she heard somebody saying hello, she had looked up to see an attractive, slender woman with blue eyes walking up to the counter. Claire had smiled a slight greeting at the lady, thinking it was odd the woman was introducing herself to Claire.

"So, are you enjoying working down at the station?" Kristin had asked.

"It's alright," Claire had answered politely.

"The boys aren't giving you too much trouble, are they?"

"They're alright."

"Even Derek Jacob?"

Kristin gave Claire a knowing smile that irritated her. It clicked then, what this woman's interest in Claire was. Claire had little doubt she was one of Derek's many conquests. She wondered if this one was going to be as rude as Carolyn had been that morning.

"He's—"

"—alright," Kristin finished for her with a laugh. "You surprise me, Dorothy. I've never known a woman to describe him in such…bland terms."

"What do you want me to say?" Claire asked as her irritation turned to annoyance. "That he's the most annoying, repulsive man I've ever had the displeasure to meet?"

"I think you actually mean that." Kristin's smile grew bigger. "I just can't imagine why you would say it."

"Because with the way he behaves, he should have been pornographer. The man is lewd, crude, completely lacking in any social grace or sense of decorum, and those are his finer qualities."

"True, but he normally charms most women. In fact, he's very good at sweeping them off their feet."

"I got the impression he was a slut." That comment drew outright laughter from the other woman.

"He most certainly is," Kristin agreed. "But most women don't care about that. In fact, it sort of adds to his allure. You're the first woman I ever met he wanted who didn't want him back."

"How do you know he wants me?" Claire scowled, feeling the blush creeping into her cheeks. Kristin was wrong about her assumption. Derek had made Claire's body sing like no man ever had and that pissed her off.

"Woman's intuition?" Kristin offered with a cocked brow.

"You appear to know a lot about him."

"I should. I'm his twin sister."

Claire had been stumped, unsure how to respond. She had desperately looked for an excuse, any reason to escape now. Kristin would rat her out to the barbarian, she knew. Claire could imagine his delight in hearing her opinions. There would be revenge.

Hello? Kate intruded on Claire's brooding. *I'm still waiting.*

"You're a ghost, just imagine how long you can be left waiting."

Come on, Claire. Admit you're just annoyed because the chief makes you hot and you thought you were better than that.

"He annoys me because he just might be our killer!"

Pardon me?

Claire clenched her jaw tight and flopped back down on the couch. Kate had pushed her buttons and she'd blurted out the very thing she was trying to keep a secret from the ghost.

Claire was still reeling from the possibility herself. It had been a shock she hadn't been expecting. Of all the insults she felt justified in lobbing at Derek, murderer had not been on the list until her trip to the library.

She had gone there looking for Kathleen. Mysteriously, Kathleen's police file had been missing. Claire had hoped her disappearance had been covered by the local paper and spent two hours scrolling through the white and black strobe of the microfiche machine on full speed.

When Claire had finally found Kathleen, she had found Derek as well.

Her boyfriend, Derek Jacob, last saw Kathleen...

Claire's hands had started to tremble as the spicy combination of panic mixed with rage began to pump through her blood stream. She had fought not to give in to emotion. Carefully uncurling her fist, she had picked up her pen, forcing herself to jot down the information before reading on.

The days following Kathleen Harper's disappearance were chronicled in the Wilsonville Times. The disappearance of a teenage girl may have been statistically normal for the country at large, but for Wilsonville it was an anomaly.

The limited details of the case added to the ominous air of the articles. Kathleen had been out on a date with Derek. They had driven down a makeshift dirt road to a secluded spot to look out at the night sky over the marsh.

They had a fight—the details of the argument were not revealed — and Kathleen had run off. Derek had followed her and, realizing how upset she was, had gone back to get the truck.

Apparently he'd intended to pick her up in his truck and take her home, but, when he'd driven back, he couldn't find her. Derek had searched, the cops had searched, and bloodhounds had tried to track her. There was no trail to track. Kathleen Harper had simply vanished.

The articles did not provide any more facts. They focused instead on speculation and opinions. Nathan Harper was widely quoted for his belief in Derek's guilt. The police chief at the time, Ned Olsen, was just as widely quoted for his belief in Derek's innocence. Why Nathan believed in Derek's guilt was obvious. Why the chief did not, was never explained.

Claire could take a guess. She would have bet money Ned Olsen was a were, too. He had probably relied on his ability to scent deceit and cleared Derek. The "good, old boy" tradition, with a twist.

She spent almost an hour making as many notes as she could. Even if something didn't appear important at the time, there was no telling how future light would change that. She couldn't focus too much on the information itself, not yet ready to confront the possibility Derek was a killer. So, she simply transcribed it all.

Claire?

"What?"

You want to expand on how you get from jerk to murderer?

"You want to mind your own business?"

You know that's not going to happen.

"Well, then, you can just wait there expectantly, because I don't have anything to say to you."

Too bad. I have a lot to say to you. Want to hear it?

"No."

Then perhaps you should be the one talking.

"I'm going to have Alyssa exorcise you and send you back to whatever hellhole dimension you crawled out of to torment me."

Good. Then, when Agakiar has his way with you, I can torment you for all eternity.

"Fine! If you must know, I went to the library and looked up the details of Kathleen Harper's disappearance."

And?

Claire quickly went over the details of what she had learned.

Well, shit.

"That was helpful. I feel so much better now. Thanks."

Come on, Claire. You can't honestly think the police chief is a serial killer.

"Why not? He had motive and opportunity with Kathleen. He had access to her missing file."

Claire, he's a werewolf. Werewolves normally rip their prey to pieces when they go rogue. They don't turn into serial killers.

"Normally is not always, and nothing bars them from becoming serial killers. They're still part human."

You're serious. You are really considering him a suspect.

"I can't afford not to."

Derek is not Agakiar.

"What the hell does that have to do with anything?"

Oh, don't play dumb with me. I know what you're doing. You're sitting here wondering if you made the same mistake twice.

"Dumb?"

Making a mistake kills you, but making it twice? What are you going to do? Get out the whips and chains?

"What do you want me to do, Kate? Ignore the evidence? Just pretend it doesn't exist and remove Kathleen from the list because it would make my life easier? I can't do that."

Come on, Claire. Think about this. What do you need to prove his involvement or lack of it?

"I need to get into his house."

What are you looking for?

"Trophies, the missing police file, something of Kathleen's I could get a vision from."

Okay, so we get you into his house. That shouldn't be a big deal.

"Maybe you should go."

Why?

"It would easier for you."

If he is the killer, I doubt he left anything out in the open. That would mean I'd have to open and go through things. That takes a lot of energy. Not to mention cleaning up. I'm not sure I can do all that in one go.

"If I go, he'll smell me and know I've been in his house."

Not if he already knows you've been in his house.

"What are you suggesting?"

* * * *

Derek took another sip of beer as he flipped through the TV channels. There was nothing good on. He had a new book waiting in his den, but he didn't feel like reading. What he wanted to do was cross the street, sweep Dorothy into his arms and carry her off to bed.

The problem was he didn't know if it was Dorothy he was taking to bed. If he hadn't been so interested in her for other reasons, he may have noticed the telling clues. It had taken the shock of her not wanting to be called Dorothy, after making love, for him to realize the obvious.

His mind had been swirling all day, trying to put all the pieces together. That move she had pulled at the park had not been a lucky toss or an instinctive reaction. It had been a finely honed, trained reflex. The same for the move she had pulled when he come upon her jogging. That could have been a lucky hit, but taken with the toss, it was obvious Dorothy had some martial arts or self-defense training.

Where did a little assistant get that kind of training? Perhaps an older brother had taught her those moves or she had taken a few classes. It could be nothing, but he didn't think so.

He hadn't caught much of her phone call in the truck, but he had caught the scent of rage and fear. It had been just as strong as the odor of her deception earlier today. He had thought at the time she was mad at him, but now he wondered.

Derek's cop brain instantly jumped to the idea she was running from somebody. Probably a man, given her stubborn resistance toward the relationship developing between them.

Whatever the reasons for her odd behavior, he was going to find the answers. It was too bad his day had been so filled with meetings he hadn't had time to get her file from the personnel office. He would take care of that in the morning. Then he would start investigating.

That he had to go to such lengths irritated him. He didn't want any secrets between them.

A pounding at his door broke him out of his thoughts. Derek rose and lazily went to answer the angry, incessant pounding. He paused when he heard her voice, anticipation stirring in his blood.

"Open up, you rodent!" Dorothy fist hit the door in another series of bangs. "I want to talk to you!"

She exploded across the threshold the second he opened the door. Pushing the thick wood out of her way, she began to poke him in the chest hurling accusations with each hard jab. Derek winced away from her finger.

"Listen you…you rodent from hell." Dorothy advanced on him as he backed away from her jabbing finger. "I should rip you from limb to limb!"

"What have I done now?"

"What?" Dorothy shrieked. "Fucking me over your desk, does that ring a bell?"

"You're getting around to that now? That was this morning."

"Yes," Dorothy snarled. "I'm getting around to it now. Unlike *some* people, *I* know how to be a professional at work! Unlike *some* people, who abuse their authority to *humiliate* their employees by *sexually* molesting them in their office, *I* prefer to wait until an *appropriate* time to handle the matter."

Dorothy stabbed him in the chest with her finger with every sneered word. Derek had back away until he pressed against the wall. With nowhere to go, he grabbed her finger.

"That hurts!"

"It's supposed to." Dorothy yanked her finger out of his grasp. "You should be lucky I don't deck you after what you did."

"Deck me?" Derek snorted before puffing up his chest. "Go on, little bit. If it will make you feel better, hit me."

"Don't tempt me," Dorothy growled. "You sank to your lowest level today."

"You didn't appear to mind at the time." Derek shrugged, unrepentant.

"How dare you!" Dorothy shriek.

"I understand. You don't want to admit you're just as lewd and perverted as I am. So, if it makes you feel better, by all means, blame me."

"Where did you get your psychology degree? A box of cereal?"

"Actually, it came as a prize with my six-pack," Derek corrected her in all seriousness.

Her response was instantaneous. Without warning her fist slammed into his chest, thumping him back into the wall. Derek gasped for breath as he stumbled back.

He knew he told her to hit him, had taunted her into doing just that, but he hadn't expected it to hurt. Gingerly, he rubbed the throbbing spot on his chest as he glanced at her hand. It must have hurt her, too.

If so, she was hiding it well. She looked pleased with herself as she studied him with a smug little smile, her eyes shining with satisfaction. Her arms were crossed over her chest, her hips jutting out slightly as she waited for him to recover.

"What the hell did you do that for?" Derek demanded when he finally caught his breath.

"You told me to. What's wrong, Beevis? Were you expecting a little girlie slap?"

"Well, yeah!" Derek straightened, stepping away from the wall. "Where did you learn to hit like that?"

"None of your business."

"You're a real piece of work, you know that?" Derek asked shaking his head.

"Me!" Dorothy fell open. "Perhaps you should look in the mirror, Butthead."

"Hey, now that's an idea." He snagged her wrist and started to drag her down the hall.

"Let me go!" Dorothy struggled against his hold.

Chapter 9

Claire managed to get a quick glimpse of a study, then a room with exercise equipment, before she found herself in a bedroom. It was obviously Derek's from the oversized, dark wood furniture. Everything screamed male from the simple bed coverings to the plain wooden blinds covering the windows.

There was not a bit of frill or softness to the room. Even the woodsy-spicy smell was elementally male. It fit the image of the hard-bodied police chief beside her, but it lacked the teasing, irreverent attitude of the man within.

Claire scowled. She had known when she let Kate talk her into this insane idea they would end up in his bedroom. Part one of the plan was done. Now it was up to Kate to live up to her end and pull off a distraction that would pull Derek out of the house before things went too far between them.

"What? Expecting a messy bed and dirty underwear thrown on the floor?" Derek chuckled, misreading her expression.

"You forgot the pictures of naked women tacked up on the walls." Claire forced a growl into her voice.

As much as she didn't want to like Derek, as much as she had fought against it, she couldn't disguise the fact it was exhilarating to be near him. Swapping insults and comebacks, anticipating whatever insane thing might come out of his mouth next. In every way, trying to deal with him was a challenge.

He could not be the killer. She could not be wrong about him.

"Now, over here," Derek walked her over to the large, cedar-framed mirror that dominated the wall over his dresser. "This is what we're looking for."

"I guess it's a good thing you don't need glasses or we just might have missed it."

"It's because of my poor eyesight, I got such a big mirror." Derek moved behind her as he spoke. He leaned in close to whisper. "That way I can see every detail."

Claire understood immediately what he was implying. The mirror was set directly across from the bed. Whatever Derek did, with whomever he was with, he'd be able to watch a tantalizing show.

"I'm surprised you didn't put it on the ceiling over the bed."

"Too heavy." His breath tickled against her ear causing her stomach muscles to tighten and quiver.

"So you went with a camera, right?" Claire retorted, her hoarse voice betraying her desire.

"You are just one shock after another." Derek hugged her close. "I never thought of that."

"As depraved as you are?"

"I'm not the one who brought up the idea," Derek whispered huskily. She could feel his cock growing, stretching against his jeans to fill the small gap between them and brush against her bottom.

"You would have thought of it eventually."

"Possibly."

He turned her to face him, locking his arms around her waist to hold her pressed against him his hardness. Heaven. Everything about the way he felt was heaven, Claire thought, savoring the fit of their bodies.

"Tell me, would you let me film you?"

"Uh, no."

Already her body was beginning to respond to the warm pressure of his. He was doing that subtle rubbing thing he had done when he'd pinned her against the wall in the lagoon. It had a devastating effect on her defenses.

She could not stop herself from melting into him, cuddling his erection and returning the subtle rubbing motion. She ached with need, had been suffering that fine pain all day, despite her attempts to deny it.

"Come on, sweetness."

"Never going to happen."

Derek was looking down at her with that feral, hungry lust darkening his blue eyes. No one had ever looked at her with such an open, honest expression of need. He was irresistible. He drugged Claire's senses, making rational thought impossible and leaving her willing to agree to anything.

"Don't get shy now, honey." Derek head lowered. His hot, husky voice brushing against her nerves, enflaming them with desire. "Have you ever watched yourself being pleasured?"

"No." Her answer was barely audible.

"I think it's time we correct that."

"Derek."

"We'll start with a kiss. One little kiss, where's the harm in that?" He coaxed, brushing his lips against her in light, fleeting caresses.

"You know what you're kisses do to me," Claire whispered not truly protesting.

"And you knew when you knocked on my door I'd be kissing you before you left. Didn't you?"

"Yes, I knew."

"You hunger, the same as I do. There's no point in fighting it." He had pulled back to meet her soft, sultry gaze with his hungry, needy one.

"No point," Claire agreed, reaching up to trace the curve of his mouth with her fingers.

He opened his mouth, biting down on the tip of her finger before soothing the small hurt with a lick of tongue. Claire trembled under the teasing caress and instinctively pulled her hand back. He caught her wrist, holding her still as he nipped and kissed his way to her wrist.

Searing heat burned from her palm, through her arm and spread out her body until her breast tightened, her nipples puckered, and her pussy clenched. The need to feel him stroking into her overwhelmed all other considerations. Whatever the price, this moment was worth it.

Derek gave her plenty time to object, to escape, but Claire was beyond pretending to protest. When his head dipped, she met him halfway, moaning as their lips touched. Catching her bottom lip with his teeth, he tasted her slowly before slipping his tongue between her parted lips to deepen the kiss.

Quickly the kiss flamed out of control. He tasted of beer and man. Delicious. The taste made her head spin with the need for more. She caught his tongue between her lips and she sucked on it, eliciting a moan from him.

Her hands gripped his shoulders as she tried to mesh their bodies through the layers of clothes. She wanted to be pressed against him, skin to skin. Her nails bit into the cotton of his shirt, digging into the hard muscle beneath, wanting to rip the offending fabric out of the way.

She had never felt such overwhelming need before meeting Derek. It was undeniable and left her desperate for more. Of their own volition, her legs lifted, encircling his waist and putting his cock just where she wanted it, needed it, pressed right against her weeping pussy.

Derek helped, his hand slipping under her ass to hold her in place so he could grind against her. The hard edge of the dresser pressed against her lower back as he began to thrust into the cradle of her thighs. He stroked his tongue into her mouth in rhythm with each thrust, pressing his cock against her cloth-covered mound.

His kiss took on a new level of savagery, devouring her mouth as if he were starved for the taste and feel of her. He plundered her moist interior, tasting, stroking, twining his tongue with hers, and driving her need higher.

The need for oxygen finally drove them apart. Forehead to forehead, their panting mingled as they attempted to catch their breath. Her lips tingled, her body burned and her mind was absent any lucid thought.

"Ah, sweetheart," Derek whispered raggedly. "You tempted me as none ever has. There are so many things I want to do to you right now."

He lifted his head and Claire swallowed hard at the intensity of his gaze. She licked her suddenly dry lips. Derek's eyes dropped to her mouth, darkening as they followed her tongue's movement. He groaned, leaning in to trace the path her tongue had just taken with his own.

Claire trembled under the gentle assault. The back of his fingers caressed her from cheeks to lips, his tongue following. They traced over her trembling lips, his mouth settling on top of hers a moment later.

This time the kiss was a slow savoring. Claire opened her mouth and let Derek take control. His hands had smoothed their way down her neck and closed gently over her breasts. Instantly, her breast swelled, begging for his touch.

Claire sighed into his mouth, arching her back to increase the pressure of his hand on her swollen flesh. Derek took the offering, his thumb reaching out to brush her nipple. The hard nub seemed wired in a direct current to her clit.

As her nipple tightened and tingled, so did the tender numb hidden in her moist folds. Again and again his thumb moved and her clit pulsed until her cunt clenched, sending a spasm through her inner muscles and a wave of arousal soaking into her panties.

Her bottom unconsciously wiggled, changing the motion of her hips, grinding into his. The slow side-to-side motion had his hand tightening slightly over her breast and her silently cursing the shirt interfering with his intoxicating touch. She wanted to be skin to skin, to feel his rough hands against her soft smoothness.

He pinched her nipple hard in response. She broke the kiss to gasp as he repeated the assault on her tender nub. The painful sensation quickly turned to excruciating pleasure and she begged for more.

Derek gave it to her, rolling and pinching her nipples roughly through the fabric of her shirt. His mouth nibbled a path to her ears as she cried out her pleasure.

"So responsive, so passionate, and mine. Only mine," Derek growled. "Say it."

"Only yours," Claire stuttered, unaware of what she was saying.

He bit down on her earlobe in response. The bite was hard enough to make her moan before he sucked on the small hurt. His tongue snacked out to trace the delicate shell of her ear before dipping in.

"Please." Claire heard herself whimper, not sure what she was begging for.

"Please what?" Derek murmured into her ear.

"Touch me. Please."

"Where?"

"I don't know." She did, she just couldn't bring herself to say it.

"Tell me where you want me to touch you?" Derek insisted. Her only response was to moan and rub herself against him.

"Here?" Derek twisted her nipples making her writhe with the pleasure. "Or somewhere else?"

"I...I...oh, please," Claire begged, her hips pushing against his with heightened urgency.

"Here?" Derek slid a hand down to cup her mound. Claire's eyes fluttered closed as her hips arched, thrusting her crotch into his palm.

"This is where you want me to touch you?"

"Yes, please. I need it."

"And if I give you what you need, what will you give me?" Derek bartered as his hand slid up to the waistband of her jeans. Claire's stomach tightened at the feel of his fingertips. The small motion made a gap that allowed him to easily slide his hand under the denim and over the cotton of her panties.

"What will you give me, sweetness?"

"Anything you want, just...please..." Claire begged, beyond caring what she was saying.

"Anything?"

"Yes, please. Anything you want." Claire hips jerked trying to force him to pet her weeping flesh.

"And what if I want you at my beck and call? What if I want you whenever I demand it, in any way I want it? Will you give me that? Will you submit to me?"

"I..." Claire blinked as his words slowly registered.

He was asking for total submission, the right to command her passion at his free will. He wanted to master her. Was she not enslaved already in her desire for him?

"Give me what I want, sweetness, or I'll deny you."

"You wouldn't?" Claire swallowed hard.

"Wouldn't I?" Derek began to rub his fingers over her sodden panties. Unerringly finding her clit, he began to torture the small nub with light, teasing strokes. "Can you afford to take that risk?"

"Please, Derek."

"You know the price."

"Yes, fine. Just, please, touch me."

Claire no longer cared what she was agreeing too. He was driving her mad with his fingers. She needed more, needed to feel his fingers on her pussy, buried in it.

"As you wish."

Derek's hands slipped beneath the elastic band of her panties and slid into the wet folds of her pussy. Claire sobbed with delight as he found her clit and began to rub it. He matched the motions with the nipple his other hand had trapped, whirling the two sensitive nubs faster and faster.

First one, then two, then three thick fingers penetrated her clenching core. Relentlessly he began to fuck her with his fingers. Claire cried out as her hips began to pump in rhythm with his hands.

In minutes, her body was exploding with ecstasy. Claire screamed as her body convulsed with the power of her release. Her eyes clenched tight as her body arched on the lash of pleasure. A second later she collapsed against him, completely satiated.

"Mmm."

Derek's murmured sound of satisfaction had her eyes fluttering open. She felt her cheeks heat with a blush as she watched him suck her cream from his fingers.

"Tasty. I want more." His tone was almost inhuman, guttural and low. "Time to pay, sweetheart."

"Pay?" Claire's voice was little more than a squeak.

Derek just smiled and stepped back. Her legs fell from his hips to the floor. The rubbery limbs were useless and she sagged against the dresser for support. Her stomach began to tighten with the intent look in his eyes.

"Undress for me."

"Wha…what?" Claire blinked, her mind still a riot. Her body was still shimmering with the aftershocks of her release.

"You promised, anything I want, whenever I want it. Now, I want you to undress for me."

Her mouth opened to protest, but no words came out. She trembled under the demand she found in his eyes. He appeared larger, harder, dominating. Heat flashed through Claire's body and she shivered, nervous about making herself so vulnerable to him.

"Take off the shirt," he ordered.

Of their own volition, her fingers moved up. They trembled with fear and anticipation as she reached for her first button. Slowly she began to unbutton her shirt. Derek's eyes narrowed, his jaw tightening as he watched her slow progress.

By the time she undid the last one, her whole body was shaking with alternating pulses of cold fear and hot desire. Her breath was coming out in shallow pants, her nipples straining against the fabric of her bra, begging to be free, but her hands hesitated, uncertain of her actions.

She felt vulnerable, out of control and controlled, all at the same time. Never had she been the submissive type, but, then, never had her lover been dominating. There was no missing the feral look of power mixed into his lust filled eyes.

"Take it off, now."

The hard edge in his tone held a thread of threat, warning his patience was wearing thin. The sound had her body tightening with erotic fear at the idea of disobeying him. What would he do?

Claire was not ready to find out. With one last nervous glance at him, she shrugged off the shirt. Her stomach tightened painfully as she felt self-conscious in her plain, white cotton bra. She was sure Derek was used to more sophisticated styles of undergarments on his women

She had never been one to spend money on nice underwear or sexy lingerie. It had never bothered her before. Now, though, she wished she owned one nice panty and bra set.

The heat in his gaze didn't dim, though. Just the opposite, his eyes were near black, his face flushed with lust, his lips pulled back in a savage snarl. The knowledge he wanted her, wanted to see more, gave her the courage to undo the clasp at the back.

A moment later the bra fell to the floor, leaving her bared to his gaze. Claire shivered, feeling more exposed than she ever had before. A hidden part of her spirit awakened and begged for Derek's praise.

As if sensing what she needed, he reached out to cup her breast. Claire sighed and leaned into his touch. He caressed her breast for just a moment before he pulled away. She would have followed him but the hard look in his eyes had her stilling.

"You're the most beautiful woman I have ever seen." Derek smiled with masculine satisfaction and approval. "I want to see more. Take the rest off."

Anxious to please him, Claire heeled off her canvass sneakers before reaching for the button on the waistband of her jeans. As she lowered the zipper, his hand moved to grip his jean-covered cock. She watched him stroke himself through the fabric as she shimmied out of her jeans.

They pooled at the floor around her ankles leaving her in nothing but her plain white, granny panties. His gaze followed her hand to her hips and she slowly pushed the panties down until they fell to the floor.

Derek's hand tightened over his cock as he stared at her glistening honey-colored curls. She was shaking all over, tremors of anxiety mixed with anticipation. For a moment the only sound was her labored breathing.

"Turn around."

Claire closed her eyes and turned, unable to look at her naked image with Derek's fully clothed one behind her. She started when she felt his hands settle on her shoulders. He slid his hands down her arms.

When he got to her wrists, he pulled them forward so she was bent over the dresser top. Those hands were lifting her by the hips, moving her back. The position forced her to lean more of her weight on her hands and they curled into fists, imagining the picture she made.

"Spread your feet." His voice was hard with command, his thigh forcing its way between hers, making her obey.

Cool air hit the fluid coating the top of her thighs and she instinctively tried to close them, to hide the evidence of her recent release. Instantly he smacked her ass, sending sharp sparks of pain that vibrated to her clit, making it throb with pleasure. Claire cried out over both the humiliation and the thrill.

"Do not close those thighs," Derek growled the warning. "Or I'll punish you. Understand?"

"Yes," Claire squeaked.

"Good. Open your eyes."

Claire could feel the heat of her blush as she slowly lifted her lids. Embarrassment and arousal flushed her face as she looked at herself in the mirror. Her wanton image looked back, her breasts hanging and her legs spread in invitation.

Derek was behind her, fully clothed, his features tight with lust. Her muscles clench with the erotic image they made. He was forcing her to watch her own submission. There would be no denying later it was freely given.

She moaned and started to close her eyes. Another sharp smack had her ass blazing, her clit tingling. She could see the flash of lust cross her features as her lips parted on another groan.

"No," Derek commanded. "Watch."

With no warning, he dipped his fingered into her cunt. He rubbed her already slippery clit for a second before slipping down into her weeping channel. She watched as his fingers fucked in and out of her cunt. In seconds her hips were countering the thrust of his fingers, increasing her pleasure until she thought she was about to come again.

He stopped, making her whimper and cry with disappointment. Her hips thrust back, pushing her ass into the large erection pressing against her. Instead of heeding the command of her body, he cupped her mound possessively with his palm.

"I want you to shave this sweet little pussy," Derek growled. "Next time I fuck you in front of this mirror I want you bare. I want to see everything."

When she didn't respond to his command, he lifted his hand. Before she could guess his intent, Derek slapped her pussy hard. He angled his hand so her clit took most the impact. Piercing shards of pleasure ripped through her tender numb, making her whole body spasm with scorching pleasure. Shocked by the sizzling sensation, she cried out.

"You are going to shave this pussy," Derek repeated in a hard, commanding tone.

"I don't know how," Claire whimpered, her voice barely audible.

"Then I'll do it for you."

Chapter 10

Before Claire could respond to that shocking, embarrassing idea he dipped his fingers back into her slit. Gathering her juices, he lifted his hand to one of her hardened nipples. He pinched and pulled the nipple before moving on to the other one. The discarded nipple glistened with her juices and puckered against the cool air.

He squeezed and rolled her other nipple before moving down her body to again bury his hand between her legs. This time he ignored her weeping entrance and focused on tormenting her clit. He circled, rubbed and pinched the sensitive nub sending waves of electric pleasure up her spine.

Pleasure as she had never felt with any other man had her muscles trembling, tightening, as the blood roared through her body pushing her toward an orgasm. She wanted a bared pussy now, to be able to see the tanned fingers toying with her pale, pink flesh. The erotic sight would push her over the edge that Derek was skillfully keeping her on.

"You're so hot, so wet and slick with your need," Derek whispered against her ear. "I can smell your pussy and it makes my cock ache to be buried in it. Nothing has ever felt as good as stroking into your tight little cunt, feeling it grip down on me."

He plunged three thick fingers into her sheath and Claire felt the walls of her cunt grip down, trying to hold him inside her.

"Ah, just like that." Derek sighed. "It makes my cock throb with demand just to feel you gripping my fingers. You like that don't you, baby?"

"Yes," Claire whined, her hips thrusting forward trying to recapture his fingers as they withdrew.

"Ah, such temptation," Derek groaned. "The last two times, need overwhelmed me and I gave into the urge to fuck you. Not tonight, tonight I'm going to enjoy you, feast on you."

Claire met his eyes and she could read the hungry desperation in them. She realized he might be controlling her, but he was no more in control of the situation than she was. He was being driven by a need, a lust, as desperate as hers. Derek was at the mercy of his body's desires, the same as hers.

Fear and excitement twisted inside her as she watched him lower to his knees behind her.

"Wider." His hands trying to force her legs open further followed the command. "Show me your pussy."

Claire didn't fight his command, excited by his words. She spread her legs wider, arching her back to give him a better view of her swollen slit. Derek growled his approval and nipped her ass. Claire cried out at the sudden assault and he soothed the small hurt with a kiss.

He nipped and kissed his way down the globe of her ass until his head dipped between the crevice and his tongue reached out to lick his way through her slit. Claire cried out at the lash of pleasure, so overwhelming it bordered on pain. Instinctively, she moved away from his mouth, seeking a moment of clarity to catch her breath.

His hands bit into her hips as he held her still for his tasting. His tongue darted in and out of cunt, licking upward to tease her clit and down to lap up her juices. Lust overwhelmed Claire and she writhed , bucking backward in an attempt to force him to give a longer, deeper caress of his tongue.

His fingers tightened on her hips as he covered her clit with his mouth. Sucking the little nub between his teeth, he flicked it with tongue repeatedly until she was pleading, begging him to let her come. When she felt the first rays of her climax detonating in her body, he stopped suddenly.

Claire growled and bucked harder against his mouth in demand. She felt like an animal, a desperate bitch in heat, needing her mate to fuck her, to claim her and master her with the rough ferocity she knew lurked just beneath Derek's skin.

"Beautiful. Delicious," Derek whispered, his breath heating her over sensitized flesh. "You satisfy me as no other could. When I'm near you, all I can think about is bringing you pleasure, taking my own. You were made for me, meant to be mine. Mine to pleasure and protect."

Claire felt her heart tighten painfully, threatening to burst with emotion at his words. Before she could respond, he licked her again, making her body clench with more than just the desires of the flesh, but the desires of her heart and soul.

As if freed from an invisible leash, he devoured her. His tongue felt as if it grew, too long to be human as it fucked into her with greedy, carnal abandon. The climax he had moments ago denied her, broke over her. Hard, consuming waves crashed through her body, making her muscles tighten with such force she was sure they would splinter from the pressure.

Derek didn't stop, didn't give her a chance to recover, but continued to consume her. His mouth worked over her pulsing flesh as she felt his teeth lengthen, nipping into her with bites that made her throb with pained pleasure. His tongue thrust deeper into her, farther than any tongue should have been able to. It swirled around, stroking her clenched inner muscles until it hit her most sensitive spot.

Claire cried out as she came again. With the aftershocks of her first climax feeding into the second, she felt dizzy and disoriented. She could feel the inner muscles of her cunt tighten down, suctioning his tongue deeper, as the lengthening marauder fucked into her repeatedly.

Another wave of icy hot shards pierced her body and she sobbed as he relentlessly tongued her with untamed abandon. Her cunt felt swollen, burning, painfully sensitive. Every taste, lick, stroke, of his magical tongue sent bolts of pure pleasure through her.

He licked his way up to her clit, lashing out at it mercilessly until she could feel her canal tighten back down, the beginning pulses of another explosion building. Two thick fingers thrust into only to retreat, tracing a slick line up to the tight rosebud hidden between her ass cheeks.

Claire tensed, knowing she should be feeling fear and not the tight clench of excited anticipation. He fucked his tongue deep into her dripping cunt as he shoved his fingers up the tight mouth of her ass. Claire screamed, pain blending almost immediately with pleasure as her world crashed in around her again.

Begging for a moment, she clawed at the dresser, futilely trying to escape, to have one second of peace, before he continued. Derek ignored her pleas. Tightening his grip until it became painful, he held her still as he continued to fuck into both her pussy and her ass. Claire was sure he was trying to kill her, at the very least drive her insane.

She came twice more before he had his fill. She lay crumpled and sobbing on the dresser's top, unable to form a coherent thought. Her eyes were open, staring listlessly at her reflection as tears and sweat mingled and her lips trembled as her lungs bellowed trying to drag in air.

She could not stop the spasms rippling through her muscles, as Derek rose behind her. She could see enough to read the savage intent in his gaze. He was not done with her. The rasp of a zipper being lower followed the pop of a button, the sounds confirming her suspicions.

Claire tried to protest, to ask for time to recover, but the words that came out were mumbled and incoherent. Her body ignored her commands to resist, too worn out from pleasure. Her limbs were weak and pliable as he positioned himself behind her.

She felt his hands lift her hips, the thick head of his cock nudging against her opening. His cock was hard, engorged, the tip moist with his excitement. Claire writhed against his hold, trying to escape as he steadily pushed into her.

"Mine," he growled, lifting her onto her tiptoes.

He rammed his cock all the way into her clenching cunt. Without hesitation, he started to violently pound into her. She cried out, boneless and weary, with the overload of carnal pleasure. Convinced she was to spent too come again, Claire gasped as she felt her body tightening, preparing for another detonation.

She opened her eyes and focused for a moment on his expression. His face was tightened, flushed with need. His lips were pulled back and two long fangs protruded, glistening with her cream.

For a second, their eyes connected. She could see the wildness recede slightly before it was snuffed out and his gaze darkened back to black. Claire closed her eyes, understanding it was not Derek who was fucking her now, but the wolf. The beast dressed in the man's body was claiming her as his.

For long, torturous minutes his sharp, guttural grunts mixed with her keening cries of pleasure. The sound was unable to drown out the slap of his balls beating into her puffed cunt lips with every savage stroke.

She burned with need as she swirled dizzyingly into another vortex. Her mouth opened on a soundless scream as pleasure crashed through her, twisting her body beneath him in wanton abandon. Colors collided against her closed lids as she came in a blinding wave of pleasure.

For a moment she could feel every perfect sensation, the feel of satin stretched over steel pushing through cramping muscles, the roughened fingertips biting into her hips as he held her up for another grinding thrust, his hot breath rasping against her shoulder, the sharp penetrations of teeth into her shoulder and then it all crashed down on her. Claire came until the world went black.

* * * *

Derek felt the wonderful, nearly painful swelling of his balls and trust deep into the wet, clinging cunt one last time. He held himself there as he exploded, allowing the pulsing sheath around his hardened cock to milk the pleasure from his body. In one long violent stream, he filled her full of his cum before collapsing on top of her.

His legs trembled as he took in great gasping breaths, as he lost control of his body. For several moments he stayed there, unable to focus on anything. Slowly the metallic taste of blood roused him from his stupor. With wide eyes, he lifted his head to look at the bite mark on her shoulder.

He didn't remember doing that. Then again, he didn't remember much of the past hour. He had felt everything, tasted everything, but it was the wolf that had been in control. The wolf did not care about laws or rules. It only cared about one thing. Claiming his mate.

Ah, hell. Derek sighed. He had mated her without her consent, or even her knowledge at what he was. Knowing he had done wrong could not penetrate his satisfaction.

Derek stroked his hand down her smooth back, marveling at the extraordinary gift he had been given. Once, a long time ago when he had been young and reckless, he had thought he had ruined his chance for this moment. In a reckless frenzy for sex, he had claimed the wrong woman.

At first, he had rebelled against the knowledge of what he'd done, but he'd quickly owned up to his responsibility. Even as he tried to make his mistake right, he had lost the opportunity. The guilt and sadness of that time assailed him for a moment.

He had never thought he was worthy of a second chance, but it had been given to him anyway. For a moment, Kathleen's face danced before his eyes and he closed them. Too often, he had seen her image in more nightmares than dreams.

Silently, he offered up a prayer and a promise. Praying Kathleen and their child were at peace, he promised he would never fail with his heart's mate. He would never see her image as nothing more than a ghost.

Opening his eyes, he stepped back, withdrawing from Dorothy's body. Gently he lifted her into his arms. She murmured a protest before settling back down. Derek grinned. Never before had he fucked a woman until she'd passed out. He was proud he had saved that treat for his mate.

Planning on fulfilling the promise just made, he laid her on his bed and went to prepare the bath. She mumbled a protest but didn't wake while he tenderly held her in his arms and bathed her. Remembering what she said and his promise, he very carefully shaved the curls from her pussy.

Derek grinned as he imagined what her response would be come morning. Whatever it was, tonight she was all sweetness. That had a lot to do with her being asleep, no doubt.

With that last thought, he carried her back to the bed. She sighed and Derek echoed the sound as he snuggled her close. As he closed his eyes, he promised tomorrow he would explain who he was, what he was, and he would make sure she did the same.

* * * *

Thursday: 2:15 am

A shrill scream had Claire's eyes popping open. For a moment she was disoriented. The bedroom was dark, but even without the morning sunlight she knew it was not her bedroom. The grumble of a masculine voice had her mind focusing.

Derek. Claire burrowed her head deeper into the pillow. The soft cotton case smelled like him. The scent relaxed her and she began to drift back off to sleep.

The sounds of clothing rustling caught her attention. He was leaving? It was the middle of the night. Where the hell did he think he was going? If she had more energy, she would have asked that question.

A moment later she felt a kiss being brushed a long her temple before the comforter was tucked more tightly around her. Claire sighted contently and snuggled deeper into the bed, warmed by his attention. A few seconds later she heard a door close in the distance, and again began to drift back off into sleep.

Claire! Get up! Kate bellowed rudely in her head.

"Go away," Claire mumbled pulling the blanket over her head.

Get your lazy ass out of bed.

"Don't want to."

I spent all night setting up this distraction while you were enjoying yourself with your werewolf. Now get up and get to work!

To emphasize her point Kate whipped the blanket off Claire. Claire shot up, growling and looking for the ghost. She did not materialize, but that didn't stop Claire from cussing at her.

Remember Kathleen? Kate snapped. *The missing girl you're supposed to be investigating?*

Claire cringed at that sharp reminder. Sad to say, she had forgotten Kathleen all together. Kate was not going to allow that to continue.

I'll keep the boys entertained for a while. You see what you can find.

Claire rubbed her eyes and yawned. Grumbling to herself, she crawled out of bed. Almost immediately, she realized that somebody had taken a razor to pussy. Her mound was now as naked as the day she'd been born. Derek, that jerk, had shaved her in her sleep. Heat suffused her face as she recalled their earlier conversations. He had asked her, no, told her to do it.

Claire cringed when she thought of how it was going to itch when the hair grew back in. He had her cornered. She was either going to suffer an itchy crotch or have to maintain it.

Duke, roused from his bed in the corner by all the commotion, greeted her eagerly, anticipating the start of a new day even if it was still the tail end of the previous one. Claire shoved him out of the way and reached for her clothes. Duke was not to be ignored.

She was tired and grumpy and not in the mood for the enthusiastic dog's shenanigans. He had a ball tucked into his mouth and when she pulled on it, he let go. Backing up he watched the ball with bright eyes and a swishing tail. The tennis ball was disgusting, coated in a thick slime of slobber with bits of dirt stuck all over it.

Quickly, Claire tossed it and, as she had expected, the dog chased it. The plan backfired when he reappeared a minute later offering the ball to her for another round. She worked her way out of the bedroom and down to the den, stopping repeatedly to throw the ball for the large, goofy retriever.

She started her search in the study. The room made Claire jealous. She had always dreamed of having a library just like this. Warm, dark wood floors contrasted with the lighter wood used in the built in bookcases. They lined the walls, spanning floor to ceiling and filled with books.

Claire couldn't deny her shock. Not that she thought Derek was illiterate, but she hadn't expected him to be a reader. From the collection of books that dominated his shelves, Claire could tell his interest ran in three directions.

He enjoyed science fiction, specifically space exploration and robotics books. There was a large collection of history books, focusing on war. Then there was her favorite section, the mystery novels. He did not have any books from her favorite author Nan Grimes. Unfortunately, showing bad taste as far as she was concerned, he had almost every of one JC Colt's mystery novels.

It figured. When they did have something in common, they couldn't agree on the specifics. Well, she wouldn't hold her breath that one day he would have her book up there. Even if he did not know her real name, with his bad taste he wouldn't know good fiction if he saw it.

Claire dragged herself away from ogling his library, focusing on the search for the missing police files. Any clue would help determine his involvement in the Kathleen Harper case. A cursory glance showed little, except an old picture of Kathleen Harper, framed and collecting dust off in the corner of one shelf.

Claire studied the image. Kathleen was dressed primly in what had probably been her Sunday finest. It was disorienting to look at her. Disheartening, too. It was like looking at a picture of Claire herself at that age. Except, Claire had not had any Sunday finest.

Carefully she dismantled the frame to check for any writing on the back. There was none, nor was there anything hidden in the frame. A quick search of the built-in lower cabinets revealed a storage box with the missing reports.

There was little more in the police file than there had been in the newspaper articles. There was some background information on Kathleen but not much. Claire guessed everybody knew the details of her family. Her father had been cleared as a suspect because he'd been at a bar with several friends. Her brother had been out gigging, again with friends, and her mother was deceased.

Several witness statements claimed Derek had been seeing Kathleen for a short time. She was not his normal type. Kathleen was described as reserved and shy, where Derek had been more social and outgoing. Derek had a string of girlfriends and all indications were he had not been faithful to any one woman. On the other hand, Derek was Kathleen's first boyfriend.

An odd mix, they had started dating after she had been assigned his tutor for a calculus class. Derek, not surprisingly, had been the star quarterback with not-so-hot grades. Kathleen had been the nerd, focusing on attaining an academic scholarship to college.

Kathleen's father had been too drunk to care what his daughter did, but Nathan had objected strongly to his sister dating Derek. Apparently, Derek and Nathan had several run-ins before Kathleen's disappearance. Afterward, Nathan had outright accused Derek of killing his sister and the cops of not caring because the Harpers were poor and the Jacobs were well respected.

There was one piece of bagged evidence — the last reminder of the missing girl — her golden cross and necklace. The cops had found the necklace at the end of the dirt road. The clasp was broken and the notes indicated the cops thought it had been damaged as she struggled with her assailant.

Claire studied the object of worship through the plastic bag. It had been a long time since she'd worn one of those. She smiled sadly. It figured. The only thing she could get a reading from and she couldn't touch it, not with Agakiar's mark on her.

Um, don't mean to interrupt, Kate appeared on the other side of the desk. *I'm tiring out. If you have everything you came for, can we call it a night?*

"Yeah." Claire dropped the evidence bag back into the box. "I've got everything I need."

So, guilty or not?

"The jury is still out."

Chapter 11

The morning wore on with no sign of Dorothy. Derek sat in his grandfather's old rocking chair, feet propped on the railing, becoming more moody by the second. He was tired, miserable and at the edge of his patience.

He had been that way since he had returned late last night to an empty bed. He had gone through pains to get up early, hoping to catch Dorothy before she left for work. When he had seen the empty driveway across the street, he had assumed she had ducked him again. He had dressed and gone into work.

Fully expecting to find her there, hiding behind her shield of professionalism, he had intended on dragging her out of the office and back home. Only problem — Dorothy was not at work or anywhere else he had looked.

Ace had smugly explained she had called into Baker and claimed she was sick. Derek knew it was an outright lie. That wasn't what had Ace smirking.

Derek suspected all his officers knew that he was having difficulties corralling his mate. Even if they didn't know the specifics, they were obviously amused she was being difficult. His officers probably thought it was his penance for all the easy women who had come before her.

More than once he had competed with one of officers for some beauty's affection. Derek had always won, leaving his officers to mutter that one day he would get his. Now the day had come and they were delighted.

When he had returned home to wait for Dorothy, he had found Duke whining at the study's closed door. Derek had opened the door for the dog. Duke had immediately gone in and retrieved his ball from under Derek's desk. Derek had frowned, as he smelled Dorothy's sweet scent in the room. Why had she come in here before she left?

He scanned the room quickly, noticing the picture of Kathleen was no longer dusty. Derek had kept the picture as a reminder. Sometimes he would just stare at it and go over the details of her disappearance in his head. He never touched it. It was too hard, too emotional of an experience. Somehow touching the frame or the picture hurt. He let it sit there gathering dust.

Now, though, it was clean, the dust had magically disappeared. He followed the clean trail down to cabinet where he kept Kathleen's file. A quick rummage and he was sure she had taken nothing, but had simply looked through the files. The oddities surrounding Dorothy were no longer amusing him. The woman was up to something and he meant to know what.

It was obvious that Dorothy was a master at games. A quick call and a little sweet-talking got Sherry Randal, the personnel department secretary, to reveal Dorothy had not filled out any paperwork. Derek doubted that the efficient, by-the-books assistant had forgotten.

Whatever was going on Dorothy was his mate and he would handle it, just as soon as she got home. The very first thing she was going to explain was how she pulled off that stunt last night. It was probably not the most important thing, but it had been so strange he had to know how she did it.

The entire episode had been beyond weird. It had started with a call to 911 from a breathless woman. She had whispered she was being held hostage by her deranged husband at an old tomato-packing building on the outskirts of town. Before Officer Daniels could get any more information, the call had been terminated.

When Derek got there, a light had been on. That fact had been outright creepy, because the building was without power. Things got even weirder as lights all over the building had come on and off.

Then there were the noises. They had started as crashes and bangs, like somebody throwing things onto the floor in a frenzy, but nobody responded to their call. Soon inhuman sounds of howling and shrieking echoed into the silent night.

Derek had made the decision to call in help from the county sheriff. Sheriff McBane's brother, Caleb, worked for a company that trained tactical units for local and state governments as well as private security firms and foreign governments.

Those boys had shown up in full gear. Excited and more than ready for a real life challenge, they had taken their time setting up, then, with strategic precision, they had stormed the building.

Everybody had been disappointed when they had finally secured the building only to find it vacant. It did look as if a tornado had whirled through it, but that was all. Even the lights, that had been mysteriously working moments before, were suddenly inoperable.

What really got him, though, was when he tried to track down the mysterious caller only to recognize the number the system had recorded — it was his own cell phone. The whole thing defied the laws of reality.

He could not prove it, could not even begin to figure out how she had done it, but Derek was sure Dorothy was behind him being called out in the middle of the night. She had come over to set herself in a position to be left alone in his house.

She had gone through all that effort to find Kathleen's files. How had she known they would be at his house? What was she looking for in the files? Did she think he killed Kathleen?

There was no explaining how Dorothy even knew about Kathleen, why she even cared. Those answers were hidden in the little rental across the way. Perhaps it was his turn to do a little searching.

The idea struck him just as an old Mustang pulled into his driveway and parked behind his truck. Derek groaned. He did not need this right now.

"Derek!" Carolyn slammed the door as she got out of the muscle car. "I want to talk to you!"

Derek eyed her warily as she came flying up the porch steps. He was not in the mood for Carolyn. She was obviously already in the middle of a serious snit. She would go completely ballistic when she discovered he had mated another woman. Not that it mattered. The mating was irreversible.

"You have been ducking my calls and avoiding me!" She stormed up the steps of the porch. "I want to know the hell is going on!"

"This isn't going to be a pleasant conversation," Derek muttered more to himself than her as he rose to greet her.

"No, it's not, unless you plan to tell me you've dumped whatever floozy you picked up and plan to get down on your knees and beg me for forgiveness."

"I'm mated."

Instantly his head swung to the side from Carolyn's slap. His ears rang with her shriek. Carolyn raised her hand to slap him again, but Derek caught her wrist before she could land the blow.

"Take that back!"

"I can't, Caro. It's the truth." Derek tried to keep his tone calm, but he was not in the mood for her hysterics.

"You slimy, two-timing, jackass! How could you do this to me?" With a vicious jerk, Carolyn yanked her arm free.

"I didn't do anything to you."

"You didn't do anything to me? After everything we've been through? Who stood beside you when Kathleen went missing? Huh? Who has always been there for you? Helping you whenever you needed? Me! That's who."

"Carolyn, I never promised you anything. We're just friends who occasionally had sex. You know that. I never lied to you."

"Friend! Is that all I am to you? You're going to give me a pat on my head and send me on my way now that you no longer need me?"

"That's enough, Carolyn!" Derek growled, his temper beginning to flare. He was not in the mood for her theatrics.

"Oh, I get it! You want me to introduce her around and make her feel welcome, don't you? Well that isn't going to happen, you bastard."

"I don't expect you to show Dorothy around."

"Dorothy? That's who you mated? That fat, smart mouth? My God, Derek, what have you done? How long have you even known that slut?"

"Don't talk about her that way," Derek growled. He wasn't letting anybody, including Carolyn, insult Dorothy.

"Oh, I'm sorry. Didn't mean to offend the woman you love. You do love her don't you? That is why you mated her, isn't it?"

"You know how mating works. It's not about choice."

"Don't feed me that shit. You had a choice. Just as you did last time."

"Kathleen was a mistake."

"But you would have spent the rest of your life with her. No matter what, right? Even though you didn't love her."

"I would have grown to love her."

"Bullshit! You don't grow to love people, you either do or you don't. You would have spent your life miserable if she hadn't died. You just got lucky."

"There is nothing lucky about Kathleen being killed!" Derek roared taking a threatening step forward. Carolyn didn't even notice, too consumed by her own rage.

"No? What if she were still alive, still here? What would you have done when you met your precious Dorothy?"

"Nothing. I would have done nothing, because I would have been mated."

"I'm sure that would have been a great comfort to Kathleen. Why don't you just admit it Derek? You're incapable of loving a woman. We're all just pawns to you, something for you to use and discard when you lose interest."

"Carolyn—"

"You don't even know the meaning of love. I love you. All these years and all I've ever been to you is a good fuck!"

"Carolyn—"

"Save it," she cut him off. "Know this Derek, I'm never going to accept your mate and I'm going to make damn sure none of the other women in the pack do either."

"You do anything of the sort and you'll have to answer me."

"Oh, I see. She's too weak to handle me herself. You're going to step in and protect her. Is that it?"

"Protect who?" Kristin asked, having snuck up on them while they were arguing. Her question drew both Carolyn and Derek's gazes to her.

"Your asshole of a brother has mated another woman!"

"Oh, good."

Carolyn growled as her pale blue eyes darkened with the heated anger of the inner beast. Kristin was not the least bit intimidated. Her eyes darkened in response. Derek moved quickly. The last thing he needed was for the two women to transform in daylight and go at each other in the front yard.

"Kristin." Derek stepped between the two women. "I'm glad you stopped by. Carolyn was just leaving."

"This isn't over," Carolyn growled as she shoved past the siblings.

"Yes, it is, Carolyn. You had better accept the fact I'm mated. And if I hear anything nasty coming from you about Dorothy, there will be consequences," Derek warned her. Carolyn didn't bother looking back at him. Moments later her Mustang was squealing out of the driveway and roaring down the road.

"Well, that was unpleasant," Kristin commented as Derek settled himself back into the rocker.

"Yeah." Derek did not pay much mind as he resumed his brooding contemplation of the house across the street.

"So, watcha doing home this early in the morning?"

"Nothing."

"Nothing?" Kristen settled into the rocking chair next to him. "It's the middle of the week, don't you have a job to be at?"

"So?"

"Must be nice to be the boss."

"Yep."

"So you want to tell me about how things are going with Dorothy?"

"Nope."

Kristen frowned at her brother. The one-word answers were a clear sign something was bothering him. For a recently mated man, he didn't look too happy. She wondered if he were really that affected by the scene with Carolyn.

"You're not really upset about Carolyn, are you?"

"Nope."

She followed his gaze to the run-down house across the street.

"Problems with your neighbors?" Kristen asked after a few moments. Derek did not respond to that other than to take a long drink of lemonade. Kristen took that as a yes.

"They don't appear noisy," she commented though she might as well been speaking to herself. After another moment of tense silence, Kristen tried again.

"Are they doing something illegal? Does the husband hit the wife? The kids do drugs? What's wrong with them?" Kristen paused after every question but she got no response from Derek. "Does the woman prance around naked in her house and you're waiting to catch the show?"

That got her a quick, dark look from Derek. It clearly said he was not amused. Kristen sighed and got up. Without asking, she disappeared into his house. A few minutes later, she reappeared with two beers.

Not saying anything she swapped his glass for a beer before settling back into her chair and propping her feet up on the railing, mimicking her brother's intense gaze as she joined the study of the house across the street. He didn't look over and after a few minutes Kristen became bored with staring at the run down home.

"What are we waiting for?" Kristen asked in a conspiratorial whisper.

"Nothing."

"Then why are we sitting here waiting?"

"No reason." A two-word response was an improvement. Kristen tried to see if she could keep the trend going.

"So who lives there?"

"My mate."

"Ahhh," Kristen chuckled. "That explains it. You know, your mate doesn't like you much. You must have ignored all the advice I gave you."

"How the hell do you know what Dorothy thinks?" Derek demanded.

"She told me."

"When?"

"I bumped into her at the library yesterday."

"You bumped into her at the library and she just immediately told you how much she dislikes me?"

"Actually, I think she said you were the most annoying, repulsive man she ever had the displeasure to meet. I was just sort of paraphrasing when I said she doesn't like you."

"And why would she tell you that?"

"Well, because I asked what she thought of you." Kristen grinned. "I kind of forgot to tell her that I was your sister. Trust me when she found out she could not wait to get out of the library."

"You, of course, defended my honor." He wouldn't have bet on it.

"Of course not." Kristen snorted. "She's your mate. She's allowed to say whatever she wants about you. I would never disagree with the future head bitch."

"Thanks," Derek muttered.

"It's going to be a real feat for you to seduce that one. It's like divine vengeance."

"You think?" Derek snickered. Seducing Dorothy wasn't the problem. Getting her to be honest with him was.

"I'd really like to be there when you explain about the werewolf thing. I have a feeling your mate can outdo Carolyn when it come to tantrums."

"Believe it or not, telling her I'm a werewolf is not the worst of my problems."

"It's not?" Kristin cocked her head. "Then what is?"

"The fact that Dorothy is not Dorothy is my biggest problem."

"Not Dorothy? What the hell does that mean?"

"It means her name is not Dorothy."

"Then who the hell is she?"

"I don't know, yet."

"Don't know?"

"But I'm about to find out," Derek stated with determination as he got to his feet.

"You are?" Kristin blinked in confusion. "How?"

"Come on. I'll show you."

Chapter 12

Claire paused as she took in the sight before her. It had taken her over an hour and half of fighting through the thick underbrush of the forest to get here and now she wasn't certain if she'd made the right choice in coming.

After she had left Derek's house last night, she'd been too restless to go back to sleep. She had studied the notes she had made on Kathleen's files for hours to no effect. She had needed a break. Glancing at the address she'd written down on a slip of paper at the library yesterday evening, she had made up her mind. It was time to hunt down her demon.

It had taken several minutes for the sophisticated mapping software to produce GPS coordinates for the address. It had taken another half hour to gather the supplies she needed. It had been almost six by the time she was ready. She had seen Derek's truck lights get home hours ago and hoped he would be sleeping in. Faking a hoarse voice, she had called in sick to the station and then hit the road.

The sky had just begun to lighten when she had pulled her ratty hatchback off the road and parked on the grassy shoulder. The sound of happy insects and wall of pine trees had greeted her when she got out of the car. Shouldering her backpack, Claire had turned her flashlight on and walked into the forest.

Now, as she stared at the old southern home in desperate need of repair, she wondered if she should have stayed home. The house gave her the chills.

The wood plank siding was not only peeling white paint, but there were more sections that looked rotted through then solid. The porch appeared ready to cave in at any moment. One of the support columns had fallen and the roof dipped lower over the end. There wasn't a window that wasn't broken or shattered.

At some point, it had been a beautiful home. The hint of the craftsmanship and detail that had been used when the house was built still lingered here and there. A piece of old, hand-carved cornice, the detail in the window molding carving hanging by little more then a splinter. All over were the indications the house had been lovingly built.

Over the years, the forest had grown closer, but there was an invisible line that even the trees dared not cross. The pines littering the ground came to a sudden stop, leaving nothing but dry, dead earth surrounding the decrepit structure.

Decay soured the air and something else, something she could not name but it scared her. There was no hope for it, not now when she had come this far. She needed to know if the demon living off the serial killer's bloodlust lay here.

She needed to know its name. That was the only way they would know how to exorcise it. Sending the bastard back to hell wouldn't stop the killer, but it would weaken him.

Steeling her resolve, Claire stepped forward onto the barren yard. A stiff, cold breeze broke the still air and she could swear that she heard her name whispered on it. Reminding herself with ever breath that this demon could not touch her, not with Agakiar's brand laying claim to her body, she moved closer to the rotted porch post.

Her hand trembled as she reached out to touch it. When the brittle wood touched her flesh, she lost track of time and place. Pain seared through her as the demon showed her one horrible image after another.

Scenes so real that she could smell the blood, hear the screams, taste the girls' fear burned through her brain. It wasn't until the pain in her lungs became unbearable that Claire realized she was no longer at the house.

Leaning against a pine, she panted as she tried to catch her breath. She bent over as her stomach rolled and heaved. Thankfully, there was nothing to come up.

Whatever the pain, it had been worth the cost. She had what she needed. Claire knew the name of the demon. Urazi. She would call in a team to force Urazi out of this world and back into hell, where he belonged.

She had even gotten the best clue to date about the killer's identity. It was a woman. The fact complicated the case. She would have to go through all the notes and look for any signs of a female suspect.

Found our demon, did you? Kate's voice popped into Claire's head.

"Yeah." Claire closed her eyes and took a deep breath as shudders continued to course down her spine. "He's not a pleasant guy."

Are any of them?

"At least he was helpful."

Get something did you?

"A name to start. Urazi."

Never heard of him, but he must be strong. I can feel his essence even all the way out here.

"Really? Then it would have helped if you had shown up earlier and guided me toward the house. It took me forever to find it." Claire opened her eyes, but Kate hadn't chosen to appear.

You know I'm vulnerable to these types of demons. You wouldn't want to endanger me, would you?

"Are you sure you want to ask *me* that question?" Claire snorted.

Good point. So tell me what else you found out.

"What makes you think I found anything else out?

Because you said to start, which normally implies there is more.

"Very good. You should be a detective or something."

Are you going to tell me or not? Kate demanded.

"I will, once you tell me which direction my car is in." Claire pushed away from the tree.

South. At Claire's dour look, Kate appeared to point Claire in the right direction. Once she had started stomping through the overgrown vegetation, Kate spoke up. *So?*

"Patience is a virtue."

Not when you're dead.

"You're not dead."

And you're avoiding the question.

"Yeah, well, I'm still sorting it all out."

Maybe I can help.

"I got the sense the killer was a woman. That really screws everything up."

You're positive on that?

"The killer is angry with men, but has an even greater hatred of women. She feels superior, that she's better than most women and is really mad men don't see it."

Really mad sounds like an understatement.

"Regardless, we got one pissed-off bitch on the loose."

You sure you want to use that euphemism in these parts?

"Good point." Claire shoved through more thick underbrush. Envious of the way Kate floated along, not bothered by the vegetation in her way. "And it really throws a wrinkle into our case."

Rules out your werewolf, doesn't it?

"Always direct, aren't you?"

Don't tell me you're not happy about that fact.

"It doesn't change the fact he's an overgrown juvenile with a warped sense of humor," Claire blustered.

With a hot body and hands he can't keep off you. I'd say that outweighs any flaws.

"Whatever." Claire dismissed Kate's comment.

Don't whatever me. I saw you cuddled up in his bed the other night. You've got it bad.

"And if I do? So what? It doesn't change the fact I'm branded for the rest of my life by a demon. It kind of puts a kink into any relationship."

Doesn't mean you can't enjoy it while it lasts.

"No, it doesn't," Claire begrudgingly admitted. "But that doesn't have anything to do with the case. I can't just stop or slow the investigation because I'm having a little fun with the police chief."

I hate to admit you have a point. Kate sighed. *So our killer is a female. Where does that leave us?*

"It leaves us with Kathleen."

You saw her?

"Urazi didn't appear by accident. Somebody opened a portal for him. Kathleen was part of that equation."

You mean Kathleen opened the portal or the killer did?

"Urazi feeds on the life of newborns. It was Kathleen's unborn child that opened the portal."

So now what?

"I'll call the team to get rid of Urazi. That will just leave the killer." Claire stumbled over a root hidden in the pine straw. Her legs were weak from the running and it took her a moment to regain her balance. "Then I think it's time to investigate Kathleen Harper's life in depth. The killer probably knew her."

Perhaps, I should go check Kathleen's brother's place. See if he saved any of Kathleen's things.

"You can find him?"

I'll look him up in the phone book.

"So much for the mystical powers of ghosts."

Why don't you call Mike and give him the heads up?

"Thanks, mom. I hadn't thought of that."

Claire was talking to herself. Kate had not hung to hear her sarcastic comeback. Claire hated it when the ghost did that. Kate always wanted the last word and, with her ability to just disappear, she normally got it.

* * * *

"This is insane," Kristen hissed nervously as Derek tried the last window along the east side of the house.

"You don't have to be here."

"You realize this is illegal, right?" Kristen asked for what had to be the tenth time.

"So you said."

Derek did not sound anymore concerned about breaking the law then he had the first time she had mentioned it. Derek tried the back door. Locked.

"What are those?" Kristen frowned at a small set of metal blades and picks that he unfolded from a little cloth pouch

"Relax. Who's going to arrest the chief of police?"

"You're not really going in there?" The door swung open with a groan.

"That's why they call it breaking and *entering*," Derek retorted. "Not much point in just breaking."

"I'll keep that in mind." Kristen hesitated on the doorstep as Derek disappeared into the darkened kitchen. After a moment, she stepped into the house and reached to close the door.

"Leave it open." Derek stopped her. "Just in case we have to make a quick escape."

"That's not reassuring."

Derek checked out the kitchen and dining room, moving with an efficient speed. Kristen trailed along at a much slower pace, noting the house was sparsely furnished. There had been no attempt at decorating or personalizing the rental.

As she moved through the arched entry dividing the dining room and living room, she noticed Derek rooted to a spot in the middle of the hall. He appeared transfixed by something. Curiosity got the better of her, and she hurried to see what he was staring at.

Her legs stumbled to a stop, her whole body freezing as her eyes traveled past Derek and into the small bedroom. She stared in frightened amazement at the wall, at all the faces looking back at her.

Dorothy had pasted up dozens of pictures of missing girls in neat rows. Around the rows, she had marred up the entire surface with graffiti, all sorts of strange writing. The overall effect sent chills down Kristen's back.

Derek was feeling just the opposite as he slowly stepped into the room to get a better look at the pictures. It all made sense to him now. As if to verify his assumption, he caught sight of the last picture to be tacked up.

It hung on the bottom row, out of sequence with the others. It was where Dorothy had added Kathleen Harper. He recognized the picture as the one used in the original missing person's report.

It was a storyboard, used by detectives who worked large, complicated cases. Derek had never needed to use one, but he had learned about them. From what he could tell of this one, the case was more strange than complicated.

He stepped back and began to read the writing on the wall. One word jumped out at him, demon. Quickly, he scanned the wall looking for more strange words.

Werewolf den.

"I don't think I have to worry about her freaking out when she learns I'm a werewolf."

"What the hell is going on here, Derek?" Kristin demanded from the doorway, unwilling to step into the room.

"She's working a case." Derek moved away from the wall to study the rest of the room.

"A case?" Kristin scowled. "You sure? Because from where I'm standing, it looks as if we're going to need a straightjacket for your mate."

"No." Derek flipped through files and papers. "It's a case. She's an investigator of some type."

"Well she's not a good one, if she believes in demons."

Derek barely heard his sister. He stopped to study a list of notes Dorothy had made on the old haunted house down Bent Creek Road. Apparently, Dorothy thought the house as more than haunted. She believed it was possessed by a demon. It was also the place she suspected the killer was taking the missing girls.

Derek looked back at the wall. All the missing girls did look alike, but was that so strange? Given the number of teenage runaways every year, there was bound to be some who looked alike. Dorothy's time frame spanned more than a single year. It covered more than a decade. So why was she so convinced these cases were related?

Derek turned and walked out of the room. He had come here for answers and he was finding more questions. It would be easier to go over the information on the wall and her notes with Dorothy and that's exactly what he intended to do.

Kristin had left her spot by the door, no doubt left the house altogether. He almost did the same, but at the last minute changed directions. He found what he was looking for at the next door.

Dorothy's bedroom looked like a tornado had swirled through. So much for the neat and organized assistant. Whoever Dorothy was, she was a slob. Not that there was a lot of furniture to put things away in. There was a twin bed and a few plastic drawers.

Dirty clothes were piled in the corner. Several books were stacked on the floor her bed. There was a lamp and alarm clock on the drawers being used as a nightstand. Several soda cans cluttered the top of the makeshift nightstand.

Dorothy obviously liked to read in bed. Derek looked through the books, noticing she liked to read mysteries and science fiction. He had to roll his eyes when he saw she had several of Nan Grimes' books. The woman had bad taste in authors.

Even worse taste in underwear Derek soon discovered. He had thought the white cotton panties were just one pair, but apparently it was an obsession. All her bras and all her panties were plain and white. He was going to have to make a serious investment in lingerie.

Searching through her drawers, Derek frowned. Who put shoes in a drawer?

The last drawer was full of toiletries and make-up. In true female fashion, she had a million colorful bottles, everything from moisturizer to lipstick. He found a bottle of liquid talcum powder. That was something he had never seen before. Unable to resist he opened it and rubbed some between his hands.

Sure enough as it dried to a powder form. It smelled like Dorothy. Nice, yes, but he didn't want to smell like her. Quickly, he rubbed his hands against his slack trying to get rid of the scent.

Continuing to rub his hands, he moved on to the closet. He struck gold in the form of a small cigar box stuffed with pictures and postcards, tucked into a suitcase on the closet floor.

Derek flipped through them noticing there were no letters from a lover or cozy pictures of Dorothy and any guy. He paused on the third picture. It was of Dorothy and two men. They were all wearing bulletproof fest and Dorothy was wearing baseball hat with "FBI" embroidered at the top.

Could his mate be an FBI agent? Did FBI agents believe in demons and haunting?

The deeper he delved, the further back in time he traveled. Almost every picture was taken while she was on the job. It quickly became apparent that Dorothy was or had been affiliated with the FBI. There were many pictures of her with people wearing ATF, DEA and even GBI embroidered on clothing, but Dorothy's always read FBI.

At the bottom of the pile was the only picture of her as a child. Dorothy was standing in front of a Christmas tree barely taller than she was, holding the hand of an older woman. From the similarities, Derek guessed her mother.

Dorothy's mother could have been a hooker by the way she was dressed. From the looks of the room, the pathetic nature of the tree, the lack of gifts, it was obvious they were poor.

Despite the season, or the fact that she looked about ten, Dorothy had a serious expression on her face. Dorothy's mother, on the other hand, had an ear-to-ear grin. Derek studied the picture wondering exactly what had made Dorothy such a tense little kid.

There was something about that face that made him want to reach through time, back to that moment, and make her smile. It was Christmas — time for baked goods, specials on TV, singing carols, for merriness and laughter. A little girl should be giggling and dancing, not looking as if the weight of the world rested on her fragile shoulders.

Derek dropped the picture back into the box and lifted an old college photo identification card. There was a picture of a tense-faced Dorothy with the name Claire Hollowell beneath it.

Chapter 13

A trail of dust followed Derek's truck as it bumped its way down the dirt road. The twisted limbs of oaks and cedars grew overhead, caging the road. It felt as if they were tunneling through the forest.

He had enough questions and tired of waiting for answers. He had spent two hours on the phone today, but had learned little. Claire was a thirty-year-old Atlanta, Georgia-native. Formerly an FBI agent, she was now licensed as a private investigator in forty-five of the fifty states, including South Carolina.

Her license listed her employer as The Masters of Cerberus. Derek had never heard of the company, had tried to locate any information on what they did specifically. With an organization named after a legendary hellhound, and with Claire writing about demons on her wall, Derek wished he could afford to remain ignorant.

He was frustrated with his lack of progress. He needed to convince Claire to be honest with him and needed independent facts to compare her answers with. Those facts were going to come from McBane. He hated bringing his long-time friend into the middle of this, but he had no choice. Between McBane and his brother Caleb, they had the connections to learn the truth Claire was hiding.

Derek just had to make sure to keep them away from Claire. It was well known that McBane's breed shared their women. Even when they mated, they shared one mate between each set of twin brothers. They always mated outside the pack, normally with humans.

It didn't matter to them if the woman was already mated. McBane's breed had one shot at procreation, one woman who could bear their children. Many never found that woman. That made them desperate and more than willing to fight to the death over a chosen mate.

Nature may have handicapped them in the mate department, but it had also given them an edge over other men. McBane's breed could emit a musk that drugged women with lust. One whiff and a woman became so aroused she would do anything the man asked of them.

Derek wasn't about to let Claire be snatched away from him. He was going to keep a tight hold on his mate and make sure she stayed safe, even if he had to drag the truth out of her.

As the trees gave way to sand and marsh, Derek brought the truck to a stop. A few feet past the hood, the tall marsh grass bent and shivered in the afternoon breeze. Just beyond, the water glinted in the reflection of the sun, looking cool and welcoming in the afternoon heat.

* * * *

It was beautiful. And lonely, Claire thought, and there was a sense of isolation. They may have been only twenty minutes from town, but it felt like a world of its own.

The odor of decay and rot contrasted sharply with the beauty of the land. Death was not unknown to the marsh. It was its lifeblood, the grim reality behind the soft murmuring water, the teasing whisper of blades of grass in the wind, the occasional call of marsh birds.

This was where Derek had brought Kathleen the night she had disappeared. There was no doubt in her mind. Why he had brought her here? When he had showed up at her door only fifteen minutes ago, she had contemplated not answering.

She had already received a call earlier from Agakiar, which had been beyond the normal unpleasant experience. This time, his threats hadn't been aimed at Claire.

"Stay away from the werewolf. You only get one warning," Agakiar growled, sounding truly angered for once.

"Are you watching me?" His warning had more than freaked her out. It had terrified her. She had checked with Mike later to assure herself Agakiar was nowhere near Wilsonville. It had soothed her frazzled nerves a little, but left her wondering how he knew about Derek.

"I don't share what is mine."

"I'm not yours, you psychotic—"

"I think you need an example."

Before she could respond, the line went dead. Claire had stood there shaking, as she considered the ramifications of what Agakiar had said. Was Agakiar going to hurt Derek? How could she protect him?

The last thing she wanted was to see Derek hurt, but walking away wasn't going to save him. If Agakiar wanted to harm Derek, it would only give him an opening. Claire's only option was to keep a very close eye on him and pray she could stop Agakiar when the time came. If that meant sacrificing herself, she was prepared to do so. Never again did she want to attend another funeral knowing somebody else had died because of her.

Her only other hope was to turn Agakiar's attention away by leaving town. She might be able to pull that off soon. She had spent three hours on the phone with the team.

Sasha, priestess, and Harold, the sorcerer, would be the ones who did the dirty work. They would get rid of Urazi. Deik, the vampire, would be the protector, his job to protect the team from anything other than the demon.

Deik had already made it clear he didn't want Claire to go near the house when the exorcism was being performed. Claire had made it just as clear she was not about to be cut out of anything. If they didn't want her to be a part of the exorcism that was fine but she was tagging along.

With Urazi out of the way, she could focus her efforts on finding the killer. Kate had reported Nathan not only kept something of his sister, he had kept her room exactly as it had been when she left. It was a treasure trove and Claire had to figure out how to get access to it.

With Urazi and the killer handled, she would be able to leave Wilsonville and Derek behind. Agakiar would do the same.

"So where are we?" Claire finally broke the silence.

"I brought Kathleen here the night she disappeared."

* * * *

Derek leaned back against his door and watched her. She hesitated for a moment, probably considering her options. It disappointed him when she went with the obvious response.

"Who?" Claire inquired politely inquisitive.

"Kathleen. You know, the girl in the police files you searched through at my house."

Claire chewed her lip for a moment. Derek knew she was debating her options, trying to figure out how much he knew and how best to handle him. He was not in the mood to play games. He wasn't going to tolerate any more deceptions or evasions.

"I can see why you would be curious about her. She matches all the other women whose disappearances you're investigating, Claire."

Claire's eyes widened, her expression going from tentative to shock in an instant. It faded as her eyes turned speculative again.

"Yes, I know," Derek continued in a hard voice. "Your real name is Claire Hollowell and you're investigating a case. You're looking for a serial killer who you believe either is a demon or is working with one."

"Such a wealth of information. Tell me, how did you come by it?" There was a bite to her tone.

"Same way you came by yours. I looked through your stuff."

"You were in my house? When?" She gaped at him

"This morning, when you were off having a walk through the woods looking for the haunted farm house," Derek retorted. At her flinch, he knew his suspicion had been right. He had seen her notes about the old Howard place and figured that was where she had gone.

"You broke into my house?" Claire ignored his sarcastic comments. "You do realize that's illegal and you're a cop, right?"

"Who's going to arrest the chief of police?"

"You think you know everything, don't you?" Claire glared out over the water.

"So you're not denying your real name is Claire Hollowell?

"What's the point?"

"And that you're a former FBI agent?"

"Right again."

"And you consider me a suspect in Kathleen's disappearance." Derek could not keep the pain and hurt out of his statement. Claire hesitated before looking back at him.

"Not anymore," she begrudgingly admitted.

"So you changed your mind? Why?"

"It's complicated."

"I think I can keep up."

"Why should I tell you anything?"

"Because when you came to this town to investigate the disappearance of twenty or so women, you came into *my* jurisdiction."

"God, are we going to get into a pissing contest?"

"When you added Kathleen to the list of victims, you stepped into my business. You should have come to me."

"Like I haven't heard that one before. Tell me, Derek, what would you have done if I had come to you and explained that I was hunting a serial killer who was working with a demon? Hmm?"

She waited a moment, but when he didn't respond, she snorted.

"That's what I thought. You know the case just gets so much better from there. After all, I'm sure you would have wanted proof.

Real proof, that is, and all I have to give are psychic visions. I'm sure you would have taken me very seriously."

"That's not why you didn't tell me. You didn't tell me because you didn't trust me!"

"Really? So, you want to explain that bite mark on my neck, wolf boy?" Claire shot back. "I'm sure you tell every woman before you fuck them they're about to do a dog."

"Don't even try to distract me with insults," Derek snarled. "Right now, we're talking about your case. Now I want to know why you don't think I'm guilty."

"What does it matter?" Claire shot him a disgusted look. "I'm letting you off the hook. I'd think that you'd be happy about it."

"I want to know why? Because I'm good in bed?"

"Oh, yeah. That's how I determine whether all my suspects are innocent."

Derek took a deep breath. This conversation was going worse than he had imagined.

If they continued along this path, they would tear each other apart. Underneath all the other volatile emotions, he wanted to set things right between them. He wanted to work as partners, not as enemies.

"Look," Derek tried to sound calm and rational, "how about we make a trade?"

"A trade?" Claire's eyed him distrustfully.

"Yes. You're working under the assumption that Kathleen is the first victim, right?"

"Yes."

"I take it you believe if you solve Kathleen's murder, you'll have found the other women's killer. Right?"

"Yes." There was a little hesitation before she answered, as if she knew where he was headed and didn't want to go there.

"I can help you with that. I know everything about that case, everything about Kathleen. I know this town and its people. I'm an insider and you're not."

"What do you want in return?"

"The truth."

"What truth?"

"About who you are and how you came to be here. Deal?"

"I can't make that deal." Claire sighed and looked down. "It's not up to me."

"Who's it up to? Your company? The Masers of Cerberus?"

"I can't let you in because you don't understand what you're getting into."

"Then explain it to me," Derek pressed. He wasn't going to take no for an answer.

"I can't. It's just too dangerous. People have a bad habit of getting hurt around me."

"Why?"

"A demon. He's got a personal interest in me." Claire's shoulders slumped. He had a right to know this much. "I don't want to see you get hurt."

Derek's breath caught. It was the closest she had ever come to admitting she cared. It wasn't much, but it was a start, warming his heart and hoping that she would grow to care even more for him. First, though, he had to convince her to let him in.

"He'll use me to hurt you."

"He made that threat today." Claire smiled tightly as she looked back up at him.

"He's here? In Wilsonville?" Derek's eyes widened in alarm.

"Nope, but he doesn't need to be here to hurt you. He's got henchmen to do his dirty work."

"Why hasn't he hurt you?"

"Who says he hasn't?" Claire shot back impulsively and then instantly regretted the words. Derek's eyes darkened as a feral growl rumbled from his chest past his tight lips.

"I'll kill him," Derek snarled.

"You can't."

"Why not?"

"Because then you'll kill me," Claire explained simply.

"How does that work?"

"We're tied together." Claire sighed, not wanting to go into all the details. "Look, Derek, I know you want to help and it's sweet of you, but you can't."

"So, you just live like this? With this demon controlling your life?"

"There are others working on the problem." Least there had been, but there were no solutions. It was something Claire was learning to accept.

"So, now what?" Derek sighed.

He was not about to let the matter of this demon go. He was not going to trust people he didn't even know with Claire's safety, but he could tell there was no point in pressing the matter now.

"So, now I find Kathleen's killer."

"We find him," Derek corrected her. At her frown, he continued. "You don't really think you can stop me from interfering, do you?"

"No." Claire sighed. "You do annoying better than most."

"That I do." Derek smiled slightly. "So the deal is honesty for honesty."

"Fine." Claire caved after several tense minutes of silence. "But you're going first. I want to know about that night with Kathleen."

Derek leaned his head back and began to recite everything that happened. It had been so long since he had talked about it. All the times he forced himself to relive that night, looking for some clue, some answer, nothing had ever come to him. Nothing, except the painful reality he had failed Kathleen.

Now as he talked, he felt something shifting inside him. When he was done he was not left with the sense of isolation that normally filled him. Neither one spoke for several minutes. Derek assumed Claire was digesting everything he had told her, but when he opened his eyes he saw her glare. She was annoyed with him and for the life of him, he didn't know why.

"What?"

"I got all that from reading the police file. I was hoping for something new," Claire stated pointedly.

"There is nothing."

"Now who's holding back?"

"What?"

"The fight — what was it about? Let me take a guess. You fought because she was pregnant."

"How did you know that?"

"All the other girls were pregnant. It's part of the profile. I guess you just skimmed my notes."

"So she was pregnant. So what?"

"I know this must be hard for you," Claire stated quietly, after a moment of silence. "But you're missing the big picture here. Kathleen isn't just the first. She's the one who set the pattern. Tell me about the fight."

"She was upset because she had learned that I was a werewolf," Derek began, looking away from Claire. "She was afraid because she was pregnant. Never mind that her chances of going to college and getting out of this tiny town were blown, she was terrified that her child was a monster."

Claire didn't respond to that. She could sense there was more to the story, but she didn't want to press. It did not require a werewolf's ability to sense emotion to see it hurt him.

"Truth was, I didn't want to be a father at that age." Derek rubbed his head. "I didn't want to be mated. I was having too much fun to be tied to just one woman. It just sort of happened. When we got here that night, she confronted me with the fact and I didn't handle it well. She was all freaked out about me being a werewolf and I was all freaked out about her being pregnant. The situation just sort of exploded."

"It must have been hard for you all these years, knowing that your last conversation was a fight," Claire stated softly.

"Yeah," Derek sighed heavily. "She ran away from me because she thought I was some crazed beast who would hurt her."

"It's not your fault, Derek."

"No?" He smirked at that.

"She was pregnant with your child. You had to tell her what you were."

"What?" Derek scowled at Claire. He didn't like the look on her face.

"I didn't tell her."

"You didn't?"

"No. She already knew. That's why she wanted an abortion."

"Then who did?" Claire scowled.

"How the hell would I know?" Derek scowled back at her. "It wasn't an important question to me at the time."

"Haven't you ever wondered?"

"Of course, but what does it matter now?

Chapter 14

Several minutes passed in silence while Claire considered the implications of what Derek had said. He might not think that it mattered, but whoever had told Kathleen what Derek was had terrified her.

They must have done something more than simply tell her, too. They had to have proven it in some way, some way that frightened her.

"Well?"

"Maybe it was Nathan."

"Nathan? Who's Nathan?" Derek's annoyed growl brought Claire's eyes back to him.

"Excuse me?"

"I don't know what you're talking about, but it's time for you to 'fess up."

"'Fess up?"

"Dorothy versus Claire? Assistant-versus-investigator? Some company named The Masters of Cerberus? Any of that ring a bell?"

"Well, you already know I'm not Dorothy and I am an investigator who works for Cerberus, what else it there?"

"Claire."

"Alright." Claire rolled her eyes. "What do you want to know?"

"What should I know?"

Claire turned her gaze away from him, unable to face him anymore. If she had any guts, she would tell him about Agakiar and the reason she had been fired from the FBI. The words just wouldn't come out.

"Tell me why you never smiled as a child." Derek surprised her with that question.

"Who says I didn't?"

"I saw the picture of you and your mother. A kid that doesn't smile at Christmas doesn't smile. Why was that?"

"I just wasn't a smiler."

"You're not really good at this sharing thing, you know that?"

Claire looked through the windshield and into the past. It was not a place she liked to go.

"My dad left when I was little. My mother wasn't real…responsible. She had a problem with alcohol and pills. There wasn't much to smile about."

"How old were you when your dad left?"

"Five or six. It's hard to remember."

"You ever see him again?"

"No." She had never looked for her dad. He hadn't wanted to be a part of her life when she was a child. She didn't want to be part of his as an adult.

"So where is your mom now?"

"Dead."

"I'm sorry." She felt Derek shift beside her and knew what was coming next. "How did she die?"

"One of her…clients beat her to death."

"Jesus."

"He panicked, wrapped her in a sheet and dumped the body in the garbage bin of our apartment. I guess he thought it would be picked up the next day."

Derek didn't respond for several moments. When his hand settled over hers, she realized she was clenching them together. Claire looked at her white knuckles as he pried her fingers apart, intertwining them with his.

"The cops caught him?"

"I told them." Claire closed her eyes. "I was under her bed the whole time."

"You saw."

Claire didn't know how to respond to that last statement, at least not with Derek. Normally she dismissed comfort and sympathy. That didn't feel right this time.

"Everything. I saw everything." Claire opened her eyes, feeling almost undone by the compassion she could see in his. "Later I testified to...everything."

"How old were you?"

"Fourteen."

"You had a lot of guts for fourteen." Derek smiled slightly. The small gesture broke her intensity, making her relax slightly. "That's why you became an FBI agent."

"I guess we have that in common, huh?" Claire took a deep breath. She did not like to go back into the past and as quickly as she could leave it, she did. "We both ended up in law enforcement, because we lost someone we loved."

"We're just some true blue cops on a mission to revenge the victims."

"Don't make me sound so noble."

"If you find Kathleen's killer, you'll be a hero in this town."

"You think they'll build me a pedestal?" Claire asked.

"Pedestal?" Derek gave her a strange look.

"Yeah." Claire smiled. "So I can stand on it and all can admire my glory."

"How about your picture in the paper? Will that do?"

"I don't know. I really had my heart set on a pedestal."

"So — partners?" Derek squeezed her hand.

"I'm not sure you want to be my partner." Claire hesitated.

"Why not?"

"I doubt you'll believe in my methods."

"What methods?"

"Psychic visions."

"Visions?" Derek tasted the word. "Well, I'm a werewolf, we're hunting a demon and you have visions. What's not to believe in?"

"It's not a joke, Derek."

"Didn't think it was."

"Well, if you're going to be so open-minded about everything, I guess I should tell you about my partner," Claire stated with a straight face.

"You have a partner?" Derek scowled. "Where have you been hiding him?"

"So macho." Claire rolled her eyes. "It happens to be a her and she's not hiding, not technically. She's a ghost."

"A ghost?" Derek laughed outright at that. "And I thought I had strange friends."

"I thought you were being open-minded?"

"I'm sorry. If you say you have a ghost helping you, who am I to disagree? So what is this ghost doing?"

"I'm not done." Claire wasn't sure what Kate was doing, but she would bet the nosey apparition was listening in on their conversation.

"What do you mean?"

"There's more."

"More?" Derek raised an eyebrow at that. "Let me guess your boss is a unicorn."

"A dragon, actually," Claire responded dryly. "But that's not it. It's about my visions of the killer."

"The killer?" Derek cut in. "What? Is he a robot from the future sent back through time to—"

"The killer is a woman." It didn't surprise Claire that cut Derek's humor cold. It took him several minutes to digest it.

"A woman. How's that possible?"

"Women do kill."

"Yeah, but this…a serial killer stalking teenage girls. That doesn't sound like a woman." Derek let go of her hand to run his through his hair.

"Well it is."

"Are you sure about this? I mean, how do you know?"

"I told you my visions."

"Forgive me." Derek shook his head. "Can't blame me for being a little suspicious. After all, you've done nothing but lie since I met you."

"It's called acting," Claire retorted.

"The difference escapes me."

"I admit it's a fine line," Claire conceded. "But lying is when you attempt to deceive…that is, when your intentions are not…it's just different. Besides, you're a werewolf, aren't you suppose to be able to sense lies?"

"I can sense a lot of things." Derek eyes heated as they swept over her. "Your scent distracts me."

"You're the one trying to distract me." Claire could feel her ears start to heat. "We're supposed to be talking about the case here."

"So are we going to be working as partners?"

"You didn't leave me a lot of choice, did you?"

"Well then, partner." Derek slid closer across the seat. "I think we should officially seal our agreement."

"Derek." Claire forced a frown. "We're supposed to be focusing here."

"I told you I was distracted. Got an itch that needs to be scratched before I can concentrate on anything else."

"And your sister said you were all charm, sweeping women off their feet." Claire rolled her eyes.

"It's not in what you say, sweetheart. It's in what you do," Derek whispered in her ear before his finger settled under her chin. Claire did not resist as he turned her face toward his.

Their lips met, parted, and, for a moment, they gently pressed into each other. Derek's arms came around, pulling her closer into his embrace as his tongue slid to into her mouth. Claire no longer wanted to resist the heat and attraction that existed between them.

Her tongue forced his back into his mouth as her followed to duel and tangle with his, demanding more. She kissed him with all the hunger and need riding her body, leaving no doubt she wanted him to possess her body and her soul.

Derek was not going to be dominated as he forced their love play back into her mouth. Holding her tightly to him, he plundered her sweetness, tasting her with a roughness that was his own silent message. He claimed her mouth the way he intended to claim her body.

They were both flushed and breathing hard by the time they were forced to separate so they could breathe. Claire found herself on his lap, her legs straddling his thighs and wondered when he had done that. Already he was beginning to take control.

As much as Claire wanted his loving, this time she wanted to control the situation. She wanted to be the one who teased and tormented him until he was out of his mind with desire. Perhaps then he would be the one to beg her.

Claire smiled at the idea and placed her hands over his as they began to work the buttons of her shirt free. They stilled and his eyes darted to meet hers. She could read the annoyance there, the expectation she was going to try to deny him. That was the last thing on her mind.

"Let me."

Claire leaned back allowing her hands to slide between them. He growled, not liking to be denied. After a moment, he began to relax as she began to pull each button of his uniform free.

As his shirt slowly parted, and more smooth flesh was revealed, Claire gave in to the urge to follow the teasing line of his shirt edge with her mouth. Leaning forward, she traced the crease of pectorals with her tongue.

The rough hair on his chest tickled her nose and she rubbed her cheek against him, enjoying the contrast of smooth, hot skin against the cool, rasping curls. Even as her hands undid the rest of his shirt, her mouth sidetracked.

Working across his chest, she kissed a trail to one of his flat, brown nipples. Using the same technique he normally used to torment her harden buds, she caught his nipple between her teeth and began to tease the sensitive nub with her tongue.

Claire could feel the fine tremors rolling through his body. She smiled, encouraged by his response. Closing her eyes, she murmured her satisfaction, as she tasted her way toward his other nipple. He tasted good, like salty, sweaty man.

Derek's breath caught on a groan as she began to suck and nibble on his other nipple. His stomach muscles contracted, allowing her hands to free the button at the waistband of his trousers. The zipper was harder to get lowered as his erection pressed outward, stretching the fabric.

Finally, she got the metal fly down. Her hands slipped in to find his cock surging against the soft cotton of his boxer briefs. She worked her hand inside, sighing when she felt his velvety hardness.

For several minutes, she explored his length with a tentative touch, before her hands tightened around the thick knob at the top. She sucked hard on his nipple as her hand squeezed down on his sensitive head, pulling it slightly. She could feel the wetness leaking, as his breath became a ragged pant.

"Here."

Derek lifted his hips, forcing her off to the side so he could pull down both his pants and his boxers. He squirmed for a moment, toeing off his shoes and kicking his clothes aside.

Claire's eyes were riveted on his hard cock. It was so hard and hot, covered in smooth, soft skin and it was all for her. Her pussy clenched, wanting to feel his thickness stretching her wide. Just the thought had her cunt weeping with need.

Claire pulled back and smiled at the picture he made. He was hard and aching, ready to beg. She was sure of it. Never before had a man begged for her. Especially not one so mouth-wateringly sexy as Derek.

It was a heady sense of power, one that made her lightheaded and giddy. She felt like giggling and she never giggled. Never had she felt so lighthearted, wanting to tease and play with a man.

Derek growled, the sound of the beast within sensing the shift in her mood. Claire leaned back and scooted across the seat. Instantly his hand shot out to latch on to her arm.

"Let me." Claire pulled back on her arm. "I want to undress for you."

His eyes narrowed, his distrust obvious, but he let her go. Claire made a slow show out of undoing the buttons of her shirt, letting her hands run down the sides as the material parted. She slipped her hands under the fabric and began to massage her breast.

"You said you liked to watch," Claire reminded him, her voice low and sultry as she shrugged out of her shirt. "Let me give you something to watch."

His eyes darkened to midnight blue. They followed every movement of her fingers as they slipped under her bra cups to rub against her nipples.

"Take it off," he growled, the sound barely human.

Claire smiled. She had him just where she wanted him. The beast inside was barely restrained, just as he had been last night.

With a seductive smile, she reached behind her back as if she were about to undo the bra's clasp. Instead, her fingers latched onto the door handle. She only had one chance at escape.

Derek was primed and ready, he would lunge on her the second he realized her intent. Not that it mattered, he'd capture her soon enough. Claire just wanted to draw out the game, make sure that when he caught her, he was too far out of control to think about anything but fucking her senseless.

"Now!"

The beast was impatient, wanting to see his woman now. Claire laughed and yanked the door handle open. She all but fell out of the truck and, just as she expected, Derek sprang, barely missing her ankle as she managed to get both feet on the ground.

She heard him growl, the sound echoing out of the truck and silencing all the noisy marsh critters. Every living thing knew what Claire knew — a predator was on the prowl. Quickly she backed away from the truck as he unfolded himself from the seat.

Chapter 15

The sunlight painted his naked form as a golden god as he paced forward. A savage god from the lean, hungry look hardening his eyes. The full heat of the wolf's mating fever was riding him and it thickened his already bulging muscles until every move made his body ripple with strength.

"Surrender now and I won't punish you," the wolf demanded, wanting the total submission of his mate.

"Where would be the fun in that?" Claire taunted, backing away from him.

She reached behind her and undid her bra clasp, letting the material fall to the ground. Just as she intended, his eyes dropped instantly to her breast. The heated look felt like a caress, making her already puckered nipples tighten even further.

Smiling seductively she let her hands come back around to hold and fondle her breasts. Pinching and pulling on her nipples, she moaned as the pleasure she gave herself ricocheted through her body, making her pussy clench and spasm with delight.

Keeping her eyes locked on his, she lifted one breast and tilted her head down. The late afternoon sun warmed her skin, but the inferno of desire she could see in his gaze seared her flesh as her tongue snaked out to lick her nipple. The flame licked right through her skin and straight to her clit as she saw his features tighten.

She would never get enough of the way Derek looked at her. Always they shined with the lust he felt for her. It didn't matter how many times they came together. That look would never die. It made her shiver with longing and need.

As her hand lifted one, and then the other breast to her waiting mouth, her other hand slid down over her stomach to the snap of her jeans. Derek didn't appear aware of what she was doing until she wiggled, allowing her pants and panties to fall to the ground.

Then his eyes dropped, narrowing on the smooth, naked flesh of her cunt. Claire knew it glistened with evidence of her desire, but widened her stance to make sure that he saw the cream coating the tops of thighs.

"This what you want to see, right?" Claire purred. "That's why you shaved me, so you could see every inch of my naked pussy, isn't it? Or did you want to see something else? Perhaps, you wanted to see me touch myself, watch me as I pleasured myself."

Claire matched her actions to her words, allowing her hand to slide into the wet folds of her cunt. She sent him a small challenging smile as she began to rub her clit. Moaning with her escalating desire, Claire pumped three fingers into her aching slit.

Derek snarled as he watched her. She thrilled at the rough, ragged sound. His lips were pulled back and she could see his canines beginning to lengthen.

"All the way baby," Derek commanded her. "Make yourself come."

Claire had no mind left to deny him. It was so erotic, pleasuring herself in the outdoors while he watched. Faster and faster, she fucked her fingers into her clenching core. She whimpered and arched her hips up, trying to deepen the thrust of her slender fingers.

Her whole body flushed with her spiraling desire. She rubbed her clit harder as her second hand abandoned her breast to join the other. Then she was crying out his name as her body jerked violently with her release.

Panting hard, she raised lids that had lowered during her climax and saw him watching her with a smug, satisfied expression. The cocky bastard did not even have to touch her to control her. Claire stiffened slightly as she realized she had lost the upper hand.

Her legs, now weak and rubbery, would be little good for out running him. The beast within him, which had appeared on the edge of springing free, now glowed contently under control in his nearly black eyes. That simply would not do.

Raising her hand, she slowly sucked the cream from each finger. Derek watched her the way a cat watches a mouse it's about to devour. Claire smiled at him when she was done, letting her hand come back to rest on her bared mound.

"Hmm," she purred. "I don't know if I need you anymore Derek. I'm feeling quite satisfied."

"I don't know, sweetheart. Normally, when I'm done with you, you're barely able to speak, let alone walk."

Claire matched his every step forward with one backward as he pursued her. Claire smiled at him, intending to flee down the road, but she could see that he was prepared.

Feigning right, she quickly switched to the left when he moved to block her. She just barely made it around him and was circling the back of the truck when he tackled her. Even in his heightened state of arousal, he was protective of her, turning as they fell so he took most of the impact.

Claire struggled, her fight only adding to his excitement. He turned, crushing her beneath his weight. Before she could take a breath, his mouth was on hers. For all the hunger and need, it was not a bruising kiss.

He was still in control as he sent his tongue in to taste and stroke hers. Claire whimpered, disappointed her plan to push beyond reason had failed. She lost track of the thought as he continued to devour her mouth.

The feel of his tongue filling her mouth made her pussy ache with a sense of emptiness. His tongue fucked into her mouth, stroking her with motions that matched the rock of his hips against her own. Claire's legs spread, making a place for him between them.

As his hardened cock rubbed against her sensitized clit, she groaned and arched her hips upward, forcing the small nubbin against him. Taking control, she ground her pelvis into his, stroking the fires of renewed desire.

Her lips closed over his tongue, sucking it into her mouth. Derek groaned and his cock thumbed against her in approval. Derek tore his mouth away and leaned up.

"I think you still need me for something, baby."

He teased her by forcing his thick length between her swollen cunt lips and stroked against her. Claire moaned and arched her back.

"You like that don't you, baby."

"You know I do." Claire could barely get the words out. "Please."

"Please what? What do you want?" Derek nipped his way down her neck while the head of his cock found the clenching opening of her slick channel. Slowly he pushed against it, allowing the thick head of his cock to stretch her opening wide.

"Yes." Claire gasped, her hips raising, trying to force more of him into her.

"That's what you want? If so, then say it?" Derek arched his hips away, letting his cock slip free of her clinging warmth.

"Please, that's what I want."

He had worked his way to her breast and was teasing her nipple. Tracing the edge of her areola with the tip of his tongue, he ignored her aching tip. The need to feel his mouth more firmly on her was driving her insane.

"You want me to fuck you, don't you, baby? Admit that's what you need."

"Yes, I need you to fuck me. Now, damn it!" Claire growled, annoyed at the game he was playing.

"Not yet. There's still the little matter of your punishment."

"P..pu...punishment?" Claire blinked, her mind struggling to understand.

Derek did not explain. Instead his head dropped, his lips sucking the hard peak of her nipple pass the rough edge of his teeth. Claire groaned and arched more fully into his mouth. Pleasure shot directly out from her breast to her pussy.

His cock came back to tease her clit, parting her fold with his thick length and sliding over the little nub with increasing speed. Claire cried out as the vise of ecstatic pleasure tightened over her body again.

It was more intense this time since her whole body was sensitive to the feel of his moving on top of her. Just as the waves of ecstasy were about to crash down on her, he stopped. Claire groan turned to a snarl as he failed to continue. She wiggled against him, trying to force her throbbing clit against his hardness.

"Sorry, sweetheart," Derek groaned and settled down on top of her, stilling her movement.

For long moments he rested there, bear skin against bare skin, his chest against her breasts, hard cock laying against her soft, weeping core. Claire's body still shook with the build up of her pleasure and he seemed to absorb the small tremors. His muscles began to quiver with small shakes.

"Please," Claire whispered, hoping to inspire him to forget the punishment and get on to the fucking.

His only response was a groan as he lifted his head and began to kiss his way down her body. Claire knew his intention and prayed that he would not tease her again, because she wasn't sure if she had sanity left for that.

His lips latched onto her clit as his fingers delved deep into her tight channel. Claire cried out, her body jerking violently from the electric pleasure that she nearly dislodged him. Derek shifted, settling more firmly between her spread thighs as he began to lick, lave and suck on her tender flesh.

His hungry groans turned into primal growls as the beast rose up to taste the sweet cream pouring from her body. He nicked her with teeth grown long and sharp. Claire flinched from the tiny pain, only to arch into his mouth as he began to suck on the playful wound.

He licked his way lower, tunneling his elongated tongue into her clinging channel. Claire sobbed, sure that her body would splinter into a thousand fragments from the piercing pleasure radiating out of her pussy as he fucked his tongue repeatedly deeper into her.

Again, just when her body began to shake with her impending release, he stopped. Claire cried and begged him to continue as her hands fisted into his hair, trying to force his face back between her legs.

"Who do you belong to?" He snarled, the heated sound grating on her already excited nerves.

"You," Claire answered immediately. "Please, Derek, I need you."

"You won't ever run or fight me again?"

"I was just playing."

"And I told you to surrender." Derek gave her another long lick, straight up her creaming pussy. "Do you surrender now?"

"Yes, yes. I surrender. Please, Derek, fuck me!"

He growled and rolled off her. Claire's eyes flew wide open, her body tensing to force the matter if it came to that. Before she could issue a protest or another plea, he lifted her off the ground.

Claire found herself suddenly facing the tailgate of his truck. Quickly, with firm hands he backed her hips up so she was nearly bent over. His leg forced hers wide and he reached around to stretch her arms forward. Forcing her hands around the edge of the metal frame, she felt his hard shaft slide between her swollen cunt lips.

"Hold on, baby, because I'm going to give you one hell of a ride."

With that warning, he bit down on the tender skin of her shoulder and slammed himself into her. Claire cried out at the sudden penetration and held on to the truck as he began to fuck her fast and furiously.

Her whole body shook with pleasure as it flowed from her pussy up her spine and out to her limbs. Mindlessly, she cried out as he took her with a savagery that left her only able to focus on his thick cock slamming into her repeatedly.

Her heart and soul sang out as he filled her, possessed her, making them one perfect being. He rutted on her until they were both writhing, desperately reaching for the climax that lay just beyond.

Suddenly her world exploded and Claire bucked beneath him, helpless to control the movements of her hips as ecstasy consumed her flesh. Still he did not stop.

The exquisite feel of his cock thrusting into her stroked her climax higher and higher, until it condensed before erupting into lava flows of fire through her. Claire screamed as her world went black.

* * * *

Derek withdrew and thrust back into the wet heaven of her pussy, glorying in the way her hips pumped backward, meeting his thrust with her own demand. Instinctively, his mouth went to the bite mark on her shoulder.

As his fangs sank into her soft flesh, a sense of masculine triumphant went through him heightening his pleasure. More than her words, his mark proclaimed to the world she was his.

Claire suddenly bucked into him with the ferocity of her climax. Derek knew he should pause and give her a moment, but he was lost in his own driving pleasure. White-hot flames ate their way from his balls toward his cock, warning him that his release was moments away.

The intensity of his own pleasure had him pistoning even faster, harder into her tight depths until Claire's back arched and her scream ripped through the serenity of the marsh. Her tight channel fisted tight around him, holding his cock deep within her for a moment before it spasmed with her pleasure.

Derek closed his eyes, savoring the feel of her warm tight channel milking his cock. He fought for control, wanting to hold back his release and enjoy this moment for as long as possible. It was impossible and he felt the liquid jets of his release ripped from his balls with ecstatic agony as his entire body went up in flames of pleasure.

He crashed into her, smashing her into the tailgate. After a moment, he shifted and lifted his head.

"Sweetheart?"

There was no response and he could tell from her limp body that she had passed out again. Derek smiled with masculine satisfaction at having pleased his mate so well.

Carefully, so not to disturb her, he slipped from her body and lifted her into his arms. His legs wobbled slightly, weak from his recent release and his grin widened. Claire wasn't the only one who had been drained from their love play.

Chapter 16

Derek sighed and stretched his arm out along the back of the seat. Curling his palm around Claire's shoulder, he pulled her into his side. Now this was why he had bought a truck with a bench seat.

It felt nice to drive off into the night with Claire cuddled against him. He stroked her hair away from her face, his fingers tangling in the silky tresses. The feel of it sliding through his fingers was the sweetest caress.

Derek felt his cock harden in a rush and had to mentally shake his head at his body's unruly reaction. It did not matter they had spent the past four hours making love. He should be worn out, but here he was, hard and hurting all because his mate was close.

Claire sighed, resting her head on his shoulder. Her eyes fluttered closed as her breathing evened out. He had worn her out obviously. Perhaps after he got some food into her, she would be reenergized and be ready for another round. If not, he would not complain. Either way she was sleeping in his bed tonight.

Derek glanced down at her. Her black lashes were long and sleek against her cheek. She looked small and delicate when she was asleep. Derek smiled when he realized what a con that was.

He bet their kids would pull the same con. They would probably look like angels when they slept, but one could only imagine what kind of devils they'd be when they were awake. Between Claire's determination and his tendency for mischief, their kids were going to keep them on their toes.

At least, they would have his parents to help guide them through. He knew his parents were going to love Claire. Right now they were somewhere out west, taking a tour of the country in an RV. Once he told them about his mate, they would turn around and head home.

His mother had been waiting for the day she got to plan her first wedding. When that was done, she would begin to nag about grandchildren. Derek grinned thinking back over the day.

Grandkids would be no problem. He had every intention of getting Claire pregnant before he even married her. It would take his mother over a month to plan a wedding and he just had a week to go before the full moon.

As he pulled into the Firehouse's dirt parking lot, the truck bumped over the uneven surface. Claire groaned as her head bounced. Slowly straightening, she blinked as she looked around. It was late for dinner by Wilsonville standards and the lot was mostly empty.

Derek parked close to the door and helped Claire from the truck. She still appeared a little foggy as he led her into the small restaurant. They didn't talk until after the waitress had brought them sweet tea. Derek ordered two dinners despite Claire's frown at his presumption.

"Okay, Miss FBI, why don't you catch me up on the details of the case?" Derek had decided they might as well get through the dirty work.

"I thought we already talked about that."

"We need to talk about it again. Why don't you tell me about how you plan to track down Kathleen's killer?"

Claire heaved an extravagant sigh before she began to talk. There wasn't much to go on and the killer being a woman had set Claire back to the beginning of having to formulate theories.

The food came and Derek dug in as Claire began to nibble on her fries. She continued to talk about what her approach was going to be. He could not object to the idea of investigating Kathleen's life and her friends, but, as he pointed out, Kathleen had not had a lot of friends.

"And we have to look at you." Claire's nonchalant statement had him choking on his last bite of burger. Quickly, he washed down the heavy mass with a gulp of tea.

"I thought we already agreed that I wasn't a suspect."

"Not as a suspect." Claire waved a fry at him. "But as the antagonist."

"Antagonist? I didn't antagonize a killer into taking Kathleen."

"You sure about that? Look at the case. We have a shy girl without a lot of friends, no enemies, who is about to take you off the dating market."

"So?" Derek's glass hit the table hard enough to make the ice clink.

"So, we have a female killer. A boy who dates a lot and undoubtedly left a trail of broken hearts."

"I did not."

"Really? Why don't we ask her?" Claire nodded to a woman over his shoulder.

Derek glanced back and cursed mentally when he saw she was referring to Carolyn. The blonde was rapidly approaching with fire in her eyes and Cecelia and Denise to back her up. Things were about to become unpleasant. Derek thought about interceding, but it was too late. Carolyn came to a stop, eyes trained on Claire.

"Carolyn—"

"Save it Derek. I've come to meet your mate."

"Mate?" Claire raised her eyebrow at that.

"Do you want to know what kind of disgusting, lowlife you've mated yourself to?" Carolyn's snarl drew Claire's eyes back to her.

"So repulsive you want him back." Claire smiled slightly.

Carolyn growled at Claire's happy tone before turning heated eyes on Derek.

"You cannot possibly have mated this—"

"Watch it now." Claire brought Carolyn's attention back to her. "You don't want your mouth to get you into trouble."

"Trouble? I'll teach you about trouble."

"Such a generous offer, but I'm afraid I don't take lessons from puppies."

"What did you call me?"

"A puppy. It seems fitting. As far as I can tell, you pathetically yap after Derek. Obviously, after all these years, you couldn't get him to mate you. It was kind of like you were chasing your own tail. Just like a puppy, wouldn't you say?"

"Why you—"

"Why me?" Claire blinked innocently. "I'm better in bed."

Derek groaned at that flippant response. Things were about a second from getting out of hand. As queen bitch, Claire had the right to handle the other bitches any way she saw fit. Any way, as long as it did not compromise the pack.

"Better? I doubt that."

"Really? Are you sure about that? Because, if I'm not mistaken, I stole the best fuck in town right out from underneath you."

"Smile, now, bitch, because you won't be smiling for long."

"No. Soon I'll be laughing."

"I swear—" Whatever Carolyn's threat, it was lost in a shriek as a sudden a gust of wind appeared from nowhere and blew up her skirt. As she tried to force it back down, another invisible blow sent her to the ground. Her bellow of outrage was cut off when her ass smacked into the hard tile floor.

Her two friends backed up, their expressions going from superior to distinctly wary as they looked around. For her part, Claire laughed and shook her head.

"You'll pay for that." Carolyn scrambled back up to her feet.

"Pay for the fact that you're a klutz?" Claire raised an eyebrow at that. "Please leave, Carolyn. You're annoying me."

Carolyn growled before turning and storming off. Derek had little doubt the other woman had left because he was there. Carolyn knew he would not let her harm Claire. Still Claire was going to have to watch it. He would not always be around to help.

"You shouldn't have done that," Derek quickly admonished her.

"Ah, but now I know." Claire smiled smugly as she sipped from her straw.

"Know what?"

"She's possessive and, quite possibly, disturbed."

"Carolyn may be a lot of things, but not a killer. Nobody in my pack would do what you're suggesting."

"You'll forgive me if I prefer harder evidence than just your instincts on this matter." Claire shoved her plate toward him. "Here you can have my burger."

"Not hungry?"

"Not now."

"It's talking about the case, isn't it? Made you lose your appetite."

"I'm on a diet."

"You hate it, don't you?"

"What? My burger?"

"Being an investigator." Derek bit into the double-decker in front of him.

"Being an investigator?" Claire repeated her eyes widening slightly before she shrugged. "It's like any job, there are days when you love it and days when you dream of doing something else."

"What else do you dream of doing?" Derek coked his head.

"You'll think it's silly." Claire looked down, a blush tinting her cheeks.

"That's the point of dreams, Claire. If they aren't outrageously silly and over the moon, then they wouldn't be called dreams."

"Okay." Claire took a deep breath and looked him straight in the eye. "I wrote a book."

"A book?"

"Yeah, a mystery novel." Her tone was slightly defensive. "I have an agent trying to pimp it."

"Pimp it?" Derek repeated, biting back a smile.

"It's been almost a year now. That's how long Sally, my agent, has been on the case. It took me eight months just to get her. I have an amazing collection of rejection letters. Maybe I'll let you see them sometime."

"That's great." Derek popped a fry into his mouth. "So are you going to let me read the book?"

"Not in this lifetime."

"Come on," Derek cajoled her. "I can give you my opinion."

"What makes you think I would value the opinion of a Colt fan?"

"If it's published, you wouldn't be able to stop me."

"You'll have to pay full price for it," Claire warned him. "No free copies."

"Only at the library." Derek's hand paused as he lifted another fry. "Tell me something, how did you knock Carolyn on her ass?"

"I didn't do anything." Claire wiggled her straw, trying to get to the last little bit of tea in her glass.

"Claire."

"What? I didn't do anything." Claire rolled her eyes at him. "Fine. It was my partner."

"Partner? Oh, you mean the ghost." Derek couldn't stop himself from looking around. There was nothing there. "It's here."

As if in answer to that question, his glass moved further away.

"She. Her name is Kate," Claire corrected. For a moment, she appeared to be thinking heavily, and then she smiled. "She thinks you're pathetic to have slept with that woman."

"She talks to you?"

"Yes and I can see her." Claire smiled. "All part of the curse."

"That's creepy. Hey!" Derek shouted indignantly as his empty plate flipped into his lap.

"Only the special can insult Kate," Claire admonished him. "You're not special."

"Does she hang around you often?"

"Usually." At Claire's answer, Derek suddenly had a dirty thought.

"Then she's seen us. I mean when we–"

"Kate is a real pervert. A few hundred years of not getting laid, would make anybody horny." Claire's hand tightened around her glass. "I don't think so sweetheart."

"She can move things." Derek lifted his plate before pinning Claire with a hard gaze. "Can she manipulate electricity?"

"She pleads the fifth," Claire answered after a moment.

"That's how you did it. Kate staged that incident at the tomato-packing plant just so you could search my house."

Derek's cell ringing saved Claire from answering that question. After a moment of listening to Travis, he silently groaned. It would be nice to get one night without being disturbed but those nights wouldn't come until after summer ended and the tourists went home.

As he explained to Claire that a drunk had run a red light and caused a minor pile up with serious injuries, she was already getting up. Derek slapped some money down on the table and they moved quickly to the car.

The ride home was relaxed, a pleasant silence. Derek realized there was one advantage to mating a former FBI agent. She wouldn't get mad at him because his job dragged him away all hours of the night.

She wanted to be a writer, a nice safe occupation she could do from home while she cared for their kids. Derek chuckled; knowing if Claire could hear his thoughts, she would probably hit him.

He let her inside the house and gave her a kiss. Warning her there would be hell to pay if she were not in his bed when he got home, he left.

* * * *

The team is here.

Claire turned away from the sight of Derek's taillights disappearing down the road. Kate was there. The ghost nodded to the rental across the street. Glancing at the rundown house, she saw the lights come on.

That didn't surprise Claire. While nobody else on the team could see Kate, for some strange reason, Deik could hear her. Once Deik had drawn Kate, based on a description Kate herself gave him. It had been an impressive rendition, even if Kate had emphasized certain nonexistent attributes.

Without commenting, Claire headed across the street. Deik opened the door for her. The tall, lean vampire was giving her one of his hypnotizing smiles when suddenly his green eyes narrowed. He reached out to touch her shoulder right where Derek had bitten her.

"Werewolf," Deik purred in his honey voice. "You surprise me Claire."

"Maybe you'll show me a little more respect now, huh?" Claire pushed past him and nodded a greeting at Sasha and Harold, who were relaxing on the worn couch that had come with the house. Claire never sat there; too afraid of the bugs she was certain lived in it.

"You mated a werewolf?" Sasha blinked at her.

"That's none of anybody's business." Claire wasn't about to admit she hadn't realized Derek had mated her. That jerk had charmed her into forgetting to ask about Carolyn's statement. Well, he wasn't going to get away with that twice. "You're here to help me with Urazi, not my social life."

I'm just surprised you have one.

Thank you, Kate.

One that I'm jealous of.

Thank you!

"Not to help, sweetheart." Deik shut the door. "To handle."

"A werewolf with a demon's brand is certainly an issue for the company," Sasha admonished at the same time.

She's just jealous. She's never done it in front of a mirror.

At least I have a reflection.

"See that you mention this new situation when you speak to Mike next," Sasha instructed in her prim tone.

"Can we focus on Urazi, people?" Claire implored with open hands.

"By all means." Harold stood. "We're ready to handle that matter now. All we need is directions."

Oh, they're going to love this.

"I'll show you," Claire offered.

Go on. Tell them the truth.

"You'll tell us," Deik corrected her.

"It's not that simple. The place is hidden in the woods."

Chicken.

"You don't have GPS coordinates."

Tell them.

"I did," Claire admitted before begrudgingly confessing. "I kind of left the unit at the house."

"Stellar work there, Claire." Harold laughed. "So now we get to wander around in the dark going, 'here demon, demon'."

"Try, 'here Urazi, Urazi.' It might get a better response."

"You did that on purpose," Deik complained. "Just so we had to take you with us."

He thinks you're cleverer than you actually are.

"I left it there because I was scared shitless, which is why you don't have to worry about me getting in the way."

"Make sure of that," Sasha warned her.

"Such confidence in my ability," Claire muttered, before pinning Sasha with her gaze. "So what is the plan?"

"We extract Urazi from the house and secure him in this." Sasha gestured to a large piece of pottery, "urn. Then we'll take him back to the company for warehousing."

"You're not sending him back to hell?"

You're obsessed with sending things to hell.

"Why do that? So he can come back someday?" Sasha retorted. "We'll keep him locked up and permanently neutered."

"If that's what you want to do." Claire did not agree with the plan, but there was nothing she could do about that. "We should get moving. I haven't got a lot of time."

"What, you're werewolf going to spank you if he comes home and you're not dutifully waiting for him?" Deik snickered.

"Don't push it, Deik."

"So, how are we moving?" Harold interjected before their bickering could escalate into a full-scale argument.

"Well, by air would be best if we can. Otherwise, we drive and hike."

"I can carry the dog," Deik offered antagonistically.

"I am not a dog!"

"I can carry the sorceress," Harold intervened again.

Chapter 17

Friday: 11:40 am

Derek leaned back in his chair and checked the clock. Twenty more minutes and it would be lunchtime. He thought about what he wanted to eat for lunch. Claire sounded good. Spread out on his bed like a banquet, Derek would feast on her.

He shifted in his seat, trying to get more comfortable with the steel pole rising out of his lap. He had been hard almost all morning. How much he suffered depended on how close Claire was or where his thoughts strayed.

She had been exactly where she was supposed to be when he had come home last night. Despite his best intentions to let her rest, he couldn't stop touching her.

Touching led to kissing and soon she was moaning and he was lost. Not that Claire had objected to the sex, or retreated afterward. She snuggled into him after and gone to sleep, just like a mate should.

Of course, she had awakened him to questions about their mating at the crack of dawn. He wanted to answer them, wanted to explain everything to her, but the sight of her rumpled and naked in his bed had sidetracked him. By the time he had released enough energy to focus, they had been late for work. Tonight, over a romantic dinner, he would explain everything.

The intercom beeped.

"Yes, sweetheart?" Derek pressed the talk button.

"Sheriff McBane, line one," came back in that prim, uptight tone that told him he was violating one of her professional standards.

"Thanks, sexy." Derek grinned as he picked up the receiver. That should get her feisty, add a little zing to their lunch.

"McBane, hope you have good news for me," Derek greeted the sheriff.

"Depends on your definition of good news," McBane growled back. "Meet me for lunch."

"I had plans," Derek hedged, hoping McBane would suggest another time.

"Your mate will have to wait," McBane snorted, accurately guessing Derek's plans.

"Okay, fine." Derek flicked his pen across the pile of reports he had been reviewing. "Where do you want to meet?"

"Someplace private."

"My house?"

"You got anything to eat?"

"Does beer count?"

"I want two burgers, you can call it in to Millie."

"See you in thirty, then?"

"I'll be there."

Derek disconnected and put the call in to Millie for the food. Twenty minutes later, he headed out. Dropping a kiss on Claire's lips, he told her he had to meet the sheriff for lunch.

* * * *

Derek watched McBane wolf down the two burgers without hesitation or comment. Only when he had gulped down an entire can of beer did he lean back in his chair to glare at Derek.

"Where was your lovely mate around by ten last night?"

"Why do you want to know?" Derek spun his own can of beer in his cupped hands.

"The old Howard's place burned between eleven and midnight last night. So where was she?"

"In bed."

"With you."

"I had a call on an accident about eight-thirty and didn't get home until one."

"So she could've done it." McBane stood, chunking his own empty can into the trash.

"She did not burn it down."

"Says you." JD pulled a new beer out of the fridge.

"Says me. What proof do you have to say otherwise?"

"She was sniffing near that area not two days ago. Only one to show any interest in the area in years." JD sat back down. "By your own statement she was curious about the Howard place."

"That and a buck fifty will get you nowhere," Derek growled over the hiss JD's can made as he popped it open. "So don't be accusing my mate of things you can't back up."

"What about the FBI considering her a prime suspect in another fire? Does that do it for you?"

"What fire?"

"The fire that got her fired." McBane's eyes twitched. "Nasty bit of business. I couldn't get all the details, but I got enough to know that your mate comes with some serious baggage."

"Don't keep me in suspense."

"Agent Cory was undercover working on a task force to bust a man who was importing young, foreign girls for the sex trade. During the investigation, it appears Agent Cory and a man named Peter Wall became romantically involved."

"They did, did they?" The can in Derek's hand crinkled he dented it.

"The operation went bad." JD eyed Derek's can as it crackled again. "SWAT went in, place blew up, everybody died. Pardon me, everybody but Mr. Wall and Agent Cory, who both magically escaped the flames unharmed."

"Jesus." Derek closed his eyes. Whatever he had been expecting McBane to tell him, that was not it. "So they arrested her."

"Suspended pending investigation," McBane corrected. "I guess they couldn't get the goods, because they never charged her. Eventually she was let go. They did arrest Mr. Wall on other charges, but he was released about a week ago now."

"He's free." Derek rubbed his head.

"I guess it will be no shock to you that the reason this information was hard to come by was because the FBI considers this an open investigation." McBane rubbed his chin. "Which is why I'm curious about where your mate was last night."

"Why would she burn that house?" Derek defended her out loud, but he did not doubt that she was guilty. Why was the question he planned to ask? Well, after he spanked her for deceiving him again.

"More appropriate question is how did she do it and then how did she stop it?" JD corrected. "Fire was out, out cold, not even a smoldering ash by the time the fire department managed to hike back there. Now that ain't right, not with all that dry wood around the place, that forest should have been blazing.

"If that's not strange enough, the investigator tells me this morning he can't find the point of origin. He doesn't know how the fire started. I don't like mysteries, Derek. I want to know what the hell is going on."

"I'll get you answers." Derek uncurled his fist from his destroyed beer can. "You get anything on Cerberus?"

"The Masters of Cerberus does covert operations and investigations, but they're not mainstream. They handle supernatural cases or problems." JD paused to smirk slightly. "They call their investigators handlers. That's some sick kind of humor, isn't it?"

"That actually figures." Derek ignored JD's side comment.

"How so?"

"Claire is some sort of psychic."

"Really? What? She has visions and stuff?"

"Actually, yes." Derek nodded seriously. "She came here because there's a demon living in out midst."

"A demon?" JD's eyebrow went up at that. "You buy that?"

" I do."

"Heh. You really are living in a freak show." JD lost his smile a moment later. "A demon, huh? I don't buy that. We'd know if there was some deviant scumbag living in our mist."

"Would we?"

"Goddamn right we would."

"We've missed a killer who's already claimed twenty-plus women."

"Oh, so now we not only have a psychic, a demon, but now a serial killer?"

"And a ghost." Derek thought suddenly. He would bet money Claire's friendly ghost, Kate, was around. Remembering how she had responded last night to Derek's disbelief, he hoped he could inspire her to convince JD.

"A ghost? As in Casper?" JD laughed. "You've lost it my friend."

"She's the one who set up our night of entertainment at the tomato-packing plant."

"Bullshit. No stupid little ghost pulled that off."

As if on cue, JD's plate flew off the table and slammed into his chest.

"Goddamn it!" JD peeled back the plate to expose the ketchup and mustard stains on his uniform.

"Kate doesn't like being laughed at."

"Kate?"

"That's the ghost's name."

"It figures it would be a woman, playing all those stupid ass games."

In obvious retaliation, JD's chair suddenly flipped out and he found himself hitting the floor. Derek shook his head. Kate was going to teach JD manners the hard way, which was the only way JD learned some things.

JD had picked himself off the floor and was glaring around the room. Looking for the ghost was pointless. There was nothing there. With agitated motions, the sheriff retrieved his chair and slammed it down before sitting.

"Look, you want to buy into all this mumbo jumbo, be my guest. I don't want any more fires. You make that real clear to your mate."

"There wouldn't be anymore fires. I promise."

"Good."

"So what've you got on this killer?"

Derek told JD everything, including that Kathleen was probably the first victim and Claire thought the killer was a woman. JD snorted at that. Derek did not bother trying to convince him.

"I'm not saying I buy into this female serial killer thing, but I admit your woman has some good ideas."

"I'm going to follow them up," Derek agreed.

"Well, I look around on my end. Keep me posted."

"Back at you." Derek stood and stretched. "Now if you don't mind, I've got to talk to my mate." He paused and looked around. "And don't warn her Kate."

* * * *

Claire knew she was in trouble the minute she saw Derek's face as he stormed back into the police station. Ignoring the officer's greetings, he made a direct line for her. Claire cringed inwardly, wondering what had happened.

Kate. Claire called out to the ghost, but got no response.

Kate!

Damn it! What was the point of sending Kate to spy on Derek if the ghost did not report back? Before Claire could think of a way to escape the irate police chief closing in on her, he was standing beside her desk. This was going to be bad.

Kate, damn it!

"In my office." He jabbed at the open door with his finger. "Now!"

She said nothing, though several obnoxious comments came to her mind. Silently, dutifully, she went into the small room and took her seat. He slammed the door so hard the wall shook and Claire cringed.

She watched as he settled into his seat. For several moments, he sat quietly, breathing deeply, obviously trying to calm himself. From the way his eyes were darkening, Claire didn't think it was helping.

"Do you understand the definition of honesty?"

Her stomach twisted at his words as her mind ran through all the possibilities of which one of her secrets he had discovered. She was betting on the Howard place going up in flames last night, but she couldn't be certain. Since Claire was unsure, she chose not to respond but went with a confused look.

"Don't give me that innocent look." Derek leaned forward. "I can smell your calculation."

"Honesty is—"

"Save it!"

"Well, you as—"

"We'll start with something simple," Derek growled. "Did you set fire to the Howard's house?"

"Did I?" Claire placed a hand on her chest. "No."

Derek did not respond right away but intensely studied her. The corner of his eyes twitched, surprising Claire and, strangely, calming her.

"Do you know who did?"

"Me?"

"Damn it, Claire!" His fist hit the desk and she could see the vein on his left temple bulge. "Don't fucking play games with me! Answer the question!"

"Yes." Claire shifted slightly. "I know who set the fire."

"Who?"

"Just some friends."

"You don't have any friends in Wilsonville." Derek's eyes narrowed.

"They got in last night."

"You don't mean friends. These are more employees of Cerberus."

"They're friends, too." Claire plucked at an invisible piece of lint.

"Why?"

"Why?" Claire frowned slightly. "Why are they my friends?"

"Stupid doesn't become you," Derek forced between clenched teeth.

"Well if you would ask more specific—"

"Why did they set the fire?"

"Well," Claire pursed her lips. "It was just…" He was going red in the face. "Okay, so we burned the building to keep Urazi from inhabiting it…again."

"Urazi? And who is Urazi?" Even as he stopped forming the words, he was sitting back. His eyes went wide for a moment before narrowing back to slits. "Oh, he's the demon, isn't he?"

"Good news." Claire forced a smile. "We found the demon."

"Not last night, you didn't, there wasn't enough time. That means you knew about it before we talked last night. You sat there at dinner and bullshitted me."

"I didn't bullshit you." Claire clenched her hands, trying to remain calm. "I just omitted a few facts."

"It's the same damn thing! You know what your problem is? You don't trust me!" Derek roared.

Claire cringed at that. "It's not that, Derek. It's just…"

"It's what?"

"Demon's are dangerous and I just don't want to see you get hurt."

"So, you decided to go off and handle it on your own."

"No. I'm not trained to handle exorcisms. That's what the friends are for."

The room echoed with Derek's deep breath. He had closed his eyes as he sat there, perfectly still. Claire shifted, crossing and uncrossing her legs, waiting for his response. When he spoke next, his voice was hoarse.

"So the demon is taken care of."

"Well...no."

"No?" His eyes popped open.

"He kind of escaped, but before you go off the deep end—"

"The deep end?" Derek sputtered. "Oh, sweetheart, from what I understand, you're swimming in the abyss."

"It's not like he's running free around town." Claire was quick to explain.

"Oh? Then what is it like?"

"Well...see, Urazi needs a...shrine."

"Shrine?"

"Something that's...poisoned enough to attract him."

"Another haunted house."

"Yeah." Claire nodded. "But ,see, it doesn't have to be here. He could be anywhere in the world."

"Oh, well, that's really reassuring." Derek rolled his eyes. "So, he's out of the scene."

"Maybe," Claire mumbled softy, studying the crease in her slacks.

"But you—"

"A shrine doesn't have to be a building." Claire looked up. "Could be anything that is appropriately corrupt."

"Anything? Like a car or a beer can?" Derek suggested obnoxiously.

"Or a person." Claire's words were barely audible.

"Oh, wait a second." Derek's head tilted to the side as he studied her. "You're suggesting the killer. You're saying that we no longer have a serial killer working with a demon, but we have a demonic serial killer."

"It's a possibility." Claire cringed.

"You've seen this before, haven't you?" Derek asked softly after another long stretch of silence. "Last time a bunch of people got hurt."

"The last time?" Claire could feel the blood draining out of her face and her body starting to shake.

"The last fire that you were involved in." Derek appeared unconcerned by her reaction, too absorbed in his anger. "How many died then, Claire?"

"Thirty-six." Her voice was barley audible, as she turned her attention to her lap. "Nineteen girls, three pimps, fourteen cops."

"But you lived."

"Flames of hell don't hurt me," Claire repeated softly, more for herself than for him.

"What? What are you talking about, the flames of hell?"

Claire didn't get a chance to respond. The door shook as somebody pounded on it.

"Not now!" Derek shouted.

"Uh, Derek. The FBI is here." Baker sounded unsure and nervous.

"Shit!" Derek turned his lethal glare back on her. Claire squirmed in her seat, casting an uneasy glance at the door.

"What is about to happen would go a lot better if I knew what was coming." Derek stood. "See why honesty is so important?"

"Derek?" Baker called through the door.

"I'm coming." Without a backward, glance he walked away.

Chapter 18

The deputies could smell the authority emanating from the two men dressed in the dark suits. Mixed in the odor was another smell, anger. Derek didn't flinch under their scrutiny as he walked to the front desk.

"I'm Sheriff Derek Keller." Derek's eyes went to the older of the two men in his lobby. He stood slightly in front of the other agent, his scowl wrinkling his heavy tanned face.

"Agent Perst," the man held up his badge, "this is Agent Yankovic of the Federal Bureau of Investigations. We're looking for Miss Cory. I believe she's working here."

Derek could feel the subtle shifting of his men behind him.

"Why are you looking for Miss Cory?"

"Does she work here?" Perst asked coldly.

"We only have a Dorothy Walker working here." That gem came from Travis. Derek could feel him coming closer to the desk.

"That would be Claire." Perst lips gave a bitter curl. "I'd like to see her."

"Got a warrant?" Ace demanded.

"I don't need one, she's not under arrest."

"Then she doesn't have to talk to you," Baker grunted.

Perst looked around at the officers before turning his cold gaze back on Derek.

"Chief Jacob, it is important to the FBI that we speak with Miss Cory."

An implied threat was hidden in that simple statement. Derek didn't like to be threatened. Neither did he like exposing his mate to danger. He wasn't the only one. The smell of aggression strengthened behind him as his pack members prepared to defend their queen.

"It's alright, Derek." Claire drew everybody but Derek's attention to her. "I'll talk to him."

Perst pale blue eyes narrow for a moment as his smell went from anger to contempt. Concern for his mate overrode every other consideration.

"I don't think you should talk to them without a lawyer." He turned to confront Claire as she made her way to the desk. Instantly her mouth opened and he knew she was going to reject his idea. She must have seen something in his eyes, because she hesitated and gave him a considering look before nodding.

"Alright."

Claire's agreement surprised and pleased him. He was not real sure what it meant, but Derek was certain her deferring to his wishes was a turning point for them.

"Lawyer," Perst repeated. "You have one of those?"

"My sister," Derek answered for her. "I'll call her, she can be here in a few minutes."

"Fine." Perst studied him for a moment. "Do you mind if we wait in your office?"

"Please," Derek gestured to the small wooden gate that divided the public area from the rest of the station, "step this way."

"Wait here," Derek murmured in Claire's ear before stepping away to escort the agents to his office. Derek didn't wait to see if she did as instructed, but followed the two agents into his office.

"Please, make yourself comfortable."

Before either of the agents could respond, Derek shut the door. Claire was standing in the doorway to the outer office. Her concerned gazed stayed on his office door as he reached for the phone. Derek could smell her anxiety, her fear.

He used Claire's phone to call Kristin. Keeping the details short, he asked her to come down to the station. His sister picked up on the worry in his tone and agreed to be there in a minute.

"How long will it take Kristin to get here?"

Claire's tone was professional. Derek was beginning to learn that she hid behind a wall of professionalism whenever her emotions became too much. It was her way of remaining in control.

"I don't know if calling her in was a good idea," Claire continued to talk, oblivious to the hand he had latched on to her arm.

"It will probably piss them off." Claire did not offer any resistance as he led her out of the office, past the curious gazes of the other officers, and toward the break room.

"Perst doesn't like me anyway."

"Baker send Kristin back to the break room when she gets here."

Baker nodded at Derek's instruction. Claire continued to speak, showing no awareness for what was going on around her.

"Not that he has reason to."

Derek came to a stop in the small break room and turned to face her. Claire frowned.

"I wonder what he wants."

Derek didn't respond, but pulled her into his arms. She didn't resist, nor did she respond. She just stood there in his embrace, detached as ever.

"You shouldn't put yourself in the middle. It's a dangerous place to be."

"That's the second time you've warned me about being involved with you."

"Perhaps you'll listen this time." Emotion finally sounded in her voice.

"Don't worry about it, baby."

"Perst could hurt you," Claire argued. Pulling her head back, she frowned at him.

"Don't worry about Perst. I'm not." Derek brushed her hair behind her ears. Curling his fingers around her neck, he pulled her closer until her head rested on his chest.

"He could make your life really difficult," Claire mumbled into his shirt.

"And how could he do that, sweetheart?"

"You're a police chief." Claire tried to pull back again, but Derek held her close. "If the town discovers you're harboring a suspect in a federal investigation, it could go badly for you."

"The town will understand."

"Yeah, they'll understand you threw your moral code aside for sex."

"Not just sex, but the best sex in town. Isn't that what you told Carolyn?"

"This isn't a joke."

"Look, Claire." Derek raised her chin so he could look into eyes made more gold than green with worry. "Most of the town belongs to my pack. I could run around the square naked, yelling 'down with the man' and I'd still get reelected."

"That's just…" Claire rolled her eyes. "I don't even know what that is."

"It's the truth." Derek dropped a quick kiss on her furrowed forehead. "And so is this. Anybody in my pack would defend you."

Before Claire could respond to that, Derek lowered his head and kissed her. Ever so gently, he tasted her sweet mouth. Tracing the fullness of her bottom lip, his tongue slid inside when she sighed.

Sweet tea and sweeter woman, he could not get enough of her taste. What had started as gentle reassurance quickly spun out of control as the passion between them roared to life. Repeatedly he stroked his tongue into her until she caught it with her lips, sucking on the velvety marauder.

Derek groaned, feeling his cock thump against his slacks at her aggression. The hard tips of her soft breast poked into his chest and he rubbed against them, making his little mate moan with need. The intoxicating scent of her desire filled his head.

That was what he wanted, her wet with her need for him. Derek growled, turning and pinning her against he counter. He lifted one of her legs, holding it up along his hips so he could grind his hard cock into the heaven between her thighs.

Too many clothes. Derek grunted with the thought, his fingers curling around the collar of her shirt. Before he could rip the offending fabric out of his way, a throat cleared throwing ice water over the moment or at least over Claire. She stiffened against him. A moment later, she was fighting his hold.

"Is this the emergency you called me down here for?" Kristin asked dryly.

"Oh, my God," Claire muttered before shooting Derek a dark look.

He could hear her silent words. *Without decency or decorum.* Yeah, he was and if his sister had not interrupted, he would have fucked her against the counter in the break room. He wouldn't have had a moment of embarrassment or regret.

"Thanks for coming so quickly, sis," Derek forced himself to say.

"Try it with a hint of sincerity and I just might believe it," Kristin snorted as she set her briefcase down on the table. "So what can I do for you?"

"Claire has a little problem."

"Are you in some kind of trouble?" Kristin switched her gaze to the blushing woman standing as far from Derek as the small room allowed.

"Some kind," Claire repeated softly earning her a sharp look from Derek.

"A few details would be helpful." Kristin prodded. "We could start with criminal or civil."

"Criminal," Derek answered for Claire. "There are two FBI agents waiting in my office."

"FBI?" Kristin whistled. "I've got to admit I'm impressed. She's outdone you, Derek."

"Thanks," Derek returned dryly.

"And I've also got to say I've never worked a federal case before. Sounds serious." Kristin's eyes darted over to Claire looking for a response. "Is it, Claire?"

"Don't know." Claire shrugged. "Your brother hasn't let me talk to them long enough to learn anything."

"Maybe you should go find out what they want, Kristin," Derek suggested.

"I could—"

"That's just going to piss them off."

"What do you care?" Derek turned on Claire.

"They're just doing their job." Claire frowned at him. "This isn't about the past. Something else has happened. I want to know what it is and help if I can."

"Pardon me." Kristin waved a finger at them. "What past?"

"Claire is at best considered an accessory and at worst a conspirator in a fire that killed a lot of people."

"But they never charged you?" Kristin looked at Claire who shook her head. "How many is a lot?"

"Thirty-six," Derek answered when Claire remained silent. He caught her flinch out of the corner of his eye. "And it included more than a dozen cops."

Kristin just stood there for a minute just absorbing that.

"She's not guilty, Kristin," Derek snapped.

"I…I didn't say that, but forgive me if this is a lot to take in all of a sudden." Kristin took a deep breath before casting a hard look at Claire. "Derek is probably right, you shouldn't talk to them until I know what is going on."

"I want to talk to them."

"Claire—"

"Look, Derek, I know you're trying to help me and appreciate it." Claire took hold of his hand and gave it a gentle squeeze. "But I want to talk to them."

"Fine." Derek relented. "But if Kristin says don't answer, then don't. Agreed?"

"Agreed." Claire stretched and gave him a horribly chaste kiss on his cheek.

"Well then, let's get this over with." Kristin picked up her briefcase and headed for Derek's office.

* * * *

The two extra chairs in Derek's office were both occupied by the agents. Not expecting them to give up their seats, Claire dragged in another chair for Kristin. Neither agent spoke while Claire took Derek's seat at his silent insistence.

Derek chose to stand as everybody waited for somebody to start speaking. Claire thought he probably enjoyed towering over the two agents, while Kristin quickly went through the introductions.

"So what brings you to Wilsonville?" Not in the mood to waste time with the preliminaries, Claire cut straight to the matter at hand.

"When was the last time you were in contact with Agent Howard?" The younger agent, who had been introduced as Agent Yankovic, had a legal pad resting on his knees and pen ready in his hand.

"Max?" Claire had not expected that question. "I talked to him on the phone a few days ago."

"When specifically?" Yankovic pressed.

At Yankovic's insistence, Claire went over the details of her phone call with Max. The agent used her answers to turn the conversation to Wall and the real interrogation began. For five minutes, he pumped her for information about her phone conversations with Mr. Wall. When he started to turn up the pressure, Kristin interceded.

"I have to interject here." Kristin cleared her throat. "I know an interrogation when I see one. As Claire's lawyer, I'm going to suggest she not answer anymore questions until you explain exactly why you are interrogating her."

Yankovic blinked at Kristin, as if surprised she was speaking. Not sure what to do, the younger agent turned to his superior for direction. Perst had not once taken his frosty gaze off Claire.

Claire had not returned his look, knowing what she would find there. Now she did, keeping her gaze just as detached and emotionless as his. For a moment, they studied each other, once respected colleagues and now competitors.

"Take a look." Perst hefted his briefcase onto his lap.

The pop of the latches echoed in the small office. A moment later, he slapped two vanilla folders in front of her. Claire glanced down at the folders. Each label was filled out with a name. Max Howard and Denise Marshall.

Max Howard, once her partner, then her lover, and the only man who could have set the record straight about what happened the night of the fire. Denise Marshal was the mother of one of the missing girls. A woman so filled with grief and guilt she had come to Cerberus as her last opportunity to find her missing daughter.

Neither had anything in common but Claire. Now they had one more thing. People didn't get their name on one of these special folders unless they were victims of crime. It required no great guess to figure out what type of crime.

Claire felt grief and fear try to overthrow her control. She closed her eyes and took a deep breath, fighting back the sensations. The last thing she wanted to do was to open one of those folders.

"Don't want to see?" There was a touch of condescension in Perst's challenge.

Bracing herself mentally, she reached down and opened the first file. Slowly she took in the images of horror laid out in front of her. As if he needed to add to the pictures, Perst spoke up. His tone filled with loathing and disgust.

"Both victims were discovered bled dry. As you can see, the killer burned the word 'one' on Marshall's chest and the word 'warning' on Max's. Does that mean anything to you?"

You only get one warning.

Wall's words echoed in her head. Telling Perst would make him more suspicious of her. Not telling him would be interfering in his case.

"The last time I talked to Wall, he said I would only get one warning." Claire looked up to meet Perst's eyes.

"One warning? He said that?" Perst pursed his lips.

"That's not enough," Yankovic commented, but he wrote her comment in his notebook nonetheless.

"What was he warning you about Claire? Was your conscience getting to you?"

"He was warning me," Claire took a deep breath, "to dissociate from Chief Jacob."

"What?" Kristin turned rounded eyes on Derek. Even Perst cast a look at the chief.

"The maniac who killed these people is threatening you?"

"Kristin." Derek's tone was hard.

"Don't 'Kristin' me," Kristin snapped. "I want to know!"

"We'll discuss this later," Derek growled.

Kristin looked ready to object and, for a moment, Claire thought she was going to. Instead, Kristin resumed her seat, her rigid posture clearly broadcasting her displeasure.

"So, Wall calls you and threatens your lover." Perst spoke as if nothing had just happened. "And to assure you get the message he kills your former lover. Who, then, is Denise Marshal?"

"A client."

"A client," Perst repeated. "Max and she had no association, nothing in common, but for you. Right?"

"Right."

"Why kill your client?"

"Ask Wall."

"So you don't know."

"I can't speak for his motivation. He made no threat against her."

"Did you tell him she was your client?"

"No. The name Denise Marshal never came up in our conversations."

"Did you mention Denise to Max?"

"No."

Perst continued questioning her in rapid fire. Claire answered as best she could. It wasn't much, because she didn't know much. It was obvious Perst believed her short answers to be intentionally misleading and not truthful.

"Look at those pictures, Claire. He's dead because of you. Brutally murdered. The least you can do is answer my questions honestly."

She felt Derek shift, the tension thickening suddenly. Perst sensed the change in the chief at the same time. His eyes darted to the larger man. Before things escalated, Claire shot Derek a hard look. She could read the anger in his navy eyes. He did not like Perst attacking his mate. She was sure that the agent had received the message.

Turning her attention back to the folders, she carefully examined the pictures. It was easier to avoid taking in the horror of the pictures by breaking them down, studying only small sections and never allowing her mind to focus on the overall picture.

When she was done, Claire neatly stacked the pictures and closed the files. Without allowing any emotion to show through, she handed them back to Perst.

"I can't help you."

"Can't or won't?"

"Claire, we need your help on this." Yankovic stepped in, probably sensing the personal undercurrents between Perst and her.

"I wish I could, but I told you all I know."

"You're sure? There's nothing else you can tell us?"

"I'm sorry."

"No, you're not." Perst stood. "But one day, you will be. Chief." Perst nodded to Derek before turning to Kristin. "Madame, I suggest you watch out for your brother."

Yankovic mumbled his good-byes and followed Perst out of the office. Claire bit her lip as the door shut with a finality that had her wishing he had left it open. What she wanted more than anything was to have a few minutes of privacy but she doubted it was on the agenda.

"Okay." Kristin slammed her briefcase down on the desk and stood. "One of you start talking and I mean NOW!"

Chapter 19

"Kristin," Derek growled. He knew his sister had a right to be upset, but he didn't want her adding to Claire's problems.

"Don't Kristin me!" Kristin snapped. "Did you not hear what I just heard?"

"I heard."

"Did she tell you your life was in danger?" Kristin pointed at Claire, who was staring down at the desk, her hands curled into fist. "That you have a psycho threatening you because of her."

"That's enough!" Derek came away from the wall.

"I've only just begun!" Kristin stepped forward, meeting him in the middle of the room.

"I won't have you upsetting Claire."

"Upsetting her? How upset will she be when you're dead?"

"What would you have me do?" Derek held his hands up.

"Send her away."

"Never!" Derek barked. "She's mine and she goes nowhere."

"It wouldn't have to be forever, Derek." Now it was Kristin's whose hands came up.

"It's not going to happen." Derek turned away from his sister.

"Maybe it's what she wants, if she really cares about you. Why don't we ask her?" Kristin demanded as Derek moved to Claire's side.

"No." Derek did not give Claire a chance to respond. Crossing his arms over his chest, he glared at his twin. "I'm not letting her go. So get used to the idea."

"So what are you going to do? Sit around and wait to be killed?"

"We'll figure something out."

"Figure something out," Kristin parroted back snidely as she yanked her briefcase off the desk. "Like funeral arrangements!"

Kristin got the last word when she slammed the office door behind her. For a moment, Derek stared at the door, shaking with rage. He could not believe Kristin would suggest sending Claire away. The mere suggestion was repulsive. Claire was his to love and protect, and he was not about to fail in either regard.

The problem was that Kristin's idea might motivate Claire. He was already fighting enough battles between serial killers, FBI and the fact he still hadn't explained to Claire she had less than a week before her transformation under the full moon.

Derek looked down at her. She was still staring at her clenched hands, her eyes remote and emotionless. Claire had withdrawn from the office into whatever safe place existed in her mind. Determined to see to his mate's needs, he lifted her out of the chair and led her from the station house.

* * * *

"You're crying."

The brush of fingers against her wet cheek followed Derek's comment. Claire touched her face with trembling fingers, feeling the evidence of her overwhelming emotions leaking through her defenses. She had thought she was beyond tears.

"Come on." Derek pushed open the truck door and dragged her across the seat.

Claire didn't object, still lost in her thoughts. She just couldn't wrap her mind around the fact that Max was dead, that Wall had killed him. Derek was next.

Duke jumped up the minute she stepped through the door, his big paws slamming into her middle. The extra pressure weakened her control over her rolling stomach. She shoved Duke out of the way, barely making it to the toilet in time.

A wet cloth appeared in front of her when she had finished. Claire accepted the rag and wiped her face. As she stood, she intentionally avoided looking Derek in the eyes. Embarrassed by the moment, she silently went to the sink and vented her emotions by vigorously brushing her teeth.

The reflection in the mirror taunted her. Her face looked pale, her eyes sunken, lifeless. This is what Agakiar wanted, to wear her down to the bone. Claire closed her eyes, not able to look at herself anymore.

She didn't help as Derek began removing her clothes, her mind lost to regrets. She should have told Max she hated him. That he disgusted her and she never wanted to see him again. She should have spit in his face, keyed his car, anything to keep him away from her. It may have hurt him, but at least he would be alive to feel the pain.

Now there was Derek. Agakiar would make Derek's death special, more painful and gruesome. She would not be able to protect him. The only hope was to turn him against her, to severe the bound that was forming between them.

She shied away from those thoughts, not wanting to think about it now. Claire let her head fall back on Derek's shoulder, enjoying the feel of his hands smoothing over her body as he bathed her. For just tonight, she wanted to forget and savor this time with Derek.

Too soon, the shower was over and Derek was wrapping her in an oversized towel. He carried her to the bed. He placed her on her stomach and pulled the towel back to her waist. His hands settled on her shoulders and he began to message the tense muscles there, forcing her body to relax if not her mind.

"Aren't you going to ask me about Wall?" Claire asked after a while.

"Do you want to tell me?"

Claire didn't want to, but could see no other choice. Derek was involved now, whether she liked it or not. In a halting voice, she told him the whole story. She started with meeting Wall while undercover and falling for his charm and concern.

It was hard for her to admit to having fallen for Wall's seductive charm. She tensed, expecting Derek to respond. He didn't. He just continued to massage her back with firm even strokes.

After that, it was easier to talk. She told him how, when she had arrived at the sting set up to bust the man smuggling in young girls to be sold to the pimps waiting, Wall had appeared. Just after she had given the signal to the SWAT team, the warehouse had exploded into unexplained flames.

The fire had consumed the warehouse and killed thirty-six people. That was when Max had seen her exit the fire unharmed at Wall's side. Max had not admitted what he had seen to Perst, too worried about becoming a suspect himself.

Perst had arrested her and taken her in for questioning. A lawyer had appeared almost by magic and freed Claire from the clutches of the FBI. Then he had introduced her to the company that had hired him, Cerberus. They had taken her into their fold and explained about Wall.

He wasn't human, but a minion, a vessel for the demon Agakiar. Sleeping with Agakiar had branded her. Now her flesh was damned and Agakiar would work to darken her soul as well.

"So we get rid of his mark and his tie over you is gone, right?"

"If only it were that easy. There is no way to get rid of the brand."

"There must be, the brand is already fading."

"It can't be."

"It is, go look." Derek pointed to the bathroom.

Casting a doubtful look at Derek, she scrambled off the bedroom and hurried into the bathroom. It was not the easiest spot to see and she had to use her handheld makeup mirror to get a good look. Claire scowled at the mirror, turning and twisting, unable to accept what she was seeing.

"It's fading, isn't it?" Derek demanded smugly from the door.

"We need to go across the street. I have to talk to Deik."

"Who the hell is Deik?"

* * * *

Deik turned out to be a vampire with a superior glint mixing with the distaste in his slanted green eyes. Derek felt the hairs on the back of his neck raise. Vampires and werewolves weren't automatically enemies, but they were not friendly either.

"Deik." Claire grasped the bloodsucker's hand, pulling him into the living room. "I need to ask you about something."

Derek forced back the growl. He didn't like his mate being so close to a vampire he didn't know, one he had no reason to trust.

"What can I do for you my lovely?" Deik draped a friendly arm over her shoulders.

"I need to know what it means if Agakiar's brand is fading?"

"Is it?" That broke the vampire's smug smile.

"It appears to be."

"Show me." Deik stepped back.

That was it. Derek interceded as Claire's fingers curled around the hem of her shirt. There was no way Derek was going to let his mate strip from the waist up for the vampire's examination.

"You can trust us," Derek growled, pulling her hands away from the shirt.

"And you are?"

"Oh, I'm sorry." Claire flushed slightly, as if finally sensing the tension between the two men. "Derek this is Deik. Deik this is Derek, the chief of police."

"Her mate," Derek corrected. Police chief, indeed. It was insulting to be introduced in such an impersonal way.

"What is going on in here?" A short, raven-haired woman demanded from the hallway.

She paused there to glare at Derek and he could feel a slight cooling in the air around him. It felt at though a million little fingers were brushing over him before the sensation died. Her violet gaze turned from him to Claire as Deik spoke.

"Claire claims that Agakiar's brand is fading."

"It is?" The woman's eyes widened with surprise. Just as quickly, they narrowed back on Derek. "Hmm, interesting."

"I don't need interesting, Sasha. I need answers," Claire snapped.

"Perhaps we should discuss this in private." The woman gestured down the hall.

"You might as well talk in front of the wolf."

Deik relaxed back into the couch, apparently amused by the events unfolding in front of him. Derek cut his gaze from the petite woman glaring at him to the bloodsucker, surprised the man was defending him.

"After all, it's probably the wolf's fault the mark is fading."

"What say you, Deik?" Sasha frowned at the vampire.

"I'd say that one mark is erasing another. Come Wednesday, when the final act of mating is completed, then Agakiar's mark will be completely removed."

"Final act of mating?" Claire scowled in confusion at the vampire. "What are you talking about?"

"You are planning on finishing the mating, are you not?" Deik ignored Claire's question to ask Derek one of his own.

"Of course."

"Derek what is he talking about?" Claire turned her frown on him.

"I'll explain later." Derek was not about to go into details in front of two strangers. It was bad enough the vampire appeared to know them. He would not embarrass Claire by speaking of them in front of others.

"You best explain it soon." Deik's snotty advice broke into Derek's thoughts. "You have what? About five days left."

"Please." Sasha stepped up to grasp Claire's hand, interrupting the argument brewing between Derek and her. "Let me examine you. Come."

With one last scowl, Claire allowed the tiny woman to lead her away from the two men. Derek watched her disappear down the hall before cutting his gaze back over to the vampire. Deik was watching him with an amused expression.

"So you haven't told our little Claire what lies ahead? Wonder how she'll react when she learns what you intend to do to her."

"She's not 'ours', she's mine." Derek refused the seat the vampire gestured to with his hand. "I guess I have you to thank for the fact I no longer have a demon and a killer running free, but a demonic killer?"

* * * *

"It is fading." Sasha didn't sound happy with her conclusion as she allowed Claire to finally to roll back over on her back.

"Gee, Sasha, don't get ready to have a party or anything." Claire tugged her shirt down. "That's just the best news I've ever heard."

"I'm sorry." Sasha smiled slightly. "I'm just shocked."

"Well, if I had known all it took to get rid of the brand was to have a werewolf bite me, I would have asked Mighty Mike a long time ago."

"I don't think that would have helped." Sasha gave her a small smile.

"It would have been worth a try, at least." Claire grinned. "So how long do you think it will be before the whole thing is gone?"

"I don't think it has anything to do with time." Sasha stood. "I think Deik is right, one mark is replacing another. Agakiar's mark will be gone when your werewolf's mark is in place."

"I thought it was in place." Claire shot Sasha a curious look. "How many times does he need to bite me to make it permanent?"

"It's not that." Sasha gave a small laugh. "What am trying to say is that when you're fully mated to…Derek, right?"

"Yeah, Derek."

"When you fully mate with Derek, your soul will bond to his and Agakiar will, in essence, be cut off."

"So, how do I become fully mated?"

"Each breed of wolf has their own rituals. I suggest you ask Derek for the details." Sasha shrugged in ignorance.

Claire eyes narrowed. Everybody knew something and nobody was willing to tell her what it was. That could only mean one thing. Whatever the final mating ritual was, Claire was not going to like it.

"I will say, though, now is very dangerous time for you." Sasha lifted Claire's chin so their gazes met. "Agakiar will sense his mark fading. What we know of him indicates he will do whatever he needs to keep you."

"He's already made moves." Claire shivered, realizing she had misread Agakiar's intentions.

She had thought Agakiar had been jealous, but things were worse than that. Agakiar was fighting to keep a possible minion, to keep her. Minions were the lifeblood of demons on earth. They could not affect this reality on their own. They needed humans to fulfill their desires.

Quickly she explained everything to Sasha, from Agakiar's phone call to her conversation with Agent Perst that afternoon. She tried hard to remain detached as they went over the details of Max's death.

The lifelong shield she had used to protect herself suddenly had cracks. She felt herself trembling, hearing tears in her voice, though she managed to stop them from falling from her eyes. With a shuddering breath, she finished the story.

Sasha insisted they contact Mike. Mike listened silently while Claire explained what was going on. He made no sound until she finished telling him everything, then he wanted a conference call with the team.

The women found the men waiting in the living room. Deik and Derek were standing on opposite side of the small room. Derek had his arms crossed over his chest, while Deik's hands were curled at his sides.

Claire shivered at the cold tension emanating out of Derek and wished he felt more comfortable. Whatever his concerns, the team was there to help. They had nothing to fear from the company or from Deik, as annoying as he was.

Claire came to stand by him, hoping her nearness would help calm him. It did. His arm snaked around her waist, pulling her closer. A moment later the com-unit on the coffee table buzzed. With a nonchalant flick of his wrist, Deik activated the small machine.

"Everybody present?" Mike demanded instantly.

"All here, including an extra," Deik confirmed.

"Extra? What extra?" Mike sounded annoyed.

"Claire's furry friend." Deik snickered and Claire felt Derek tense for a moment. She shot Deik a hard look. Deik enjoyed riling up people and had focused his interest on Derek.

"Oh, well I guess he can stay." Mike's begrudging acceptance didn't help ease Derek's straining muscles. "Okay, let's get on with this. Claire?"

For several minutes, they discussed Claire's fading brand. Mike wanted to put Derek and her into a safe house. Derek refused, not willing to leave his town or his pack in danger. Mike argued hard, but had no choice in the matter. With ill-grace, he conceded the matter.

Turning to the next issue, Mike ordered Claire to back off the search for the serial killer. He didn't want to complicate the problem with Agakiar anymore than necessary. Claire didn't agree, but she kept that opinion to herself.

"Now, just for shits and giggles, why doesn't somebody catch me up on the matter of Urazi. I got Deik's message the house had been destroyed, but I did not hear Urazi had been eliminated."

Mike paused, waiting for a response. Everybody in the room shifted slightly except Derek. Claire cast a look over at Sasha and Harold. It was up to one of them to explain the details.

"I don't like silence."

"Urazi morphed out of the building," Sasha finally answered. It was for the best. Mike would be hard pressed to cuss at her.

"Morphed? Where the hell did he morph to?"

"Our best guess?"

"Is that all you have, Harold? A guess?"

"It's as good as it gets for now," Deik snorted.

"Shut up, Deik," Mike snapped. "Tell me about this guess, Harold."

"I'd say he went into the killer."

Mike's response was expected. He cussed for several minutes before barking out questions. Nobody had answers. Urazi was not supposed to be strong enough to fully posses a minion.

It was a mystery that would have to be solved after Claire's mating. Once she was fully mated, the company could eliminate Wall without consequences. Until then the team's focus would be on keeping Claire and Derek safe, all other issues would have to wait.

"Deik, I expect a status report every night."

"Can do."

"I'll leave you guys to sort out the details of keeping Claire and Derek safe."

"Talk to you later boss." Deik signed off, before turning a smirk at the couple. "Well I guess I'm in charge of you two now."

"God help us," Claire muttered.

Chapter 20

Claire stretched her arms over her head and yawned as they entered Derek's house. The team had spent the past hour going over how to best keep her safe. Mostly it had been Derek and Deik talking. They had found common ground in keeping her safe.

"Tired, sweetheart." Derek wrapped his arms around her from behind.

"Mmm." Claire sagged against him.

"Too bad." He nibbled on her ear. "I was hoping for a little entertainment."

"I'm tired," Claire murmured.

"We haven't been going out for a week and already she's tired," Derek grouched good-naturedly. "Well, then lets get you to bed so you can wake energized."

Derek led her down the hall to the bedroom. Claire flopped down on the bed and closed her eyes, ready to pass out fully clothed. A rustle of clothing had her peeking open her eyes.

She had to stretch her neck to look back at where Derek stood on the other side of the bed. Her gaze was level with his waist and she admired the way his black uniform slacks emphasized his narrow hips and muscular thighs.

Claire's breath caught at the site of the massive erection straining for freedom. His hand reached for the edge of his shirt and she rolled over on her stomach to watch silently as he stripped. As he dropped his navy T-shirt to the floor, Claire felt her heart skip a beat before erupting into a fast-paced tattoo against her chest.

He was magnificent. All smooth, bronzed skin stretched tautly over muscles. A dark thatch of hair covered his chest, narrowing as it trailed over his stomach and disappeared into the waistband of his jeans.

The idea of tracing the path of his hair down to his cock had Claire's mouth going dry. She licked her lips and watched as his erection visibly jerked against his jeans. Her eyes cut up to his and she found him watching her with a heated look.

Pointedly, Claire lowered her eyes to where his hands waited on his hips. When her gaze fell on them, they moved to lower his zipper. A moment later, he slid both his slacks and boxers down so he stood in all his naked glory before her.

"Are you sure you're tired?"

As she watched, he wrapped his hand around his shaft and stroked it slowly, pulling the already taut flesh even tighter. A glistening bead of pearly white liquid seeped from the top.

"Hmm, I might be up for a little bedtime snack."

She crawled across the bed, lured closer by the desire to taste him. She glanced at his face and watched his look of pleasure as she licked the evidence of his desire from the head of his cock.

His face tightened, his eyes glinting with carnal sensuality, his lips pulled back in a feral snarl, as she licked him again. A wave of feminine satisfaction moved through her. She wanted to be the one to give him pleasure.

Closing her eyes, she nuzzled her cheek against his hard cock while her hand came to explore the hot masculine flesh. Sliding her cheek down, along the length of his long shaft, she caressed his balls gently.

She opened her eyes to watch his expression. With a tender touch, she learned the way he liked to be touched. Another drop of arousal slipped from the head of his cock and Claire lovingly lapped it up. He shuddered. Wrapping his hands in her hair, he nudged her lips against the head of his erection.

"Lick it," he growled, the sound more animal than human.

Claire had not given a lot of blowjobs in her life. They had always been something she felt pressured to do.

Now, though, she found herself wishing she knew more about how to satisfy a man. She looked up at his face again, watching for any indication she was failing or succeeding as she stuck the tip of her tongue out and began to explore the naked length of flesh before her.

She tasted the slit along the top of his cock, savoring the salty fluid gathering there, before licking her way down his cock. Experimentally, she scraped her front teeth along the sensitive skin and saw his stomach muscles tighten and quiver at her actions.

Kissing away any hurt she might have caused, Claire made her way to the base of his erection. Unsure of herself, she carefully licked one ball and then the other. When she heard his breathing roughen to a chop she grew bolder, sucking lightly on his testicles.

Derek's hands tightened almost painfully in her hair with a groan. Claire felt her body reacting to the knowledge that she was bringing him pleasure. Her breast tightened and her pussy began to hum.

With growing confidence, she licked and sucked her way back up to the head of his cock now purplish red from all the blood circulating there. Claire opened her mouth, sucking the bulbous head into her mouth and trapping it there.

Licking and sucking on his caged flesh, she showed him no mercy until he was shuddering. Sometimes she would open her mouth just enough to let her tongue slip out and tease the sensitive underside of his cock.

"Suck it now, Claire," Derek demanded.

Not waiting for her to obey, he jerked his hips forcing her to take more of him. Relaxing her lips, she allowed him to work as much of his hardened shaft into her mouth as would fit. As the head butted against the back of her throat, she swallowed and heard him groan.

"Again."

Claire swallowed again and, as he jerked, all control was lost. He held her head exactly as he wanted it as he began to fuck in and out of her mouth with forceful strokes.

Quickly his thrusting became wild, his breath labored, his body shaking until he convulsed with pleasure. He roared out his release as Claire tried to swallow the jets of hot liquid flooding her mouth.

She held him through his climax, not allowing his softening flesh to go until he pulled back on her head and slipped from between her lips. He stared down at her with the look of a sated beast admiring his mate. One calloused finger traced her lips, cleaning the evidence of his desire.

"Baby," his rough, gravelly voice sent shrills of pleasure over her body, "you're in for it now."

He lifted her off the bed. Setting her on her feet, he made short work of her shirt and bra. Desire darkened his already navy eyes to black as he stared at her breast. The soft globes ached with need, her nipples painfully tight.

Claire groaned as his large palms came up to cup her tender flesh. Expertly he rubbed her nipples, making her cry out, her back arch, thrusting the sensitive tips deeper into his hold. Derek showed her no mercy as he squeezed and pinch the sensitive tips until her body was shaking with need.

Derek bent his head, rubbing his closed lips teasingly against the tips until it was Claire threading her hands into his hair, trying to force him to suck on her. Derek chuckled, his hot breath tantalizing her.

Claire watched in heated fascination as his lips opened, closing over one needy peak. Sizzling heat shot out from her breast, burning a path straight to her clenching cunt.

Derek gave her what she needed, suckling on one breast and then the other. Each pull of his mouth, every velvety stroke of his tongue, sent burning pleasure arching through her, intensifying the need in her pussy.

While she lost herself to the erotic rasp of his mouth on her breast, his free hand slid over the quivering muscles of her stomach to slip beneath the waistband of her jeans and under the elastic edge of her panties, until his hot palm was cupping her weeping mound.

His fingers teased her needy flesh, sliding along the seam of her nether lips, only to slip into her folds for quick, light touches. Claire strained against him, her hips squirming, shifting up and down in silent demand for more of his touch, begging for deeper exploration.

With his thumb, he brushed back her folds to press against her clit. Claire gasped, grinding herself against that digit. As he licked and sucked the flushed bud at the tip of her breast, she mimicked his motions with her hips, bringing herself pleasure.

Sensations overwhelmed her, and Claire felt her legs give out as her body burst with starlight. With a gasp, she trembled, her hips falling still. Derek took over, not giving her time to catch her breath.

His hand moved. His fingers slipping pass her folds to stroke into her still quivering sheath. He rotated his palm so it pressed against her clit, rubbing against the ultra-sensitive nub as he began to relentlessly fuck her with his fingers.

Her eyes opened, unseeing, as lights swirled before her, faster and faster until they exploded and her body was racked with another storm of shudders. Claire screamed her pleasure as her hips jerked against his hand.

"That's two," Derek growled as he shoved her jeans and panties down, out of the way. "I think our record is six."

"W...what?" Claire stuttered as she felt him lifting her off her feet.

"Last time we played this game, you came six times." Derek set her limp body down on the edge of the bed. Her tailbone almost hanging off as he positioned her knees, bent and to the side.

"Let's go for eight."

"No, wait—" Claire's denial was washed away by a scream as Derek knelt between her legs and sucked her aching clit into his mouth.

He was merciless. She thrashed about trying to escape the pleasure he was forcing on her but could not escape his firm grip. Claire's legs windmilled, trying to find purchase on his shoulders to force him back.

Derek ignored her struggles, easily holding her legs wide. He continued to work his tongue in and out of her dripping cunt. His tongue grew with the length of the wolf, its savage desires feeding his lust. Tasting, delving into her in ever deepening exploration, he forced her to climax again and again.

Claire had no choice but to accept his intimate kisses, crying out as her world dissolved into a rolling sea of ecstatic waves. When he finally lifted his head she was gasping, clutching at the bed sheets as her hips erratically jerked from the intense sensations still coursing through her system.

Claire whimpered as he stretched over her, the hard wall of his chest rubbing against her breast, his coarse hair chaffing her overly sensitive nipples. Her eyes, wet with tears, opened to look at him as she felt the thick head of his erection nudge against her pussy.

He rubbed his cock against her weeping slit sending agonizing bolts of pleasure through her. Claire jerked and whimpered again.

"Please," her voice hoarse and faint, "no more."

"Ah, baby. Just one more." Derek's smooth, honeyed voice did little to soothe her frazzled nerves.

* * * *

Derek felt his heart clench as she looked up at him with big eyes made green by a mixture of anticipation and exhaustion. She was the most exquisite woman he had ever touched. The only thing more beautiful than her body was her character.

Slowly, gently, he brushed his lips over her quivering ones, breathing in her soft panting breaths. His heart clenched as she sighed, adjusting her position so the head of his cock lodged against the opening of her cunt.

Her body rose off the bed, arching against him as he slid into her welcoming heat. It was the sweetest welcoming on the planet. Derek felt sweat trickle down his back as he tried to go slowly, seating himself fully into her clenching sheath.

He tried to leash the uncontrollable need boiling through his blood, to curb the wild hunger of the beast within, but as her inner muscled flexed and her hips arched, she shattered the remains of his control. He was consumed by the need to feel her tight, clinging heat along every inch of his shaft.

He began pounding into her with increasing force as her legs wound around his hips. Heedless of her cries, Derek fucked her hard, plunging deeper and deeper into her pussy with every stroke. He felt her body still for a second, her inner muscles clamping down tight on his inflamed flesh for one sweet moment before her body convulsed beneath his.

The feel of her climax made him snarl as his own bore down on him. For a moment, everything was perfect, beautiful. Then the world ripped apart around him, and an inferno of lust consumed him. Derek felt the flames of ecstasy sear through him as his seed was ripped from his balls.

Roaring out his release, Derek fell on top of his mate, satisfied, panting, drained of all thought and the ability to move. After several minutes, when their breathing no longer chopped through the air, Derek forced himself to lift his weight off Claire. Her eyes were closed and he wondered if she had passed out again.

"Sweetheart?"

"Hmm?" Claire eyes fluttered, opening slightly. "What?"

"Did I hurt you?" The breath Derek hadn't realized he'd been holding released with a sigh at her droopy smile.

"Are you going to ask me that every time we make love?" Claire yawned, stretching beneath him.

"I wasn't too hard on you, was I?" Derek pressed, rolling on his back and taking her with him.

"No, not too hard." Claire snuggled into his embrace. "But perhaps we should stop at eight."

"I don't think so, sweetheart." Derek nuzzled her ear. "Next time we're going for twelve."

"You'll kill me," Claire groaned.

"We'll schedule it for a whole day."

"We're going to schedule sex now?"

"How about tomorrow?"

"Tomorrow?" Claire rested her head on his shoulder, her hand coming up to play with the hair on his chest.

"It's Saturday. We both have the day off. We're supposed to keep a low profile. You can't get lower than spending the day in bed."

"I say we worry about it tomorrow and go for a shower right now." Claire lifted her head. "Then to *sleep*."

"Oh, a shower. Maybe we can get two more in."

Whatever her response it was lost as Derek sealed their mouths together for a long, slow kiss. He was pleased to see her eyes going green with desire when he pulled his head back. Without another comment, he lifted her into her arms he carried her off to the bathroom.

Forty-five minutes later after they had run out hot water and Derek had fulfilled his promise of two more. This was the life, he thought, as he settled into bed beside his mate. The only thing that could make things more perfect was for Claire to be round and ripe with his children.

By the next full moon, hopefully she would be pregnant. Derek wondered which of the two extra rooms he would have to give up for a nursery. He wanted more than just two kids, at least four if not more. Perhaps they should look at buying a bigger house.

"Derek?" Claire's barely audible whisper roused him.

"Hmmm?"

"What did Deik mean by the final act of mating?"

* * * *

"Don't worry about it, sweetheart," Derek murmured huskily.

Don't worry about it her ass, Claire thought. Something was afoot and he was deliberately not telling her. It made her uneasy. Whatever would motivate Derek to try to be tactful was probably something that she would more than object to.

"Derek?"

"We'll talk about it later." Derek yawned loudly.

"I want to talk about it now," Claire demanded, not buying into that yawn.

"I thought you were tired."

"I think you're ducking a direct question."

"I'm not ducking. I just think it would be better to discuss this at a more appropriate time."

"When is this appropriate time? Right before whatever is going to happen happens, so I don't have time to object?"

Derek sighed and turned, forcing her onto her side. She could feel his erection poking her in her lower back. Whatever was going through his mind was turning him on.

"Trust me, you won't object when its time," Derek growled softly in her ear.

"Just tell me what is going to happen on Wednesday."

"Well, about ten we'll take a drive out to the pack's hunting grounds."

"The pack will be there?"

"No, it'll just be us." Derek gave her a comforting squeeze.

"So we get there and…?" Claire prodded after Derek fell silent.

"We undress."

"We do? Why?" Claire asked suspiciously.

"Because otherwise, you'd rip your clothes when you change into a wolf."

"Okay, okay, I get it. We get there, strip and then turn into wolves."

"It's called transforming."

"Okay." Claire rolled her eyes. "We *transform* into wolves. Then?"

"Then we do what wolves do."

"What? Like run and hunt?"

"Mm-hm."

There was more to it than that. After all, Deik had called it the final mating act, not the final transformation, or the first hunt. Mating meant sex.

"Oh, no," Claire whispered to herself.

"Oh, no, what sweetheart?" Derek murmured.

"Don't you 'sweetheart' me," Claire snapped trying to wiggle away so she could turn and confront him. His arms were steel bands not allowing her even an inch of distance from him.

"Now, Claire—"

"Don't 'now, Claire' me either." Claire cut him off. "I'm not fucking you as a wolf!"

"It's natural."

"There is nothing natural about it!" Claire snapped. "It's sick, it's depraved, it's…it's…I don't know what the hell it is, but I'm not doing it."

"Don't get all worked up, honey. It may seem objectionable now, but when its time you'll enjoy yourself."

"No I won't! I can't believe you would hide something like this from me!"

"It just is. Just like we are now. Just as we're attracted to each other as humans, we'll be that way as wolves. It's the way things work between mates."

"Don't try to rationalize your perverseness. I won't do it. You can't make me!"

Derek growled for real this time. The sound echoed deep in his chest and along her back. Claire shivered, knowing she had pushed too far. Anticipation boiled with erotic fear through her blood, making her stated body awaken with renewed desire.

"You want to know what is going to happen? Fine. I'll tell you. After you transform, you'll scent my desire and you'll run, because that's what every good bitch does."

"Derek—"

"I'll track you through the forest and when I catch you, I'll force you to the ground." Derek matched his actions to his words, forcing Claire onto her stomach.

"Please, I—"

"You'll try to throw me off and I'll bite down on your shoulder to pin you in place. Your ass will be in the air, your pussy open and vulnerable." Derek's hands on her hips lifted her ass, his legs forcing their way between her thighs.

"The smell of your desire will fill the air as it does now. The sweet smell of your juices will drive me insane and I'll slam into you."

Claire screamed as he penetrated her suddenly, filling her tight sheath to the max with thick, hard, hot cock.

"Then I'll show you no mercy. I'll fuck you anyway I want, because you're mine."

Biting down hard on her shoulder, he held her still for his hard, fast fucking. Beneath him, Claire moaned and panted, bucking back into each thrust, driving his lust, his need to dominate higher.

"Soon," Derek growled into her shoulder as he moved his hand, gathering the juice from her pussy to lubricate her tight back entrance. "I'm going to fuck you here."

With that dark promise, he slid his fingers into her making her cry out with the painful pleasure. Quickly, the sensations combined, the feel of his cock filling her pussy as his fingers filled her ass. It was too much and she screamed and convulsed around his cock, squeezing his orgasm from him.

Darkness overtook her even as she felt the hot jets of his seed filling her body.

Chapter 21

Wednesday: 8:30 pm

Claire's eyes darted to the clock and she felt her stomach tighten. It was eight thirty, an hour and half left before it was time. She sighed and looked back down at the notes she had been trying to concentrate on all evening.

It was useless. She could feel the strange restlessness in her growing, her muscles cramping painfully. Derek had said everything she was experiencing was normal. She had been glad when he had been called out on an accident more than three hours ago. He had been driving her nuts, hovering over her, constantly asking how she was doing.

How she was doing didn't really matter, considering that the only cure would be found later under the full moon. As unnerving as it was to think that she would grow a tail and walk on all fours, it wasn't that idea that had her nervous.

It was what was to come after. Though she had not brought the topic up with Derek again, it haunted her. Even as her mind rejected the idea, her body warmed to it every time she thought about it.

Of course, her body was warm a lot these days. Over the past five days Derek had kept her so well loved she was amazed she could still walk. He had been true to his word and then some, keeping her in bed all Saturday and most of Sunday.

It was hard to believe how much her life was changing. Derek had made no secret he expected her to quit her job with Cerberus and settle into life in Wilsonville. They had discussed the matter of their future at some length.

Claire did not mind quitting Cerberus, but she didn't want to depend on Derek for money. While he had offered her the chance to stay at home and work on her book, it had quickly become apparent what he really wanted was for her to stay at home and raise the kids.

That was one thing there was to be no discussion on. Derek wanted lots of kids. The idea was foreign to Claire, frightening actually. She did not know anything about kids, much less how to be a mother.

Derek assured her his mother would help her with anything she needed to learn. That was another thing that intimidated her, Derek's family. Kristin had been polite the past two times she had seen her, but there was no denying Derek's sister was not pleased Claire was endangering her brother. One could imagine what Derek's mother would think.

Claire would know soon enough. After Derek had told them on the phone about her, they had apparently changed their plans. They would be home within a week. At least by then, Agakiar would be history.

By tomorrow, the demon would no longer be on the psychical plane, nor would she be branded anymore. The idea filled her with such relief she feared believing it. She didn't think about it, forcing herself to accept whatever fate came her way with the raising of the new sun tomorrow.

It would be what it would be.

"Stop worrying." Deik's annoyed voice broke through her morbid thoughts. The vampire lingered in the study's doorway. He watched her whenever Derek got called out at night.

"I could feel your anxiety all the way in the living room." Deik moved into the room, settling into the overstuffed leather reading chair. "You're making it impossible to enjoy the baseball game."

"Sorry," Claire apologized dryly.

"So what you worrying over? Agakiar?" Deik raised an inquisitive eyebrow. "Or getting banged when you're furry?"

"Jesus, Deik!" Claire glared at the vampire, exasperated by his irreverent attitude.

"What?" Deik looked innocent. "Personally, I'm kind of curious about that. I love a good wild, animalistic rut, but I never actually rutted with an animal. Hey!"

Deik dodged the book Claire beamed at his head. Giving her an injured look, he held his hands up in surrender.

"Okay, okay, we won't talk about fucking when you're on all fours."

"Deik!"

"Look at this way, at least you're not worrying over Agakiar anymore."

"I'm always worried about him. Only when Mike calls tomorrow and says Wall is dead, will I stop worrying."

"No, you won't. Then you'll just start worrying about Urazi."

"I'm ahead of you on that one." Claire nodded to the piles of papers on the desk. "I've been looking into that matter as much as possible."

"Oh, don't tell me you're mate is hindering your way." Deik settled deeper into the recliner.

"You just want to watch us fight."

"I must admit the arrogance of your wolf, does inspire me to see him aggravated." The vampire grinned, showing off his fangs.

"It's because of that kind of thinking you're lonely, Deik."

"I don't suffer from lack of companionship. I like being alone."

"You know who would be perfect for you." Claire gave him a taunting smile. "Kate."

Gee, thanks.

"I heard that," Deik called out loudly.

"Aren't you supposed to be watching Derek?" Claire asked the unseen spirit.

He's on his way home and listening to country music. Talk about boring. He's only fun to watch when he's with you.

"Have you been spying on me?"

What are you two up to now? Sixteen in six hours?

"Why you little—"

"Sixteen what?" Deik asked.

"Don't you—"

Orgasms.

"You're just jealous," Claire taunted the ghost.

Hell, yeah! I'm jealous. That man really likes to eat-

"That's enough." Claire pinned Deik with a hard glare when it looked as if he were about to say something. "From *both* of you."

"Hey, I'm jealous, too. I'd love to find a woman who likes to suck—"

"Deik!"

"No wonder you've been so mellow these past few days."

"This discussion is over."

"What's over?" Derek asked from the doorway.

"Speak of the devil," Deik snickered, though he gazed at Derek with a glint of admiration.

"Are you bragging about me?" Derek came over to drop a kiss on Claire's head.

"Kate is."

"The ghost is here?"

"Unfortunately," Claire muttered.

"Well, if she wants a real show, tell her stick around."

Derek's smug comment elicited a chuckle from Deik. It earned him a hard hit from Claire who flung her hand into his stomach. It was bad enough knowing what was coming, she didn't need an audience.

"That's enough," Claire decreed. "Our sex life is not open for conversation or viewing. Kate?"

You're no fun.

"Speaking of which, I'm going to get a few things together and then you and I should head out. Alright?"

"Do I have a choice?"

Derek gave her another kiss on top of her head and swaggered out of the room. Claire looked over at Deik's amused expression and scowled.

"Don't look so constipated, Claire," Deik advised. "Sex is always fun, anyway you can get it."

"I don't know why it has to be my sex life we're all always discussing."

"Because you're the only one who has one right now." Deik chuckled. "You know how petty jealous people can be."

"Let's talk about something a little more important. Security."

"It's all been handled."

"How?"

"I don't think you want to hear the details."

"Whenever Derek or you say that, my stomach knots up."

"Well, if it makes you feel any better. Derek knows the details."

"No, actually that doesn't make me feel any better."

"Why don't you just leave it to us this time? Anytime you think Agakiar is near, call for me. I'll hear you."

Deik's reassurance was not comforting. It implied that he was going to be near enough to hear, close enough to watch. Claire was already certain Kate was going to be catching a peek. She didn't need the smart mouth vampire getting one too.

"Ready to go?"

Derek's question prevented Claire from questioning Deik about just where he was planning on being. Claire let the question go unasked. Whatever she said would not stop Deik from doing whatever he wanted.

"Yeah."

Claire rose and turned to find Derek waiting for her in the doorway. He had a sports bag slung over his shoulder. The sight only added to her nerves, but she refused to ask what it was for. Any more details and she just might chicken out.

Derek drove her a half-hour out into the country, before turning down a dirt road that led into a pine tree forest. It looked like a farm, with all the trees in perfect rows and a maze of dirt roads cutting through.

Derek explained the pack owned the land. They used the area to run, hunt and, when the occasion called for it, mate. He kept up a running monologue as they drove, happily explaining about the history of the pack. Claire sat silently, broodingly.

The first time was the hardest for a human undergoing transformation, Derek explained. After a while it became second nature and a person could transform at will, with or without the moon.

After tonight, she would be a real werewolf, capable of smelling things she had never smelled before. Her night vision would be enhanced, as would her hearing. Even her reflexes would be quickened.

When she had drolly asked if her metabolism would increase, Derek had laugh and said he hoped not. He enjoyed her round and curvy, as he called it. That was good thing. Claire had never been one to bemoan the fact her body liked to store fat, giving her what some called a full-figured look and others, like that bitch Carolyn, called pudgy.

"Well." Derek cut off the engine and gave her an engaging grin. "We're here."

Claire swallowed looking at where here was. There was no way to tell here from there in this forest, as every spot looked the same.

"Don't worry, sweetheart." Derek turned her face toward him with a finger under her chin. "Nothing bad is going to happen."

"You're excited about this." Claire didn't move to open the door.

"What makes you say that?" Derek pulled her closer.

"There is a big bulge in your jeans."

"There always is when you're near," Derek murmured right before he kissed her. Claire relaxed slightly as the kiss went on and slowly she began to respond, kissing him back.

"I have an idea," Derek whispered against her lips. "Let's go for one right now."

"Derek!" Claire tried to pull away from him, but, as usual, his iron grip held her close.

"What? It'll help relax you," Derek teased.

"One always leads to two, and two always leads to three, and, before you know it, it will be morning. By the time you're done, I wouldn't have any mind left to transform with."

"You're probably right." Derek gave an extravagant sigh.

"Besides from what you told me, you're going to be getting yours in just a few minutes."

"Trust me, baby, you're going to get yours, too. Now get out and get naked."

Claire hesitated. There was no real choice though. What was coming was coming despite her apprehension, and turning into a wolf in a truck cab sounded highly uncomfortable.

With a sigh, Claire climbed out of the truck. Derek met her at the back where he lowered the tailgate to the truck and dropped the bag he had brought.

"I want to talk to you for a moment." Derek settled down on the tailgate and patted the spot next to him. "Have a seat."

"What?" Claire sat nervously on the edge of the gate.

"I know we discussed everything already, but I want to go over it again, one last time. Do you remember what I said about how to start the transformation?"

"To close my eyes and imagine a wolf," Claire repeated on cue. They had been over this daily.

"And when it's time to change back?"

"I imagine being a human."

"You need to try and not be afraid. Fear—"

"Will make the process harder," Claire finished for him.

"Kind of tired of hearing it, huh?"

"Just a little."

"I just don't want you to get stuck as a wolf."

"That can happen?" Claire turned alarmed eyes on him.

"Just kidding."

"Now is not the time for jokes, Derek." Claire shoved him. He swayed from the force but didn't budge from his seat.

"You need to relax sweetheart, it's going to be difficult enough without your anxiety complicating the matter."

"Can we just do it now?" Claire demanded. "All this talk and no action is adding to my anxiety."

"Alright, let's strip," Derek agreed.

Claire felt a little weird about stripping naked in the outdoors. Glancing around constantly, she carefully removed and folded her clothes. When she was finally as naked as Derek, she felt her stomach tighten until she felt as if she were going to be sick.

What if she could not do this?

Again, there was that no choice problem. Closing her eyes, she took several deep breaths, trying to calm her frazzled nerves. It did not help. Her muscles ached. Her bones felt like they were cold in the center, the sensation was piercingly painful.

"It's alright, sweetheart," Derek murmured soothingly, appearing to sense her pain. "Just try to relax and don't fight it."

"It hurts," Claire whimpered.

"I know, baby, but it won't hurt for long," Derek assured her. "Just picture a wolf in your mind and let your body do what it wants."

"I'm trying." Claire panted, feeling her muscles contract painfully.

"Concentrate, sweetheart. Start with a wet, little black nose and cute little fangs and work back over the snout to hazel eyes and full main of honey brown hair. She has a full coat, with a big bushy tail and slender legs with dainty paws. Can you see her, sweetheart?"

Claire could not respond, could not form words around the fangs she felt burning through her gums, growing and lengthening as the rest of her body was contracting painfully. Strange, painful whining animal noises came from deep inside her.

Her bones and muscles felt as though they were on fire and Claire thought the pain would consume her when it suddenly stopped. Claire panted, trying to regain her equilibrium as the world suddenly came into focus.

The night appeared brighter. The slight movements of grass in the wind were sharp and clear to her eyes. The noises that moments before had been a muted song blended together and were now distinct sounds she could hear with clarity. Something scuttled off in the nearby brush, a bird took off, its wings making a soothing whoop noise as they flapped with flight.

Everything seemed clear and inviting. The wolf, now in control, did not allow her to rationalize or think about anything. It merely identified sounds, scents, and movement, following what instinctively attracted it. The wolf shifted its attention to the man staring down at her with a grin and growled, uncomfortable with human companionship.

In the next instant, the man was no longer there. Instead, a large, black wolf was looking back at her. The male wolf smelled of aggression and arousal, making the fur along her body stand up.

Claire had no control over her own actions as her wolf side responded instantly to the sight and smell of the dominant male. She hunched down growling. He growled back, his muscles rippling in warning. A warning she did not heed as she launched herself at him, with a powerful lunge she slammed into him trying to knock him down.

The male wolf rolled with her, throwing her off. For several moments they fought, he kept biting her head and neck. Despite the powerful jaws, his teeth did not break her skin or crush her bones. The message was clear. She could not win the battle, so she kicked him away and took off.

His howl silenced the night of all other sounds. It was a challenge, a forceful declaration that the master of the night was free and all creatures should hide, Claire included. The wolf growing in her recognized the sound for what it was and picked up speed.

Leaping over fallen debris, she cut from side to side, trying to throw off the massive beast bearing down on her. She knew she was being toyed with, that he could easily have over taken her. She didn't know what he was waiting for, but, after twenty minutes, she began to tire out.

Not sure how much longer she could keep up her pace, she looked for some way to lose the massive wolf hot on her trail. There was none, just endless rows of pines. When suddenly the forest broke open into a massive field, she mustered her strength and tried to outrace him.

The field must have been what he was waiting for. Picking up speed, he caught her halfway across the field. Pouncing on her, he sent her into a tumbling roll. She came up on all fours, intent on defending herself but it was already too late.

He pinned her to the ground in seconds, his massive weight forcing her down. She could smell her own nervous arousal and feel its effect on the male. The wolf's erection grew harder, long, thumping her in the back. The fight left her body as desire took over and she instinctively lowered her head, rumbling softly in submission.

The large male used his superior strength to maneuver her into position. He let out a piercing howl as he plunged deep into her wet channel. Clamping his jaws down on her shoulder to hold her still, he rode her to climax, twice, before he gave in to his own shattering need.

Chapter 22

Thursday: 6:15 am

Claire didn't know when she shifted back to her human form. Sometime during the night she guessed. Her last memory was of amazing pleasure as she climaxed in her wolf form before blacking out.

As she woke, the night sky was still black above but the moon had disappeared behind the tree line. Her front was cool from the night air, damp from the moisture gathering on the grass. Her back was warm, snuggled into Derek's body.

Her body was sore, particularly her legs. She had pushed it with the run last night. Why she had run from him, Claire wasn't certain. Everything she had done had been instinctive, as if she had no choice in the matter and her body was just reacting as it should.

Oh, well it was done. Claire sighed. After worrying for the past five days about the final mating, Derek had been right. What had sounded objectionable had turned out to be quite natural.

Now she was a fully mated werewolf and Agakiar no longer owned a piece of her soul. Claire blinked as that thought settled into her mind. His brand should be gone!

Claire twisted in a rush to see her smooth lower back. It was impossible without a mirror. Derek grunted when she accidentally elbowed him. Blinking his eyes open, he glared at her.

"What are you doing?" He grouched.

"Is it still there?"

"What?" Derek blinked in confusion. "Where?"

"The brand! Is the brand still there?"

"Oh." Derek's eyes dropped to her lower back and he scowled.

"What?" Claire shrieked. "It's there, isn't it?"

"I don't know how to tell you this, sweetheart," Derek began sadly.

"Oh, God I knew it!" Claire wailed.

"Now, baby, don't overreact."

"Overreact? Overreact?" Claire shrieked. "How should one react to finding out they're going to turn into a demon?"

"Claire—"

"This explains everything." Claire was no longer paying attention to Derek. "No wonder Agakiar hasn't made a move, there was no need to."

"Claire—"

"I should have known it was too good to be true. All that talk about home and family, I let it all fog my thinking."

"Claire—" Derek shouted.

"As if that was ever going to happen." Claire snorted, still talking to herself. "I should have known better."

"Damn it, woman, listen to me!"

Claire suddenly found herself flat on her back with an annoyed Derek breathing in her face.

"What?"

"It's gone."

"What?" Claire scowled in confusion.

"The brand, it's gone."

"But you...oh, I could just—"

She did not finish the threat. At the sound of his chuckles, she lunged up, rolling with him to end on top. Derek quickly reversed their positions. Claire struggled against him, but he easily caught her wrists in one of his hands, stretching them over her head and out of the way.

"Damn it, Derek! If you ever do that again, I'll—"

Again, she didn't finish her threat, though this time it was Derek's kiss that stopped her. His mouth settled against hers. The kiss was slow and sensual. Each touch of his tongue was an exploration. He tasted her as if she were a delicacy he must savor.

She felt him settle more of his weight on her, his skin hot and smooth, deliciously naked. She wrapped her arms around his neck, pulling him closer so she could rub against him, enjoying the electric sparks of pleasure the friction of the flesh against flesh caused. His erection thumped her hip, telling her without words he liked it, too.

She sighed in disappointment when he pulled back, not wanting to let the moment go.

"Derek..." She breathed.

"Yes, sweetheart?" There was no denying the smug quality to his husky voice. It snapped her back to the moment and the fact she was supposed to be annoyed with him.

"Don't think a little kiss is going to get you off the hook for that one," Claire grumped without any real heat.

"Oh, and what will it take to make you forgive me?"

"Your promise to treat me like a princess from now on."

"I can do better than that. I'll promise to treat you like a queen. My queen, the queen bitch of the pack."

"Queen bitch. I'm sure the rest of your pack would love to hear that."

"They already know it."

"Why do I get the sense you're not joking?" Claire eyed him suspiciously.

"Because I'm not. Queen bitch is now your official title."

"Well, that sucks. Why can't I be first bitch, or head bitch?"

"You can call yourself whatever you want, sweetheart."

"So do I get privileges with my title?"

"Of course." Derek settled down beside her. "Let's see, you have to give your approval before any of the women can mate."

"They can't have sex without my approval?" Claire asked, the disbelief obvious in her tone.

"Mating, not sex."

"You're telling me the women in the pack have to get my approval to mate? What century do you people live in?"

"It's the way it is. The men have to get my approval."

"Why?"

"Historically, it was to make sure that if the guy chose a human, she would be able to handle what was expected of her in the pack."

"Expected?"

"How about we do the history lesson later? My mom can tell you all about it."

"Have you ever turned anybody down?" Claire asked after a moment, finding it hard to believe that he had.

"I turned down Travis and Ace when they requested you."

"Travis *and* Ace. Is this whole pack perverted?"

"Don't sound so horrified. They were going to fight for the right to mate you," Derek corrected.

"Fight? Over me?" Claire had never heard anything so ridiculous.

"I wouldn't let them."

"What about my opinion? Didn't any of you arrogant males think about asking me what I want?"

"You got what you wanted." Derek grinned. "Me."

"Are you sure about that?"

"Positive." Derek turned her face to his so he could brush light, teasing kisses across her lips. "You're just too stubborn to admit how wrong you were."

"And how wrong was I?"

"Have I told you that I love you?" Derek rubbed his nose against her.

"You might have mentioned it," Claire murmured, unable to keep the grin from her face.

"Well, you haven't even done that," Derek complained.

"I haven't?"

"No."

"Hmm."

"Well?"

"Well what?" Claire gave him an innocent look.

"Claire," Derek groaned exasperated.

"I'm thinking."

"Yeah? What are you thinking?"

"I'm thinking you are still a depraved juvenile at heart who lacks any sense of decorum."

"That's alright, you have enough decorum for both of us."

"Your sense of humor drives me insane."

"Better than not having one," Derek offered. At her snort, he changed tactics. "You're ducking the question."

"You're pushy, too."

"And you're evasive," Derek growled. "Tell me you love me."

"Even if it's a lie."

"It isn't."

"No, it isn't," Claire whispered.

"What isn't?" Derek pressed, an expectant gleam in his eye. Claire knew he wanted to hear the words.

"That I love you."

"You just love me because I got rid of the demon's brand."

"No, I love you because you love to fuck."

"Really?" Derek's grin took on a lecherous look. "Then, I've got a surprise for you."

Claire frowned slightly, watching as he turned and grabbed the sports bag he had packed last night.

"Where did that come from?" Claire eyed the bag nervously.

"I retrieved it after you fell asleep."

"You went all the way back for the bag?"

"We're not that far from the truck."

"We ran for over a half hour."

"Yeah, but I ran you in circles."

"You did not."

"I did. It's a hunting technique. You'll learn it when we go hunting with the pack."

"What's in it?"

"The bag?" At her nod, he chuckled. "You'll see. Now be a good and obedient mate, and stay still."

"Still? Still for what?"

"First." Derek unzipped the bag, making sure she couldn't see what was in it. After a moment of rummaging, he produced a bolt of black cloth. Claire watched nervously as he folded it over.

"What are you going to do with that?" She eyed the cloth apprehensively as he turned to her.

"I'm going to blindfold you."

"Blindfold?" Claire squeaked feeling her heart begin to race with fear as her pussy began to moisten with desire. "I'm not sure about this. What are you up to?"

"Trust me." The gleam in his darkening eyes didn't help her nerves.

"Why? What else do you have in that bag?"

"You'll see."

"No, I won't, not with a blindfold on."

"True, very true."

"Derek."

"Relax, sweetheart. This is my surprise. Now be a good little mate and be quiet or I'll have to gag you."

"Gag me?" Claire glared at him.

She could see the humor mixed with the lust in his eyes. He was teasing her, riling her up so when he finally did touch her it would be more explosive. He might have said it as a joke, but Claire would not put it past him.

"Fine." Claire gave a dramatic sigh as she closed her eyes. "Get on with it then."

She heard him chuckle as she felt the soft cloth settle against her cheeks and forehead, blinding her. He tied it at the back, loose enough so she could slip it off if she wanted.

Claire obeyed his silent command of his hands on her shoulder and lay back on the soft grass. The sound of him pulling things out of the bag punctuated the stillness of the predawn air. Her new heightened senses were working and she could detect the faint odor of wood and the scent of fresh dirt.

Her stomach quivered with anticipation as he lifted her wrist. Instinctively her muscles tightened, jerking against his hold. He murmured something soothing as he held her steady in his grasp. Claire tried to force herself to relax, but it became impossible when she felt him wrap a tie around her wrist.

"Derek?" Claire's voice broke.

"Shh, baby. I promise, you're going to enjoy this," Derek purred in a husky voice. "Now just relax."

That was easy for him to say, Claire thought to herself as he pulled her arm over her head. A moment later, he released his hold on her, but her arm wasn't free. He had tied it to some form of stake.

Claire tried not to flinch as he moved on to her other arm, but knowing what was coming made it harder to stand still. As excited as her body was by what he was doing, her mind was rolling with objections. She knew he wouldn't hurt her, but giving up control was a hard thing for her to do.

She felt a blush heat her skin, from her neck to the edge of her hairline, when he pulled open her legs. The smell of her arousal filled the air, drowning out all other scents. Claire knew he could see what she felt, the glistening cream of her desire at the top of her thighs.

He was looking, Claire knew. He was still, somewhere out in the darkness, watching her. The idea made her breath catch and her body tighten.

* * * *

She was perfection, so beautiful and all his. The sight of her bound for his pleasure made his body harden with a rush of desire. Derek fought to force back his need, wanting to savor what was coming.

He was not the only one who was aroused by her binds. The evidence of her desire drew his gaze. How he longed to touch her there, to taste the sweet cream of her desire, but if he did he would give in to the beast's desire to fuck, and the man's desire to play would be washed away.

"Are you comfortable?" His voice sounded raw, raspy to his ears.

"Yes." Her response was barely audible.

"Good."

He ran a hand up the outside of her leg, watching the goose bumps following in the wake of his touch. Her nipples tightened as his hands slid further up her side, barely caressing the edge of her breast. Her breathing grew shallow, her breath a soft, sexy pant forcing her chest to expand and retract hypnotically.

"Derek—"

He pressed a finger to lips, sealing in her breathy plea. He recognized the uncertainty hidden in the excitement of her voice. She was worried, no doubt, about giving up control.

Her concern made him smile. He may not have bound her before, but she'd never been in control of their lovemaking. As much control as he managed to maintain during their foreplay, he accepted his own was stripped away every time he sank into her tight, clinging sheath.

He leaned over her, intending to brush her lips with a slight, fleeting kiss, more to reassure than inflame. At the feel of his body against hers, Claire gasped and arched up, increasing the pressure.

Derek held himself still, closing his eyes against temptation as she rubbed provocatively against him. His hard and aching cock settled between her legs, nestling into the wet heaven waiting him there.

Claire groaned louder, rubbing harder. She moaned as she moved her hips, spreading them slightly so he could feel the hard nub of her clit pressing along his shaft. Faster and faster, she worked her hips, grinding her clit into him, striving for climax. Derek felt his control slipping and quickly jerked back.

"No," Derek ground out. "This time you come when I let you. Understand?"

"No," Claire whined as her hips arched, blindly seeking him. "Please."

It was a temptation Derek didn't know if he had the will to resist. He lifted his hand, holding it for a moment over her spread pussy before he smacked her, making her cry out. Her hips jerked beneath the blow as another gush of liquid poured out of her cunt.

"Again." Claire gasped.

"You," Derek smacked her, making sure her clit received most of the blow, "do not give orders."

He slapped her pussy after every word. She cried out with each hit. He could see the tears running down from under her blindfold. Not tears of pain, but of frustration, he was sure.

The evidence of her desire was obvious by her clenching pussy, silently begging to be filled. He watched the small opening contract and grinned, shaving her had definitely been a good idea. The view was stunning.

"Now be a good girl, baby, or I'll make you wait a long time before you take your pleasure," Derek warned her as nipped at her neck.

Claire sighed her acceptance and turned her head away from him, offering him more of her neck. Derek declined the offer and rolled off her, reaching for his bag. It took him a moment to pull out the jar of oil he had purchased just for this occasion. As the lid popped open, the strong odor of mint wafted out.

"What's that?" Claire whispered, obviously scenting the oil.

Instead of answering, he dipped his finger in the oil and then turned to message it into her collarbone. The oil warmed beneath his touch and he watched Claire shiver when he removed his hand and the spot cooled in the early morning air.

Derek leaned down to lick the spot he'd just touched. His eyes closed as he savored the flavor of sweet woman and mint mixed together. Derek dipped his hand back into the oil jar and began to slowly message her body. His mouth followed his hands, licking and nibbling all along her body.

Carefully, he avoided the sensitive peaks of her breast and the sweet treat between her legs. Instead, he focused on other delectable areas of her body, the inside crease of her elbow, the soft skin of her inner thigh, the smooth area where her neck and shoulders combined. By the time he was done she was squirming, panting, begging him to touch her, taste her, where she most needed it.

Turning his attention to the soft, full globes of her breasts, he began to message the scented oil into them. His mouth followed as he lapped and licked his way around first one, then the other breast, coming close but never touching the puckered bud at the tip.

Finally he gave her what she wanted, just a teasing lick for each nipple, just enough to make her moan and arch her back. He blew on them, making them tighter, fuller when he was done. Covering her breast with his hands, he lightly rolled and pulled on wrinkled tips while he settled his head between her legs, planning on a true feast.

He attacked her weeping flesh with savage intent, wanting to drive her completely out of control with her need. He licked around the entrance to her wet entrance, lapping up her cream before moving to the hard nub of her clit.

Sucking the little nubbin into his mouth, he began to tease and torment her, swirling his tongue around and around the sensitive button. As he tortured her clit, his fingers pulled and plucked her nipples with growing strength and speed. He felt her body tighten, heard her breathing increase and knew she was moments from climax.

He withdrew and she let out a scream of frustration as she writhed and fought against her binds. Derek gave her a moment to settle, just enough to let the pleasure tightening her body recede from the apex he had driven it toward.

When her breathing slowed to a fast-paced pant, he lowered his head again. This time he wasted no time teasing her, but fucked his tongue deep inside her cunt. Stroking in, again and again, he felt her muscles tighten, seeking to increase the pressure, the pleasure.

He growled with approval and desire as he felt her pussy clench and another wave of sweet cream rush out to meet his invading tongue. Her cunt clenched again, beginning to spasms with the first quake of her oncoming orgasm. Again he withdrew. This time her cry of denial echoed through the forest.

Derek leaned back on his knees, watching her flail about, fighting the binds. He again waited until she settled before caressing the outside of her legs down to where her ankles were tied. With slow movements, drawing out the motions to heighten her excitement, he undid the binds around her ankles. Immediately she pulled her legs up, widening them in invitation and giving him an intoxicating view of her wet, pink pussy.

Derek shook his head, fighting the beast back. He grabbed her by the waist and turned her over. They were going to get to the fucking soon, real soon, but first there was something else he wanted to do.

Chapter 23

Claire did not wait to be told what to do once he turned her over. Quickly she scrambled onto all fours, anticipating his desires. Her wrists were still bound forcing her scoot upward and away from him so she could rest her weight on her hands.

She knew he wanted her in this position. Derek liked to take her from behind. She had no objections to that plan, as long as he did it soon. She was dying with need.

"Shoulders down." A hand pressing her down into the grass followed the hard command. "Raise your bottom. That's it. So sexy. Spread those legs and show me your pussy."

Claire felt her stomach clench hard, her pussy pulsed with arousal at the image his words invoked. He didn't wait for her comply before sliding his hands along the inside of her thighs, then pushing them wide. She shivered as his callous roughened fingertips teased the swollen folds of her cunt and slid even higher, right between her ass cheeks.

Those fingers bit into her flesh, holding her bottom cheeks wide open. Fear rose in a thick wave over her spine as she began to guess what his intention was. She wasn't ready, not for that, and she tried to clench her cheeks closed against his hold.

"No." His barked command was followed by a sharp slap to her ass. The stinging pain sent crystal shards of pleasure up her back and down to her pussy.

"Be still or I'll spend an hour eating at that delectable pussy and not give you the satisfaction you need."

Claire flinched, knowing that he was not making an idle threat. To make sure she believed him, he fucked three thick fingers into her pussy, thrusting deep. Twirling and swirling them, he carefully avoided touching the sweet spot hidden within her sheath.

Just as Claire felt her body instinctively pushing back, to deepen the penetration he pulled back. She breathed deeply as he spread her ass cheeks again, trying to relax. The fear though would not leave, but it was tinged with excitement. She felt him shift slightly, a moment later a greased finger coming back to circle around her back entrance.

She shivered from the potent combination of apprehension and sinful pleasure his finger slowly began to penetrate. A second lubed finger pressed into her making her bite her lip to hold back a groan. Her back entrance felt stretched, burning. He widened his fingers, forcing her entrance to expand and making her gasp with the painful pressure.

Claire bit her lip hard and felt the metallic taste of blood when he added a third finger. She shifted, unable to stop her body from trying to escape the pain and the uncertainty. She didn't think she could take anymore.

She jerked when his free hand came around to toy with her clit. The mixture of pain and pleasure washed through her, fusing into a confusing blend. For several minutes, he kept her bouncing between pain and pleasure until the tension eased and her body began to accept his fingers buried insider her.

Derek's thick fingers retreated and she felt his body twist between her bent knees, reaching for something. A moment later, she felt a thick, cool gel filling her rear. She gasped at the sudden sensation. It was cold against her heated flesh.

"It's just lubricant, sweetheart." Derek soothed her, squeezing more of the liquid into her. "I don't want to tear you."

His words, meant to reassure, had her flinching. Tear did not sound like a good thing. The pain so far had been tolerable, but tearing? Claire would not be able to take that.

Over the last week he had talked about fucking her there. Everything he had said had excited her, but now that he was talking about true pain, Claire was quickly reevaluating her opinion. The fear his words inspired made it impossible for her to relax and when she felt a smooth, plastic head press against her back entrance she fought against it.

"Relax sweetheart," Derek whispered. "Fighting it will only make it hurt worse. Take a deep breath. That's good, now let it out."

As he spoke, he gently pushed the lubricated plug into her. Her entrance stretched, her thighs quivered, and her mind rioted with uncertainty. The fat head of the toy forced its way past the tight ring of muscles at her entrance, making her wince.

"It's too big." Claire sobbed. "Please, I can't do this."

"Yes you can, baby," Derek crooned. "The hard part is almost over. You'll be feeling real good soon."

"Promise."

"I promise, sweetheart. Just let me get the rest of the plug in."

"Okay." Claire could barely speak.

"Good girl."

He rewarded her with a gentle stroke of her clit. Claire panted as he continued to tease her clit while he firmly pushed the plug into her body. She felt every searing inch as he slid it in. She was sure it would rip her in two, but almost as quickly as the pain appeared, it dissipated into a tingling shower of electric sparks that vibrated through her body.

When he finally seated the plug deep within her body, Claire let out her breath and tried to force her muscles to relax. The plug filled her, stretching muscles never stretched. Her bottom ached and her pussy throbbed. The odd mixture made her body spasm with delight, only to clench with the sharp bite of pain that followed.

She fought to breathe through the sensations raking over her nerves. Her fingers were tightly clenched and blood no longer circulated through them. Her back felt strained from her tightly wound muscles, and she tried to stretch.

The small movements sent a riot of sensations radiating from her ass outward. What started as pain transformed to pleasure, making her pussy clench and weep. She heard Derek chuckle a moment before he smacked her ass, making every sensation in her body intensify as her muscles clenched around the plug.

Claire cried out as her body convulsed with pure pleasure. The sound was more animal than human. Not giving her time to come to focus through the fog of erotic pleasure, he spanked her again, then again. Over and over until she thought her muscles would snap from the tension tightening them.

Bolts of electric pleasure followed every spank. Her pussy was clenching, desperate to be filled and Claire was not sure how much more she could take. Just when she was sure that she would die from the sensations his spanking evoked, her world broke apart.

She screamed out her release as her body convulsed with waves of extraordinary pleasure. Her eyes rolled back in her head and she collapsed on the ground. She did not move until her breathing began to return to normal and the world came back into focus.

"Don't ever say, I don't keep my promises," Derek murmured, the satisfied arrogance in his tone making her sigh. He had earned the right to be smug. "Come on, sweetheart, up on your knees. I'm not done with you yet."

"I'm tired," Claire muttered in protest as she felt him lifting her back onto legs that did not want to hold her weight.

"We're going to have to work on your stamina." Derek chuckled. "Now up."

He emphasized his point with another smack to her bottom. Claire groaned, not ready to be filled with the sensations that touch brought her. Hoping to avoid another smack, she forced her jelly-like muscles to work and stayed on her knees.

"It's time for your reward for letting me get that plug in."

Derek's breath caressed the swollen, wet lips of her pussy. Her cunt clinched in response, her body already beginning to reawaken with renewed desire at his obvious intention.

She moaned her objection as he ignored her and began to feast upon her pussy. Kate was right. Derek loved to bury his head between her legs and drive her insane. It was a fine quality in a lover, one she had never experienced before.

The sensations were magnified this time. Every time her pussy contracted with pleasure, her butt cheeks tightened around the plug and sent a shower of ecstatic sparks rippling through her.

Derek didn't hold back, fucking his tongue deep into her only to pull out and suck on her clit. The typhoon of pleasure whirled faster through her, making her body twist beneath the pressure. Her hips rolled back to grant him better access to her pussy, helplessly seeking more fuel for the storm.

Derek took advantage of her silent offer. Claire was sure she could take no more, that her body and mind would splinter with another orgasm, when his tongue twisted, rubbing against the sweet spot buried within her cunt.

Claire felt ecstasy wash over her in a blinding rush. Claire could not get enough air into her lungs, as she came hard. The wicked pleasure devoured her soul, stealing her ability to think. The muscles in her thighs quivered and her legs would have given out again if not for Derek holding her up.

This time he didn't give her time to recover before he was rubbing the head of his hard dick against her spasming opening. He held her hips in hard grip as he slowly penetrated her pussy. With the plug still filling her bottom, there was little room left for his thick erection.

That didn't stop Derek as he continued to forge his way deep inside. Claire moaned feeling over filled with thick, hard cock. Her hips arched, trying to adjust and make space for him as he stretched her pussy wider and wider.

It felt as if there were about to burst, but he managed to seat himself fully into her tight sheath. Claire took deep breaths, trying to adjust to being filled in both places. Thankfully, Derek gave her the time she needed, holding himself still until she finally got control over her shaking body.

She expected Derek to begin thrusting. Instead she felt the plug being turned, pulled back. The sensations were beyond anything she had ever felt. The rounded head of the toy caught on the tight ring of muscles at the entrance before Derek pushed the plug in.

Her anal muscles clenched tightly, making her pussy contract around the thick cock seated deep inside her. Claire cried out with the sensation as he continued to stroke the plug in and out of her untried channel.

Each drag of the plug pulled and pushed her against his erection, the motion slowly fucking her against his heated flesh. The combination had her cries turning to screams as her hips bucked backward, increasing the sensation.

Her body whipped again toward ecstasy. It broke over her in a blinding rush as her muscles contracted with the pleasure rippling over her flesh. The orgasm was too strong, too intense, almost painful.

Claire was sobbing, could feel her tears soaking the blindfold. She was sure that at any moment her heart would give out and she would die here from the pleasure. Derek settled the toy deep inside her and flexed his hips, pulling his cock almost completely free. Claire's eyes popped open wide with his motion.

"Derek!"

She screamed his name as he began to fuck her. It was a hard, fast fucking as he held her hips in his iron grip. He thrust harder, deeper, increasing his speed until Claire's entire body was shaking with the impact of his strokes. Every inch of her sheath was sensitized, pulsing, exploding with pleasure, as her orgasm went on and on, spiraling higher and higher.

* * * *

Derek slammed furiously into her as she bucked and writhed beneath him. She screamed his name, driving the beast to greater ferocity. The wolf was unleashed, taking what was his.

Derek snarled as her pussy contracted painfully around his cock. The sensation more intense than it had ever been because of the plug filling her ass. It left little room for his large erection, making her already tight channel almost impossible to penetrate.

With her cunt quaking with ecstasy, Derek felt the painful pull at the base of his cock and knew that release was a moment away. He wished he could freeze time and exist in this moment, with her cunt milking his cock, her head bowed in submission, her body completely his to command.

He drew back and watched as her stretched pussy swallowed him whole, her pink lips eating every inch of his darker flesh, as he gave another final thrust and let the swift rush of ecstasy consume him. The fierce, blinding pleasure was more intense than it had ever been. She was truly his, mated with him in body, heart and soul.

He threw his head back and roared out his release, filling her body with his seed. Long minutes passed before the tension holding his body taut released and he collapsed, squashing her beneath him.

He wished they could stay like that forever, bound as one, bodies slick with sweat, hearts beating in unison. Her body was still trembling with the aftershocks of pleasure. Derek grinned, wondering if she had passed out, which she normally did after one of their more strenuous lovemaking sessions.

If she had, he was going to have to carry her back to the truck, because they could not stay here. The sky was already lightening with the sun's impending arrival.

"Claire?" His tone was raspy as he was still trying to catch his breath.

"Hmm," came back her sleepy reply.

"You alive?"

"Aren't you going to ask if you hurt me?" Claire sounded pleased.

"I didn't, did I?"

"No, but you are getting heavy."

"Sorry." He brushed a kiss across her temple in apology as he rolled to his side.

She grunted as his softening shaft pulled free of her body. She mumbled a moan as he pulled the plug out, cringing and issuing a groan of complaint when the rounded head pushed free of her.

Derek watched as her little rosebud winked closed. Next time it was going to be his cock stretching that tight entrance open. His soft dick began to harden at the thought and he grinned.

His endless desire for his mate never ceased to amaze him. He would probably kill her if he gave in to the urge every time it struck him. Claire already thought he was oversexed, there was no telling what she would think if she knew how much he thought about sex or how often he wanted it.

He reached up and unbound her arms. As he lowered her limbs, he rotated one and then the other, massaging away any stiffness as he lowered her limbs. Tucking them by her side, she curled up, backing into his side, instinctively seeking him. The small telling motion warmed his heart as he undid the blindfold.

Claire did not bother to open her eyes though she murmured a complaint when he rolled away from her to repack the bag he had brought. They had never used toys before. Derek had not owned any before two days ago, when he had bought what was in the bag.

Sure he had used them with women in his past, but they had always provided the party favors. Derek was betting Claire's collection probably resembled her underwear, basic and limited. He would see to fixing that.

There were a lot of ideas he had, the idea of her putting on a show for him the premiere one. When he turned back, he found her watching him through half-open eyes. Her eyes drifted down to settle on reemerging erection. Her lips tipped up in a snicker.

"Come on sleepyhead, we've got to get moving." He prodded her.

"Move?" Claire repeated with a yawn. "I'm comfortable."

"You wouldn't be in another hour."

"Why? What happens then?"

"The sun will be fully up and the bugs will come out."

"Bugs?" She bolted upright looking alarmed.

"Come on, I'll take you home and you can go to sleep in our soft, comfortable bed." Derek stood, hefting the bag over his shoulder.

"Mmm. That sounds like a plan." Claire rubbed her eyes, making them more bloodshot.

"So, do I carry you or can you walk?"

"I wouldn't want you to strain anything," Claire muttered, taking his offered hand.

He yanked her up with a little more force than necessary for that comment. She flinched slightly when she landed on her feet and it was his turn to snicker.

"A little sore?"

She blushed instantly, from her breast to her hairline, at that question. The sight of her obvious embarrassment touched him. As wild and passionate as Claire was when she was in his arms, she was still his straitlaced assistant at heart.

"I'm fine." She glared at him. "Lead the way."

"After you." Derek gestured in the right direction, not about to miss the opportunity of watching her walk naked. Claire knew exactly what he was up to and scowled at him.

"I think perhaps you should go first."

"How about a truce and we go side by side?"

"I guess that's as good an offer as I'm going to get," Claire agreed.

He led her back to the truck and, unfortunately, her clothes. She flinched again as she pulled on her panties and then jeans. Derek sighed regretfully, she was obviously sore and that meant he was going to have to hold off on taking that ass for a ride, at least for a day. What a shame.

Chapter 24

Saturday: 4:45 pm

Derek scanned the crowd filling the park. He heard JD snicker beside him and knew the sheriff was finding humor at his expense. JD had already made several snide comments about how Derek could not go five minutes without looking for his mate.

Derek had not defended himself. JD was right. Derek knew he was hopeless and, as long as there was still a demonic serial killer on the loose, he had no intention of changing. He was going to keep a close eye on Claire.

He spotted her. She was sitting with his sister and a large group of women at the picnic tables. He had asked Kristin to escort her around, introduce her the females in the pack. His sister, relaxed now that she knew the threat against Derek was gone, had willingly agreed.

Though the fair was spread out over the entire park, he had made Claire promise to stay within eyesight while he was technically on-duty. A part of him felt guilty at denying her the fun of enjoying the whole festival, but tomorrow he would have off. He would bring her back and they could take in all the festivities.

Today, though, he was working at the makeshift command center set up in front of the park services building. Because Wilsonville had such a small police department and the festival was so large, the county deputies helped out. Derek's officers did most of the grunt work, directing traffic through the designated parking areas, doing foot patrols through the crowds, and helping wherever was necessary.

The county deputies were out on the roads, making sure nobody sped and responding to fender benders as they occurred. During the day, things were pretty tame. It was at night when too much alcohol created problems, everything from driving accidents to fights.

Derek scanned the crowd again. The uneasy feeling had been growing for the past few days. It was strange, considering Deik had told them Wall had been handled. With no other minions, Agakiar had no vessel on this plane.

Wall's mysterious disappearance hadn't escaped the FBI's notice. The pleasant Agent Perst and his sidekick Yonkavic had reappeared. After they hit the wall of evasive answers Claire gave them, they had issued a warning that they were watching her and left.

That left one problem — Urazi and their female serial killer. That pair made him nervous, mostly because Claire was going full steam ahead with her investigation. She had an entire list of suspects based on the females Kathleen had been close to.

After a little research, Claire had deemed all three innocent. That had brought Claire back to him and his ex-girlfriends. She was focusing specifically on Carolyn. As much as he understood why Claire didn't like Carolyn, Derek just couldn't accept she was a killer.

They had fought over it last night. Claire had questioned him for the hundredth time about Carolyn. When he had patiently explained, for the hundredth time, that Carolyn was not a killer, Claire had gotten that cold, superior look in her honey eyes.

"I understand what you're saying. You don't think Carolyn is capable of murder." She had turned her head back to her notes, clearly dismissing him.

"I know she's not."

"Fine," Claire said in the pissy tone that told him he had better watch his step, defending Carolyn may cost him more than it was worth. "Then you won't mind if I investigate her."

"Investigate whoever you want." Derek could not stop himself from adding, "and waste your time."

"With that investigative attitude, it's a good thing you never had any serious crime in this small town."

"Excuse me?" Derek had paused in the study's doorway. Claire had taken over the room.

"Oh, wait. You did have one big case and it was *never solved.*"

"Okay, Sherlock, give me one good reason you think Carolyn is the killer, besides the fact you just don't like her."

"She wanted to be your mate." Claire shuffled through her notes.

"So?" Derek gripped the doorframe.

"I think it's obvious she would have done anything to be your mate."

"If you're going to say she killed Kathleen just so I would be free to mate her, then there is one serious flaw in that theory."

"What?"

"You. Why hasn't she made any attempts on your life?"

"Maybe she's just waiting for the right time." Claire looked over her shoulder and gave him a sickeningly sweet smile.

"Claire, get real."

"There is another little fact you keep overlooking." She turned back to her notes, tucking her hair behind her ears.

"What's that?"

"Somebody told Kathleen you were a werewolf."

"And?"

"And I'm going to assume that only members of the pack were privileged to that information. So add one plus one and you get…"

"What's got you growling over there, Derek?" Caleb's voice broke through Derek's reverie.

"Probably a man standing too close to his mate." JD scanned the crowd as he took another chug of his beer.

"Caleb." Derek blinked at the grinning, dark-haired man who was a perfect replica of JD. "Didn't notice you walk up."

"I know." Caleb shook Derek's hand. "You were lost in space."

Caleb and JD might have been identical in appearance, but their personalities weren't similar. Caleb was laid back, with a quick smile and a way with the ladies. JD tended to be a lot more serious.

"He's mooning over his woman." JD shot Derek a disgusted look. "It's about enough to make a real man sick."

"I can't wait until you find yours, JD," Derek shot back. "I'm going to be there to make sure you suffer."

"Hey, now." Caleb's hands shot up. "JD's not the only one who will suffer when he screws everything up."

"Screw you, Caleb." JD glared at his brother.

* * * *

"Who's that guy glaring at Derek?" Claire followed her question with a nod that had Kristin looking over her shoulder to see whom Claire was talking about.

"The guy by the beer booth in the green T-shirt?" Kristin asked.

"Yeah."

"That's Nathan Harper. I guess you know why he doesn't like Derek much." Kristin turned back to Claire.

"Yeah, I know the story." Claire nodded. "He's not going to cause trouble is he?"

"Never has." Kristin shrugged. "He'll probably do what he always does, drink too much and pass out in his truck."

Kristin rejoined the conversation that several of the women were having. Claire tried to stay interested in the conversation. These women were now a part of her pack, her family. According to Derek, she, as head bitch, was going to be in charge of handling disputes between them. On the lighter side, she was also going to be in charge of organizing and managing all sorts of pack events.

Still she quickly lost interest in the conversation and turned her attention back to Nathan Harper. He was no longer glaring at Derek, but was brooding as he gazed out over the lagoon. Claire frowned, her heart going out to the man.

As she watched him finish his drink and walk off to buy another, an idea began to form. She needed to get into Kathleen's old room. Between Derek's hyperactive scrutiny and not knowing Nathan's schedule, she had not had the opportunity. She did now.

Pleading she wasn't feeling well, she talked Kristin into giving her a ride home. They separated from the table of women to make their way toward Derek.

His eyes never left her, darkening to midnight blue as she approached. She knew that look. He was horny, again. As much as she enjoyed sex, Claire was amazed by Derek's insatiable appetite. It would not have surprised her if the man had been born with a hard-on.

JD scowled at her approach. They had met briefly on Friday. He had been dour-faced then, too. The mini-giant's disposition had not been any better as he warned her next time she started a fire he would arrest her.

"Hey, sweetheart. What's up?" Derek pulled her close for a quick kiss. Not letting her go, he nodded to the two large men standing with him. "You know Sheriff McBane and that's his brother, Caleb."

"Nice to meet you." Caleb grinned, his eyes twinkling. "Kristin."

"Hey, Caleb." Kristin nodded toward the hard eyed sheriff. "JD."

JD acknowledged both women with a grunt.

"Hello." Claire gave the two men a quick smile before turning to Derek. "Sweetheart, Kristin's going to take me home."

"Why? What's wrong?" Derek was instantly concerned.

"Nothing's wrong," Claire quickly assured him. She needed him to stay behind and if he became too concerned, he would insist on going home with her. "I just got a little too much sun. I need to lay down someplace cool and dark for a while."

"Oh." Derek's muscles relaxed though he continued to scowl. "I can take you home."

"Derek, I need to lie down and rest." She placed subtle emphasis on the last word. "Perhaps, it would be better if you stayed here."

"Yeah, alright." Derek grinned lowering his head. "You go get your rest. That way when I get home, we can—"

"Derek," Claire growled, knowing he was about to say something that would embarrass her. She could already feel the blush starting.

"I'll be home when my shift is done." Derek brushed another kiss across her lips.

* * * *

"Cute mate," Caleb commented as the men watched Claire and Kristin walk away.

"At least, she hasn't burned down anything else," JD grunted.

"You don't have any proof," Derek responded dryly. "And in the future, I would appreciate it if you didn't attempt to intimidate my mate."

"The mere fact you're not trying to pound me into the ground defending her innocence is proof enough."

"What did she burn down?" Caleb inquired.

"The old Howard place," JD answered when Derek pointedly refused to.

"Oh. Good riddance." Caleb wrinkled his nose. "That place was creepy."

"See, it's that attitude that keeps you off the force." JD belched. "It doesn't matter what she burned. The point is she broke the law."

"Well, regardless, Claire won't be breaking any more laws," Derek assured him.

"So you've reformed her. I'm sure the FBI will be glad to hear it."

"FBI?" Caleb frowned for a moment before his face brightened with realization. "Oh, hey. That's the girl whose file you had me pull. Claire Hollowell."

"Forget the file, Caleb," Derek growled.

"Hey, man." Caleb shot him an injured look. "Don't sweat it. We protect our own."

"What about the other matter?" JD chunked his plastic cup toward the trashcan. "The missing girls."

"What missing girls?" Caleb scowled as he glanced from Derek to his brother. "You guys are keeping a lot of stuff from me."

"Maybe if you weren't so busy chasing every available woman, you'd be aware of what's going on."

"Hey, somebody's got to go out and find our mate. The way I see it, I'm doing you a favor, JD. I'm doing all the hard work, while you get to relax and enjoy things with Sally."

"Hard work?" JD rolled his eyes. "I don't think fucking half the women in the county is considered hard work."

"Over half now that Derek's off the market."

"Gentlemen, please." Derek held his hands up. "Leave me out of this. I'm a happily mated man."

"You're a weird one, if you call being mated to a woman chasing after a serial killer a happy experience," JD snickered.

"Hopefully we'll get that matter wrapped up soon."

Once the case was solved, everything would be perfect. Not only would he and Claire catch Kathleen's killer, but they could also stop arguing about Carolyn. With the added bonus of getting rid of Deik and the rest of the Cerberus gang, Derek was fully invested in seeing the case closed.

Claire's former teammates, as Derek like to think of them, had set up in the small rental across the street, not moving until Urazi was taken care of. Sasha and Harold weren't so bad. At least, they barely spoke to him.

It was that damned bloodsucker. He was forever showing up at night to work with Claire and make all his snide, sarcastic comments. Derek was more than ready to see the last of that vampire.

Chapter 25

Claire pulled her beat-up, old Ford to a stop under the shade of a large crepe myrtle. She had taken off for Nathan's place less than five minutes after Kristin had dumped her off at Derek's house. A quick stop across the street to inform Sasha of her intentions was all the time Claire had spared before heading out.

As she stepped out into the early evening sun, she looked around. Nathan Harper's farm was not a commercial success from the looks of the worn, old house. Some farm equipment sat in front of the warped barn doors. Rusting into the ground, the machinery looked as if it would crumble under a strong wind.

The fields beyond the house were thick with green corn stalks. From her research, Claire knew he was growing sweet, white corn, watermelons, tomatoes, and grapes. All the farm's produce was sold locally.

Her eyes cut up to the house. It reminded her of Howard's farmhouse. The style was similar. So was the decay. Instead of the evil that had haunted the Howard's house, Nathan's home wore a shroud of silence. It weighed on Claire more than the oppressive afternoon heat as she slowly climbed the creaking front porch steps.

It took a moment for her to pick the old lock on the front door and then she moved slowly through the house. It needed a serious cleaning and some redecorating wouldn't have hurt. The house was as trapped in the past as Nathan was, solemn and morbid. Nathan Harper lived in the wreckage of what had once been.

Swiftly, she made her way to the back bedroom Kate had said was Kathleen's. Mentally, she went over her notes as she moved through the house, remembering the details of Kathleen's last day. As she paused at the closed door of the back bedroom, Claire admitted she didn't want to go in there, didn't want to be here.

There was no avoiding what needed to be done and she turned the doorknob. The room breathed out a sigh of musty, stale air as the door swung in.

It was just as Kate had said. Nathan had kept Kathleen's room as a shrine to her memory. Careful not to disturb anything, she moved through the small room. It was neat and orderly, not too frilly or girly. Claire went through drawers of faded and worn clothes, finding what she had hoped to discover under several neatly folded piles of underwear.

The bed squeaked and gave up a puff of dust as she settled onto its edge to read Kathleen's diary. Conscious of time, Claire flipped to the end and began to read the small, leather journal backward.

She felt her heart begin to race as she noted Carolyn's name throughout the last week's entries. Slowly, the story unfolded, giving credence to Claire's theory. Carolyn had approached Kathleen.

Carolyn's first attempt had been to belittle Kathleen, telling her that Derek was only going out with the nerdy girl on a bet. Carolyn claimed that some of the more popular boys made a bet Derek couldn't seduce a girl like Kathleen. It was obvious the words had hurt Kathleen.

While Kathleen had doubts about Derek's motives, she had been smart enough not to trust Carolyn. Besides, what Carolyn hadn't known was that Kathleen had already slept with Derek and was pregnant. The fact terrified Kathleen and she'd been trying to find a way to tell Derek.

When her first attempt failed, Carolyn tried again. This time Carolyn had told Kathleen all about what a beast Derek was, that he was a werewolf and Kathleen was slated to be sacrificed. Not only had Kathleen not believed Carolyn, she had told the bitch so to her face.

Carolyn had then taunted Kathleen, telling her that if she wanted to know the truth, she could see it with her own eyes. Kathleen had been leery but agreed to go with Carolyn one night and spy on Derek and some of his friends. They had indeed changed into wolves and had sent Kathleen into hysterics.

There was one more entry in the diary. Kathleen had nervously agreed to meet with Derek to talk. She didn't know if she had the courage to tell him about the pregnancy, but she knew she had to try.

Well, well, well. That helps your theory.

Claire turned her head to find Kathleen sitting beside her. The ghost was leaning slightly to read the pages as Claire did.

It does not exactly prove anything except that Carolyn is a bitch. We already knew that. Claire did not speak aloud, not wanting to disturb the air. In this room, everything felt sacred.

You don't think it will convince Derek?

I think it will upset him, but convince him? I don't think he wants to be convinced.

Why not? Kate scowled. *Doesn't he want to catch the killer?*

If the killer is Carolyn, do you know what that means? It means that Derek has been sleeping with Kathleen's killer for years. All those years he gave affection and attention to the woman who killed his mate and child. Can you imagine how he is going to react to that?

The kind of pain and guilt you know all about, huh?

Everybody handles pain and guilt differently. Just because I-

Oh, God. He's here. Kate vanished right before her eyes, her scream echoing in her head. *Run!*

Claire jumped up, instinctively moving to do as ordered. She never had the chance. Carolyn was standing in the doorway. The blonde cocked her head to the side and smiled, a cold twist of the lips that froze Claire to the bone.

"So have you figured out your mystery, Claire?" The other woman purred.

"Carolyn."

"Oh, come now, sweetheart. After all this time, you don't recognize me?"

"Agakiar?" Claire's voice faltered, asking a question that she already knew the answer to in her soul.

"Very good, Claire. I was about to become insulted." Agakiar moved slowly into the room, her eyes sweeping disdainfully over the plain décor.

"But how? Wall was eliminated."

"Yes, I know and I wasn't very pleased with that." Agakiar came to a stop, her eyes coming to rest on Claire. "I guess I have you and your friends to thank for this body. It's a nice body, does some…interesting things. I've yet to fully test all the possibilities, but I have plans for that."

"Plans? You can…transform to the wolf."

"Of course." Agakiar's laugh was brittle, the frozen shard raked across Claire's nerves.

"I still don't understand."

"What's so difficult to comprehend? You forced Urazi out of the house and into Carolyn. I forced Urazi out of Carolyn when I was forced out of Wall. It's all in the pecking order."

"So you're the one who helped Urazi take her body," Claire whispered.

"Yes, with the agreement we could share it."

"You're sharing now? That doesn't sound like you, Agakiar."

"Well, as different as Urazi and I are, we do have some similarities. We like blood sacrifice. So, occasionally, I'll let him have a baby or two. No problem there."

"It wouldn't last."

"Oh, it doesn't have to. Soon, I'll have your body. Just think, two demons running loose in werewolf form. Things are going to be interesting." Agakiar moved closer.

"You can't take my body. You're brand is gone." Claire began to move to the side. Perhaps she could circle her, she didn't know if she could beat Carolyn's body in a flat out run, but she could try.

"There are many thing, you have yet to learn." She was close now.

"So educate me." Claire wasted a step back.

"I'd rather show you." Agakiar matched her step.

"Show me?"

"I had an epiphany, you see." Carolyn's hand lifted as if in praise. "I had to thank God for this one. As you know, He in His wisdom made the soul immortal. Corruptible, but indestructible."

"I'm sure He's happy to have your praise."

"Well, that's all He's going to get. He's not going to get you, because I'm going to take you."

"You can't force me out of my body."

"Not now." Agakiar nodded his agreement. "I figure once you've watched me torture and slaughter everybody you care about and, hell, maybe a few you don't even know, you'll be broken, in no shape to withstand me."

"Fuck you."

"I think we'll start with your mate. How's that sound? I got a bone to pick with him. Maybe I'll pick a few, rip them right out of his body while he's still alive. What do you think of that?"

"I think you'll have to kill me first."

Claire charged Carolyn after making that promise. She crashed into the slender woman. They went down hard with Claire landing on top. Before the other woman could respond, Claire was punching her.

She landed three good hits before Agakiar threw her off with unnatural force. Claire felt herself flying through the air a second before she slammed into the wall. The plaster cracked beneath her as her head hit with enough force to leave her dazed.

Through blurry eyes, she saw the blonde approaching.

"Nice try, Claire."

The words barely registered before pain splinted through her head and everything went black.

* * * *

"Damn it!" Derek clicked his phone close with a snap.

The sun had set and his shift was over. Around him the park was lit up with the beginning of the night's celebration. The smell of roasting meat and deep fried sweets filled the air as music from the live band drowned out the normal night noises.

"No answer?" JD asked pleasantly. His mood had improved considerably once Sally had shown up. The short brunet hushed him, sensing that Derek's mood was volatile.

"Shut up, JD," Derek snapped.

"Don't antagonize the man." Caleb grinned. He had his arm around a cute little redhead he had picked up sometime during the day.

"She must be asleep," Derek muttered, more for his sake than the others.

"She must be a sound sleeper. How many times have you called her?" JD asked dryly.

Seven in the last half hour, but Derek didn't answer him aloud. Caleb had invited Derek to join him and his friends for some dinner, drinking and dancing. Derek had been hesitant, not wanting Claire around Caleb and JD's pack.

Caleb had read the hesitation for what it was and assured Derek he was hanging out with coworkers and not pack members. Derek had decided to let Claire make the decision. She should have answered by now. His gut was screaming at him that something was seriously wrong.

"I think I'll swing…by home and…what?"

Derek turned to see what had both Caleb and JD tensing. Deik was moving through the crowd, heading straight for them. Great, just what he needed.

"Sweetheart, why don't you get us a beer?" Caleb made short work of getting rid of the human at his side.

"Why don't you help her, Sally?" JD released his hold on her waist.

"I can handle myself," Sally responded to the hidden statement in JD's request.

"I know, honey," JD assured her. "I'm just a little thirsty."

"Okay, I'll be right back. Don't go anywhere." Sally sighed.

"That goes for you too." The red head winked at Caleb.

"Wild horses couldn't drag me away."

That line would have made Derek roll his eyes and earned him a snide comment from JD normally. Neither man had taken their eyes off the bloodsucker, though. They were not the only ones taking notice. Throughout the crowd there built the faint scent of aggression and anger.

The werewolves in attendance had taken notice of the vampire in their midst. Not that Deik was trying to hide. Nor did he appear to notice the reaction of those near him.

His face was set in a grim line that had Derek's nerves. Derek did not have long to wait to wonder. The second Deik stopped in front of them he was speaking.

"Agakiar has Claire."

"What?" Derek's response was instant. He grabbed Deik by the shirt and lifted the vampire off the ground. Deik didn't resist.

"Agakiar has Claire," Deik repeated.

"I thought you guys fucking eliminated him?"

"Who's Agakiar?" Caleb asked, his voice tight with concern in reaction to Derek's anger.

"We did. I don't know what is going on. I just know what Kate told me."

"Who's Kate?"

"Kate the ghost?" JD scowled, not having fond memories of the spook.

"Kate is a ghost?" Caleb looked from JD's shrug to Derek who was ignoring him.

"Where the hell does he have her?" Derek's fist tightened on Deik's shirt.

"I don't know."

"What the hell good are you then?" Derek shook Deik. "I thought you were supposed to be protecting her?"

"It was daylight. Claire came over and told Sasha she was going to Nathan Harper's house to look around Kathleen's room. Then at dusk Kate appears screaming about how Agakiar has Claire."

"Damn it!" Derek threw Deik back. "I'm going to Harper's place."

"What the hell is going on here Derek?" Caleb demanded of Derek's back.

"Already been there," Deik yelled, stopping Derek. "She's not there. You're wasting your time."

"What the hell am I supposed to do?"

"You're supposed to shut up and listen to the rest of what I have to say." Deik remained calm as he stepped toward Derek.

"We don't have time for these games."

"Before Agakiar showed up, Claire and Kate were reading Kathleen's diary. I don't know the details, but whatever was in it solidified Claire's conviction that your ex, Carolyn, is the killer."

"Killer?" Caleb shook his head. "I am so confused."

"I'll explain it later," JD assured his twin.

"I don't believe—"

"I don't give a shit what you believe," Deik cut Derek off. "If you want to deny the obvious so you don't have to accept the fact that you've been fucking the woman who killed your mate, then you had better be willing to accept Claire's blood will be on your hands."

"Even if Carolyn is the killer, what does that have to do with Agakiar?" Derek growled, feeling his fangs aching to grow with the need to tear into the bloodsucker. He couldn't afford that time now. Claire was in danger.

"Urazi took the body of the killer, but he needed help. My guess, Agakiar's help. Why would he do that? As back up for when Wall was eliminated. He knew it was coming because he knew he was losing Claire."

"Makes sense," Derek reluctantly agreed.

"So Urazi takes Carolyn and Agakiar takes Carolyn from Urazi. So where would Carolyn take Claire?"

"And what if you're wrong and Carolyn is not the killer?"

"Well, then Claire if fucked."

"Now who is Urazi? Man, this is sounding like one messed up pile of shit."

"Shut up, Caleb," JD snapped.

"Can't Kate find her?"

"Kate can't go near Agakiar. As a ghost, she's vulnerable to him." Deik pinned Derek with a cold gaze. "Where would Carolyn take Claire now that the haunted farmhouse is gone?"

"I don't know!"

"You better think of something!"

"What about her house?" JD offered.

"No." Derek shook his head, an idea forming in his mind. "I think I may know."

"You had better be right." Deik fell in to step beside Derek who was already moving.

"Where the hell are you going?" Derek demanded, not slowing his pace.

"You're going to need help. Agakiar isn't easy to kill."

"I'm coming, too." Caleb rushed, catching up.

"Hell, yeah." JD joined them.

They piled into JD's SUV with Derek at the wheel. While he started the engine, JD used his radio to put out an APB on Claire and Carolyn and both their cars. It took long moments to navigate through the packed parking lot at a safe speed. A moment later, he squealed the tires as he turned from dirt lot onto paved road.

Chapter 26

Claire groaned, wincing from the pain piecing her skull. The pungent smell of the marsh, the cool brush of a slight breeze, the slightly abrasive feel of sand beneath her cheek, everything told her she was laid out on the ground. It took the world a moment to come into focus as she opened her eyes.

"So you're awake?"

The sound of Carolyn's voice confused her for a moment. Then it all came back. Agakiar. Confusion turned to fear as she fought back the pain and lifted her head.

"Got a little headache, huh?"

Claire refused to respond to Agakiar's snide questions. She focused instead on standing. The demon had not bound her, but her head hurt enough to make her shaky. When she finally managed to stand without swaying, she looked around.

"Pretty, isn't it?" Agakiar scanned the small patch of dirt at the edge of the marsh. "Perfect for parking a truck and making out, don't you think?"

Claire recognized the area. This was where Derek had brought Kathleen the night she had been abducted.

"You can almost feel the fond memories." Agakiar kept talking though Claire wasn't responding. "But I guess those aren't your memories, are they Claire?"

Claire bent back the side mirror on Carolyn's Mustang. There was a large bump on her forehead. Already the skin was discoloring around the injury.

"I doubt you ever parked as teenager, Claire. No, you were never that silly and frivolous girl giggling in the passenger seat while a some young stud tried to put the moves on you."

Claire flinched as she felt the bump.

"Ugly, isn't it?" Agakiar stepped close to her and instinctively she stepped back. He smiled at the telling action. "Sorry about that. I'm sure your lover will want to kiss it and make it better."

"So, that's what we're doing here. You're waiting for Derek."

"Very good." Agakiar clapped. "As smart as ever. Yes, I'm waiting for that werewolf. I figure we'll start the evening with his murder, followed by some knife work on your face, and then we're going to have a little fun with your friends back at the rental."

Claire did not respond to the provocative remarks. There was no point and she had to save her energy for more productive things, like escaping.

Agakiar studied her for a moment. "You've changed."

"Have I?"

"Yes. I can sense it. I don't like it."

"Too damn bad."

"I'll change it back."

"You think a lot of yourself, don't you?"

"Why shouldn't I? You've seen the things I've done, what I can do. Tell me that you're not impressed." At her disgusted look, Agakiar shrugged. "At least, I've disgusted you more than anybody else could. That's saying something, isn't it?"

"Tell, me what happened to Carolyn?" Claire ignored his comment, not about to be sucked into another pointless conversation.

"What do you mean?"

"Where did she go? Did you send her soul to hell?"

"Oh, no. She's in here. Trapped, just like you will be soon."

"I see." Claire nodded as she grasped the mirror in her hands. Watching Agakiar's face carefully, she twisted it, snapping it backward until one of the metal supporting bars broke. There was a flinch for a moment, just enough to tell Claire what she needed.

"It's a real shame you took that body, Agakiar. At least, Wall was halfway attractive. Now, you're stuck looking like a skank."

"One is the same as another to me," Agakiar responded, but there was a strain to the tone, as if he had swallowed something unpleasant.

"I guess." Claire shrugged. "It's just funny is all."

"What's funny?" There was a defensive tint to his question.

"You wanted me away from Derek because once he mated me your brand was removed. Carolyn wanted me away from Derek because she wanted him for herself. Now, here you both are, sharing a body."

Claire paused to give Agakiar a cool smile. Agakiar's eyes were warming slightly with growing anger. Agakiar didn't get angry. That had to be Carolyn. She just needed a little more push.

"Yeah. You both wanted us to break up and you both suffered from the same problem. Neither of you was a good enough fuck to keep what you wanted."

"Shut up," Agakiar snarled. His voice was rising, the pitch going higher.

"You should've heard the things Derek said about Carolyn." Claire laughed, her hand going back to the side mirror. As she spoke, she twisted, trying to break it free of the last bar. "She was so bad in bed he was constantly screwing other women."

"Shut up."

The mirror was not giving. Claire focused on her arm, trying to pull strength from the beast. Derek had told her that it could be done, but it took time and practice. Two things she didn't have.

"Yep. Do you know what he told me?" Agakiar's blue eyes were darkening rapidly now. "I asked him, if she sucked so much, why bother fucking her? He said she was better than his hand, but just barely."

"Shut up!"

Claire laughed again, feeling the power flow into her arm. The mirror creaked as it turned and she quickly started speaking again to cover the sound.

"I believe him, because she lost Derek to Kathleen. You're definitely bottom of the barrel if your boyfriend dumps you for a virgin."

"Shut up! Shut up, shut up, *shut up!*" Carolyn screamed grabbing her head.

"Carolyn was so pathetic. It's a shame you got rid of her. I was going to enjoy seeing Derek throw her out of the pack. That was going to be his wedding gift to me." Claire laughed again, disguising the final snap of the mirror as it came free in her hand.

"I hate you," Carolyn snarled. "I'm going to see you dead."

"Carolyn?" Claire kept her smirk in place though her stomach was rolling and her heart racing. It was do or die time now.

"He's mine and I'll kill anybody who gets in my way," Carolyn snarled, her fangs beginning to grow.

Claire didn't need any more proof. She didn't wait, knowing Agakiar could, and probably would, appear in a moment. Swinging the mirror wide, she bashed Carolyn in the side of the head. Claire aimed for Carolyn's temple and eye, hoping to stun, if not blind, the other woman.

Carolyn screamed, her hands going to her face as she stumbled back. Blood oozed between her fingers. Claire didn't wait to see how bad the bitch was injured. Turning, she took off running for the trees.

"Bitch!" Carolyn screamed.

Claire knew she had to make it to the forest. She was a foot away from the first oak when a shot cracked, ripping the silence of the night. It was Carolyn shooting or the whole area would have bloomed with fire.

An instant later, she was almost safe behind an oak when she felt a bullet sliced through her side. Her flesh seared apart, radiating flames across her stomach and down her sides. A mind-numbing wave of adrenaline kicked into soothe the pain into a throbbing ache.

Claire ignored the sensation and kept moving. Weaving through the trees, she was soon lost. Two more rounds boomed behind her, forcing her to turn. She could hear the slugs slicing into tree as they missed their target.

Splinters of wood flew into her face following the whizzing sounds. Claire swerved to her right and away from the gunfire. The sounds of a something tearing through the undergrowth echoed around her, warning her enemy was close.

* * * *

"I'm still confused," Caleb complained. "I get the short order. A demon took off with Claire. And you," he leveled a finger at Deik, "think this demon is living in Carolyn's body."

"That's the short order," JD agreed, eyeing Derek's knuckles whitening on the steering wheel as he veered down Crocked Creek Lane.

"If Agakiar is here, you need to be careful." Deik tone was tight. "He commands the flames of hell."

"Meaning?" Caleb prodded.

"Meaning he can set fires that can't be put out and he can control them." Deik cut a hard look at Derek in the review. "Meaning you shoot to kill. Pissing off Agakiar is not something you want to experience."

"How will we know if it is this Agakiar?"

As if in answer to Caleb's question, a boom echoed down the road. It was immediately followed by flash of fire ballooning out of the forest.

"That's him."

"There's no smoke." JD studied the flames as they leaped up into the night sky.

"Be thankful for that," Deik advised him. "That's hellfire. It only makes smoke if Agakiar wants it. If that happens, the fumes will be poisonous."

"Derek, pull over man." JD waited a second before repeating himself. "We need to go in armed. The guns are in back. Pull over!"

Derek hit the brakes so hard JD almost went through the windshield. He didn't like stopping. Claire was out there somewhere and every passing second made him feel he was failing her.

If she... He couldn't bring himself to think it. He was barely managing to remain sane as thoughts swirled through his head in a frenzy. There was no time for error. That was the only certainty he had.

* * * *

Claire felt a bullet whizzing past her. Another inferno erupted before her eyes. Agakiar was back and, unlike Carolyn, he was not trying to kill her. He was trying to corral her.

As much as she knew she was playing into the devil's hand, she had no choice but to turn in a new direction. He managed to get three shots off, aiming for her legs. None of them hit. She could see the clearing, the moonlight clearly illuminating the road. A short distance away she heard a car hit the dirt drive, the engine revving.

She leaped over a fallen tree, trying to turn away from Derek. Two more shots sounded from her right and the forest exploded in fire. The heat forced her back toward the road.

There was no time to pause and think, and no other direction to go. Claire could pray she could clear the road before Derek saw her. That hope died as the searing burn of a bullet ripped through her leg.

Her leg gave out and she went tumbling toward the ground. In a daze, she lay there for a moment. The sound of tires cutting through dirt and earth brought her back to the moment.

Claire tried to get to her feet. Searing pain shot up her leg and burned through her spine as she put weight on her injured leg. Deep breaths helped and she managed a few shaky steps before she felt Carolyn's arm circle her.

An instant later, she was engulfed in a bear hug. With the demon's added strength, Carolyn's skinny arms lifted her off the ground. She could feel the slow beat of the heart behind her, a stark contrast to her pounding one.

"Don't do this, Carolyn," Claire begged as the headlights caught them in their blinding beam.

"Don't waste your breath." Agakiar pressed the cool barrel of the gun into her temple. "I've got three bullets left."

"You don't want this Carolyn. You love Derek." Claire was frantic. Knowing that it was hopeless, but having no other option but to beg.

"It won't work this time, Claire." Agakiar pointed the gun at the oncoming truck.

"No!" Claire twisted, biting down on Agakiar's arm until she tasted blood.

The truck screeched to a halt and everything happened so fast, she couldn't distinguish one act from another. The sound of the gun firing was lost in the loud explosion as the SUV exploded into a fireball.

Her scream strangled on her breath as it caught in her throat. For a moment, the flames blinded her, and she closed her eyes against the knowledge that nobody could survive that.

"Claire!"

Derek's yell had her eyes snapping open. The doors to the SUV were open and she could see men moving, taking cover in the forest. Agakiar's hand latched in her hair, ripping her off his arm.

"Run!" Claire screamed, fighting Agakiar's hold.

"Stupid bitch!" Agakiar snarled.

It was hard to breathe as Agakiar's arm tightened around her chest. The pain in her leg was excruciating. No longer focused on the run, her side began to ache in a competition for which injury hurt the worst.

Agakiar trained his gun at a large oak, drawing Claire's attention. Then she saw him and knew, whatever happened next, it didn't matter. Nothing was going to change the outcome of this night. They were both going to die out here. Selfishly, she wanted to be the one to die first.

"Say goodbye to your love," Agakiar whispered in her ear.

The feel of his hot breath sent shivers of repulsion through her.

"Carolyn, don't let him do this," Claire pleaded. "If he kills Derek, you'll never have him."

"That's not going to work this time, Claire."

"Fight him Carolyn. It's me you want to kill, not Derek."

Intending to fulfill that promise, she heard the gun cock. Claire did not hesitate. She lowered her chin and mustered all the strength she had left. Gripping the arm around her chest, she bent, trying to flip him over her back.

Normally, the move would have been quick and easy, not today, not with a bullet wound in her leg and another in her side. Her legs caved and she crashed to the ground with Agakiar. Everything happened so fast. There was a moment when Agakiar and her were struggling, her to get away, him to hold her close.

The sound of a gun going off was deafening and she felt as if she had been hit in the chest by a truck. At almost at the same second, everything in her world disappeared.

* * * *

Derek sat watching Claire through eyes that burned with pain. They were too dry, too tired, and needed to rest, but refused to stay closed. A nurse had brought him some drops, but he had ignored them. Suffering the pain reminded him he was alive and Claire was almost dead.

He kept replaying the final scene, when Claire had been shot before his eyes. He had been running toward Claire and Carolyn, but too late. The sound of gunfire had barely registered, he had been too transfixed by the sight of Claire lying still as Carolyn rose to her feet.

Legs that should have been carrying him forward had gone still as Carolyn aimed the gun at him. For a second he did nothing, not wanting to be alive if Claire was dead.

Carolyn had screamed as the night erupted with gunfire.

Carolyn had shot Claire in the chest, right in front of him, and he'd done nothing. There had been an opportunity, a moment, when Carolyn had unbent her arm to aim the gun at him, he could have shot her and saved Claire.

He hadn't. He had been frozen with disbelief. Just as Deik had accused, he had not wanted to believe Carolyn was the killer. Even as she stood ready to kill him, he had rejected the truth.

His selfishness had put Claire here, breathing through machines. It was his fault Kathleen and their child had been killed. He had brought Carolyn into Kathleen's life.

After Kathleen had disappeared, he had turned to Carolyn. She had been there for him, caring and soothing his fears and worries. When he realized the mating bind had been broken and Kathleen had to be dead, Carolyn was the one who had assured him he would find love again.

Worse still, over the years he had been sleeping with Carolyn, she had continued to kill. Many innocent girls had paid for his blindness. Claire had seen through it. She had tried to tell him.

Perhaps if he had listened, been willing to believe, Claire wouldn't have gone off to Nathan's alone. Then none of this would have happened. If it hadn't, would he have believed what Carolyn was capable of?

"She's going to be alright," a soft female voice spoke from the doorway.

Derek did not turn his head to see who had come. It was Sasha. She had arrived hours ago, along with so many others. Derek had barely taken notice.

JD and Caleb had stayed behind at the marsh to handle the mess Carolyn had left. Deik had driven Derek and Claire to the hospital in Carolyn's Mustang and then disappeared himself.

Derek had called nobody, waiting alone as the doctors worked on Claire. His phone had rung, but he hadn't answered it. Eventually, Sasha had shown up, probably sent by Deik.

She had taken over, answering Derek's phone and directing people to the hospital. Kristin had been the first to arrive. She was quickly followed by officers, pack members, old friends, until the waiting room had been packed full of noise and confusion.

Everybody wanted to know if it was true. Had Carolyn really shot Claire? Derek hadn't answered. He just stared at the double doors, waiting for the doctor to appear and tell him his fate.

When the man had come, he had brought no certainty with him. They had moved Claire into the ICU and the next twenty-four hours would be critical. That was all Derek heard.

"It's weird to see her like this." Sasha was standing over Claire's bed. "She's a strong one."

Derek didn't know what to say. Claire was a werewolf now. She would heal faster than most, if she healed.

"She's blessed. Did you know that?" Sasha turned to gaze at him with soft, concerned brown eyes.

"I would have said just the opposite." Derek could hear none of the emotions boiling within, in his flat tone.

"She found you, didn't she?" Sasha offered. "For somebody lost and alone in this world, I'd say that was a blessing."

"Me? I'm the one that put her here."

"The head does not rule the heart, but I would point one thing out. The body only suffers so much. The soul can suffer endlessly." Sasha looked back at Claire. "Hers is at peace. That's because of you."

Derek watched as Sasha performed some kind of natural blessing over Claire. When she was done, she moved toward the door. Pausing before him, she rested a small hand on his broad shoulder.

"We mourn for the dead, but it's a selfish act. It may be a tragedy that so many young lives are lost to us, but it's our tragedy alone because they are at peace."

Chapter 27

Claire slammed the door to the Suburban. It was supposed to be a day for celebration. After three weeks, the doctors had ordained her speedy recovery a miracle. Of course, they didn't know about the werewolf blood lending strength to her body or about Sasha and her healing spells.

Not that it mattered. They had released her from the hospital with smiles. Claire should have been smiling too, but thanks to Derek's antics, Claire face was soured with annoyance. Derek's juvenile sense of humor and lewd mind was the reason for her locked jaw.

In five minutes, he had ruined the image of a perfect gentleman he had been working on for the past three weeks. She should have known it was an illusion he was incapable of sustaining.

She had never been so embarrassed as she had been listening to Derek ask the doctor what sexual positions were safe given her injury. It wouldn't have been so bad if Derek had used generalities. No, that was asking too much from the pervert.

Instead, Derek had gone into full detail, causing not only Claire to blush, but also the middle-aged doctor, who had, no doubt, seen and heard almost everything before. Now the stately man had a few things to add to that list and Claire had a bone to pick with Derek.

At least now, she knew exactly where he got his twisted sense of humor — his mother. Cynthia was a mischievous woman with a quick smile. His father was much more straight-laced and serious, which explained why he and Claire had hit it right off. He had been the one who actually got around to explaining a lot of the pack laws and rules.

Devon had been disappointed, but not surprised, when he realized how little Claire knew about the pack.

Of course, that was changing fast. Almost all the members had stopped by for introductions and bearing gifts. Claire's favorites had been the candy, nothing like chocolate to help recovery. The flowers, while she had smiled and thanked every bearer for them, had become more of an annoyance than anything.

Many of the women had stayed to talk, though they had spent most of their time chatting with Cynthia. Cynthia had been holding court, gleefully planning her first wedding. That was one of the more interesting tidbits Derek's father had explained.

Claire would not get to plan her wedding. That was the privilege of her mother and mother-in-law. Claire would have to wait until her daughters married to plan a wedding.

If Derek had his way, she would have many weddings to plan one day. He was so anxious for all the children they were going to have, he had gone out and traded in his truck for a Suburban. That was only the beginning of his insanity.

The man was already looking at land so they could build a home. He had originally let Claire design the house. When she'd come up with a simply four bedroom layout, Derek had gotten downright angry.

He had claimed that he was good for at least three kids. That meant five bedrooms, which had quickly expanded to seven. Then he needed a study, a game room, expand the kitchen, a media room, a wrap around porch, two-car garage plus a shop and shed. By the time he had finished, Clare had decided she was going to need a maid.

Trying to get Derek to scale back had been as fruitless as his attempting to convince her to pop out six babies. Their argument had been mediated by Cynthia, who Claire had later overheard whispering to Derek that once Claire was pregnant there was nothing she could do but have the kid.

Obviously, Claire was going to have her hands full with Derek and his mother. At least, Carolyn and Agakiar would no longer be a problem. Kate had filled her in on the details.

The ghost had only been to visit Claire twice. Once to make sure Claire was doing all right and the second time to say good-bye.

That had caught Claire completely by surprise. The only thing more shocking to Claire was the realization that she was actually going to miss the nosey apparition. As antagonistic as their relationship was, it had been one of the stables in her life over the past few years.

I always felt drawn to you. Kate had explained as she flickered around the room.

"Can't say it was a mutual attraction." Claire forced a smile that Kate reciprocated.

Yeah, you were a real disappointment to me, too. Kate snorted. *I thought you were going to help me find my body.*

"It was always on the to-do list." Claire lost her smile as she picked at the edge of her blanket. "I'm sorry we never got a chance—"

Don't get all apologetic. Being a ghost has its advantages.

"Yeah, you can spy on everybody."

Especially the men. Did you know that Deik has a tattoo?

"The question is did I want to know that?"

Do you want to know where?

"No!" Claire laughed after a moment. "I really am going to miss you."

I'll pop in on occasion.

"I'm sure at the most inappropriate time." Claire's smile faded slowly away. "So, you go going to go look for your body?"

No. I got this undeniable attraction for a woman named Samantha. Kate stood still long enough to give Claire a mischievous look. *You think you're life is screwed up, wait until you meet this girl.*

"What? She's involved with a demon worse than Agakiar?"

No, she's a disaster all on her own.

"Just the way you like them, huh?"

You know it. Kate paused next to Claire's bed. *Well, it's been interesting.*

"Don't be a stranger."

Watching Kate fade away had depressed Claire more than she would have thought. It felt like she was strangely adrift in the world. Her days of working cases were done, the few friends and acquaintances she had collected at Cerberus would fade into the past, the same as Kate had.

Even as she said goodbye to that part of her life, a new road was building itself before her feet. At her side was Derek. That had given her comfort while she had lain in the hospital bed meeting one stranger after another.

"Are you going to pout all the way home?" Derek finally broke the silence.

Claire did not respond, did not even glance away from glaring out the windshield.

"Come on, Claire, even the doctor thought it was funny."

"Funny to a twelve-year-old who still giggles over the word booby."

"I admit I took it a little too far." Derek tried to pull her hand off her thigh, but she clenched her leg tighter. "But I really was concerned. I don't want to hurt you, baby."

"You won't, because you will be sleeping on the couch."

Derek heaved an injured sounding sighed and slowed the large vehicle so he could pull off the road and into a large clearing. Claire's eyes narrowed, her jaw tightening as he parked the oversized SUV under the shade of a gnarled oak.

"What do you think you are doing?" Claire finally turned her glare directly on him, already guessing his intent.

"Well, we've got a house full of people waiting to welcome you home. I can't have you stepping through the doors all grumpy-faced." Derek turned the engine off. "And I've got just the thing to make you smile."

"Don't even think about it," Claire warned, sliding away from him until her back was pressed up against the door.

She was not ready to get over her mad just yet and knew if he got his hands on her, it wouldn't take him more than a minute to make her forget all about what a jerk he'd been. Hell, it probably wouldn't even take him a minute.

"No, silly." Derek grinned at her before turning to grab something out of the backseat. He turned back to her with a large present so horribly wrapped she knew he had done the job himself.

"I'm talking about a present."

"Don't you mean presents?" Claire nodded at the other, more professionally wrapped, gift in the back.

"Open this one first." Derek dropped it into her lap. Claire was not impressed by his enthusiasm. She was suspicious.

"What if I want to open that one?" She watched him carefully.

"This one is better." Derek nodded eagerly to the slightly heavy box in her lap.

"That means that one is going to get you in trouble," Claire corrected.

"No." Derek snorted.

"No?"

"No, it's…for later."

"Oh, God." Claire rolled her eyes. "What is it?"

"Claire—"

"I want to open that one," Claire challenged.

"Fine, but don't say I didn't warn you." Derek grabbed the other package and handed it to her.

Claire carefully undid the bow and removed the paper. Derek had slid back across the bench seat. He was now the one trying to distance himself. She had the feeling he was getting out of striking range. A moment later, her suspicions were confirmed.

"Now, honey," Derek began.

"Don't 'now honey' me." Claire lifted a thong and the matching cupless bra out of the box. The two tiny garments were completely tasteless. Bright red, with black lace and fake diamonds.

"You don't actually think I'm going to wear this?"

"Would I be in any better shape if I said no?" Derek offered tentatively.

"No."

"Didn't think so." Derek sighed in resignation. "I just wanted to buy you some sexy lingerie to celebrate your homecoming."

"This is not sexy lingerie." Claire shook the scraps of lace in her hands. "This is slutty lingerie."

"It's better than industrial white underwear."

"Keep that up and you'll be sleeping in the rental across the street," Claire snapped, shoving the so-called underwear back into the box and not bothering to look at the other pieces.

"Don't say that, sweetheart." Derek slid a little closer, no doubt sensing that most of her annoyance was bluster.

Claire wasn't about to admit he was right. Even if he did have deplorable taste in lingerie, he had a point. The plain white granny panties did have to go. Obviously, she would have to be the one who picked out more playful undergarments.

"Why don't we go on to the next gift?"

Derek didn't wait for her agree and all but tossed the offending present into the back seat. Lifting the ill-wrapped gift from the seat between them, he slid as close to her side as the gearshift allowed before handing her the heavier present.

He was wearing that big goofy smile that said he was very pleased with himself. Whatever was hidden under the brightly-colored, Christmas wrapping paper, he was sure she was going to love it. Claire couldn't help but be affected by his double dimples.

"Open it."

"Okay, okay. Don't rush me."

She glanced at him as she began to unwrap the second gift. It was heavier and more solid. Claire's mouth fell open as pulled the paper away from the laptop. She was stunned and amazed, never having expected such a gift. After a moment, she found her voice.

"Derek, you can't give me this," Claire said it, but she did not mean it. Still she had to say it, the gift was way too expensive.

"Well, I can't take it back." Derek ignored her hesitation, sensing it was more out of formality than any true dislike. "I've already uploaded all the programs, charged the battery, and I got this satellite thingy that allows you to search the Internet from anywhere."

"Thingy," Claire snorted softly. "They must have had a field day with you at the store."

"Don't worry." Derek turned the laptop toward him and began to turn it on. "I had a little girl help me make decisions."

That got him a laugh.

"Seriously, Derek, it's too much money."

"It's an investment." Derek waved off her concern.

"In what?" Claire demanded.

"Your new career. A writer needs a laptop. You can't spend all day and night at a desk hunched over. That's bad for your back."

"But you give such good massages." Claire smiled at him, warming at the memory of what his massages always led to.

Derek shot her a devilish grin before turning the laptop back to her. "You're on the internet. Isn't that cool?"

"So cool," Claire retorted dryly as she read the Yahoo homepage. "Oh, look a new study shows that taking a hot shower has been found to lead to cancer."

"Check your email."

"I want to read about how I'm killing myself with hot showers." Claire went to click on the article.

"Check your email first." There was something in his voice that had her turning narrowed eyes on him.

"Why?"

"Just do it."

"If this is another surprise, I think I'll wait until later. I'm not sure I can take anymore surprises today." Claire pursed her lips.

"Come on sweetheart." Derek leaned in to give her a quick kiss. "Just do it for me."

"Fine," Claire sighed with exaggerated patience. A moment later she sighed again with real annoyance. "Look at that. I've got eighty-nine messages."

"Wow, you really are popular."

"It's probably all junk mail," Claire muttered as she opened her inbox. The computer was fast, a pleasant change from the large, cumbrous machine she usually used.

"Hey, watch what you're doing," Derek interrupted her. "Don't delete that one. It's from your agent."

Claire frowned at the screen and focused. He was right. It was from Melinda.

"How do you know that's my agent?" Claire asked him.

"Are you going to take all day with this?"

"I'll take as long as I want."

"I bet you peel off band-aids really slowly too."

"Okay, just a minute." Claire opened the message and read, and then read it again. She turned her stunned gaze on Derek.

Chapter 28

"Congratulations, beautiful. You're going to be published." Derek grinned that goofy grin of his.

"How did you know?" Claire stared at him in disbelief.

"Sally called to tell you." Derek slid a little closer, lifting the laptop off her lap and on to his.

"I told her you were shot. She kind of wigged out." He rolled his eyes at that, though Claire knew he had done some wigging out himself. "I assured her you were on the mend."

"She called you?" Claire pulled back slightly when he tried to put his arm around her.

"I got the message and called her back," Derek continued, happily pretending Claire had not asked a question.

"What message?"

"I told her to email you and she faxed me some papers for you to look over and sign."

"How did you get the message?"

"I'm not sure about those papers. I think you should have Kristin look at them."

"Focus, Derek," Claire snapped her fingers. "The message."

"Yes?" He blinked.

"Don't even try that innocent look on me. Tell me how you got my message."

"Caleb may have tapped into your cell phone," Derek sheepishly admitted.

"Tapped?"

"Hacked? I'm not sure what the correct—"

"Derek! Why the hell did you let him do that?" Claire was completely exasperated with her mate. "You could have just brought me the cell phone. I could've checked my own messages."

Even as she asked the question, she knew the answer. Not that she expected him to own up to it, which was good, because he didn't.

"I didn't want to worry you. You were shot and needed your to rest."

"You didn't want me to get any messages from Mike," Claire corrected him.

"Now, sweetheart—"

"Don't 'now, sweetheart' me." There was no heat in her reprimand.

Under normal circumstances, she would have continued the argument. Today she had not only been released from the hospital, but also learned that her dream had come true. It was too good a day to spend mad at Derek.

"You're impossible."

"But I'm sexy," he pointed out. "That makes up for all sorts of personality flaws, doesn't it?"

"I should probably call Sally." Claire was not about to encourage him.

"Do it later." Derek leaned in to give her a quick kiss. "Right now you can tell me all about how you're going to quit your job."

"At the station house?" Claire asked with innocent confusion. "What would you do without me?"

"You know what I meant. No more Cerberus."

"Your French is getting better."

"You're quitting that job. My poor heart can't take anymore adventures."

"Fine, but only if you admit you just want me to stay home and raise the kids."

"Guilty." Derek grinned and gave her another quick kiss. "Is that such a bad thing?"

"No. Not such a bad thing," Claire admitted with a smile before turning the laptop back toward her. She reread the message from Sally again, still not able to believe the words on the screen.

"I'm a writer," Claire whispered.

"Yes, sweetheart, you are. So, are you going to let me read your book now?"

"Write your own." Claire looked up at him and grinned. "I'd think you'd make an excellent writer."

"Really? I was thinking filmmaker. I got that camera you suggested and—"

"Don't." Claire placed her finger over his lips, holding in whatever perverted thing he was about to say. "I think we've have had enough drama for the day."

"Whatever you say, baby." Derek kissed her fingers.

"Whatever?" Claire raised an eyebrow at that. "How about a little kiss then?"

"I don't know."

"Come on, just a little kiss. What can it hurt?" Claire cajoled him. She knew his reluctance wouldn't last. She lifted the laptop and slid it on the dashboard.

"Baby, we've got a house full of people waiting at home." Derek really didn't care about them, but he was enjoying being the one to resist for a change.

"So?" Claire crawled onto his lap. "Let them wait."

"That's easy for you to say. Nobody will blame you for us being late," he grumped good-naturedly.

"Your mother wouldn't complain." Claire began to kiss her way along his jaw line. "She wants grandkids."

"Only one way to get them," he agreed, lowering his head to find her lips with his.

Claire leaned in to meet him. Her eyelids fluttered closed at the first tentative caress of his lips against hers. He breathed one little kiss after another across her lips. She sighed, disappointed with the teasing touch.

Winding her hands into his hair, she held him still and pressed her lips firmly against his in a silent demand for more. Derek gave her what she was asking for and opened his mouth on hers. The kiss began as a gentle tasting and soon escalated to a heated devouring.

He tasted good, like wilderness and man. The flavor was a drug to her senses, melting her insides and pooling warmth between her legs. It had been three long weeks since she had been filled with his hardness and her pussy ached with emptiness.

She adjusted her position so her legs straddled his and she was cradling the thick bulge of his erection against her softness. Her skirt rode up and the hard line of his cock pushed into her dampening panties. The thin material slid across her clit, teasing the sensitive nub.

Claire gasped and rubbed herself into him. Sparkling pleasure radiated out from her pussy, making her stomach quiver, her breasts tighten, and her head feel light as she pumped herself harder and faster against him trying to increase the sensation.

"Slow down, sweetheart," Derek moaned, his hands biting into her hips to hold her still. "You've got to be careful of your injuries. Remember what the doctor said, take it slow."

Claire growled in objection. She didn't want to go slow. It had been three long, miserable weeks without his touch, the feel of his hands and mouth on her body, the fullness of his cock as he pumped himself into her. She wanted to gorge herself on all the pleasurable sensations only he could give her.

Derek was not about to let her go so fast. He continued his slow seduction as he kissed his way down her jaw to explore the curve of her neck. He nibbled and sucked on her sensitive skin making her shiver with delight.

Her head tilted, exposing more of neck for his tasting. His mouth paused, his tongue coming out to circle the erratic pulse he had discovered. Claire felt her heartbeat kick up, fast and hard, as he sucked on that magic spot.

He nuzzled aside her collar to find his bite mark. Tasting the sign of his ownership, he growled and Claire could feel the cock buried between her legs thump against the confines of his jeans.

Instinctively, she responded, trying to rotate her hips in invitation. Derek's hand tightened, holding her still. Claire knew his restraint couldn't last long. Her fingers bit into his arms, urging him to release her hips.

He refused the silent command, his mouth opening to bite down on her shoulder in warning. The wolf inside her recognized the command for submission from its mate, but she was unwilling to bend. She needed him, and she needed him now.

Impatient with his constraint, Claire took matters in to her own hands. With fingers that shook with need, she began to undo his shirt buttons. When it took her almost a minute to get the first three done, she gave up and grabbed his collar.

A hard yank sent buttons flying everywhere, popping her in the face and arms before falling to the floorboards. Claire did not waste any time admiring the feast of taut golden skin before she lowered her head and began to nibble and lick her way toward his nipples.

* * * *

Derek clenched his jaw against the pleasure of Claire's mouth on his body. He had been looking forward to this all damned week and had almost blown it with that stunt with the doctor. He had known while he was pressing the doctor on what positions would be safest for Claire she was slowly heating to a boil.

As usual, he couldn't stop himself. She was so sexy when she was mad. The way she pursed her full lips with indignation made his cock swell and harden.

He had no doubt what Claire would say, much less do, if she found out how much it turned him on to watch her blush, while her hazel eyes turned chocolate with her anger. Then there was the fun of seeing how long it took him to make those amazing eyes go green with desire.

Today, though, he had known he had a surefire cure for her upset. He had planned it all so perfectly, the exact spot he was going to park, the email from her agent, and he had known exactly what that was going to get him.

Problem was if she continued to nibble on his chest, he was going to forget all about the doctor's warning to be gentle. Gentle was far from what he was feeling right now. His little mate was about to push him right past his control.

"My turn."

Derek pulled her head back with one hand and shoved her shirt up to her shoulders with the other. He growled hungrily at the sight of her large breast constrained by her industrial strength bra. With an impatient flick of his wrist, he broke the fabric holding the two cups together and let the beautiful breasts free.

"Perfect."

The smooth pale globes made his cheek tingle with anticipation for the feel of her softness against his skin. The pale pink buds invited him to taste, bite and suck until she cried out her need for him. Reaching up, he cupped her breasts, holding them together so he could nuzzle his face into her cleavage.

Absently, his thumbs rubbed against her straining nipples, rolling them to harder points. Claire groaned and her hands clenched in his hair again, trying to urge his mouth toward her puckered nipples. Derek smiled and opened his mouth to teasingly lick around her areola.

"Derek."

Her breathy plea made his body tighten with desire. His cock throbbed so fiercely with need the stiff denim holding him back was painful. All he wanted to do was unzip and impale himself in her welcoming warmth.

If he did, the beast would be unleashed and he would claim her with such savagery he might hurt her. Taking a deep, calming breath didn't help. The influx of oxygen sped up his heart and pumped even more blood to his already engorged cock.

The scent of her desire was thick in the air. With every breath, he inhaled the intoxicating odor. It was like a shot of thirty-year-old bourbon—hot, smooth and potent. He could take no more. He had to taste her.

Without warning, Derek lifted her by the hips, forcing her onto her knees. Claire gave a startled cry as her hands shot out to brace herself against the back of the seat. Shoving her skirt up to her waist, he held it out of the way with one hand while the other ripped her soaking panties from her body.

The sight of her open, wet and vulnerable to him had the wolf inside him growling out its pleasure, threatening to break loose if it wasn't appeased soon. Using his hold on her hip, he force her forward, bringing her weeping pussy to his hungry mouth.

Her hips jerked and he felt her shudder at the first teasing lick of his tongue through her wet folds. A second later she was arching her back, offering herself up to him, as his breath caressed her swollen nether lips. She rubbed against his mouth like a cat demanding attention.

He groaned and gave in. The sweet cream of her desire intoxicated him as tasted her pussy once more. Unable to hold back, he slid his tongue between her folds and pushed into her clenching core. Repeatedly, he fucked his tongue into her with growing speed.

* * * *

Claire gasped. He was showing her no mercy and she could feel Derek was no longer in control. The tongue inside her grew longer, rougher as the wolf took over the man's body. With each outstroke he lapped upward, tickling her clit with the barest of touches.

The wolf inside her responded, matching her mate's movements with her own. Claire's hands flattened against the roof of the SUV, giving her leverage to ride his mouth.

She rubbed against him, forcing his tongue deeper, making the teasing touches against her quivering button harder until the firestorm of pleasure building in her pussy erupted outward, sending bolts of heat through her body.

The sensation was too much. Her pussy throbbed and pulsed as the delicious coil of tension began to break, making her body quake with ecstatic tremors. Then it hit and white-hot pleasure broke over her, making her buck and twist from the powerful force.

Still he didn't stop. With his usual insatiable hunger, Derek continued to drive her insane. Claire knew he could continue for hours, but she wanted, needed, something thicker, harder than his tongue buried deep inside her.

She ripped herself away from him, panting as she tried to regain her breath. Falling back down, her hands went to the fastening of his jeans. Her impatience made her fumble and she growled with growing frustration as his zipper stuck on his overgrown erection.

Derek shoved her hands out of the way, flexing his hips so he could get the zipper down. Claire did not wait for him to push his pants and boxers past his knees before pushing his arms out of the way and trying to impale herself on the iron pole rising out of his lap.

His broad palms came up to support her. He easily positioned her so the tip of his cock was nudging her entrance. When Claire would have driven herself down on him, his hands turned confining.

She snarled and fought his hold. It was a pointless battle, one he easily won. Controlling the pace and depth, he allowed only the broad head of his cock to barely stretch the tight muscles of her opening wide.

Claire's whimper turned to a moaned complaint as he stopped. She pumped her hips in silent demand, but he ignored her plea and gently eased her down his rod. The slow penetration had her writhing and twisting.

He stopped when he was only halfway in and started to force her back up. Despite her cries, he continued the teasing, shallow thrusts. From his billowing breaths and his taut muscles, she knew his restraint was close to breaking.

She needed it to break. She wanted the wild, savage claiming of the beast pounding into her as though he couldn't get enough. With that single thought, she leaned down and sank her teeth into his shoulder in a retaliating bite.

Claire swiveled her hips as he lowered her. The rotating motion broke his control and he began to force her to ride him with deep, hard strokes until there was nothing but the erotic slap of their bodies coming together in an ever quickening pace, striving toward total abandonment.

Claire threw her head back, screaming as the world imploded around her. Her climax ripped through her body, tightening every muscle from her pussy outward.

She felt his cock swell as her cunt clamped down on his hardness. A moment later, his roar deafened her as she felt the hot jets of his seed flood her body.

With a sigh of contentment, she collapsed against him. His arms came up to hold her close and for several moments they stayed like that. The feel of him tensing beneath her had Claire muttering a complaint.

"Sweetheart, are you alright? I wasn't too rough, was I?" She smiled at the question. He was forever worrying he was going to hurt her with his passion. It was sweet, but also kind of silly.

"I'm fine." Claire snuggled closer into his warmth. "Tired."

"You're always tired after I'm done loving you." She could hear the smug satisfaction in his voice and chuckled. He had a right to that arrogance.

"My father is going to skin my hide for being so late," Derek predicted lazily.

"I promise to tell him we were working on those grandkids your mother is so desperate for."

"That wouldn't help."

"Tell him we were delayed due to medical reasons."

"Medicinal sex?"

"Mm-hmm." Claire smiled slightly against his shoulder. "I read an article that said they'd proved that orgasms help fight cancer."

"You're making that up." Derek laughed as he threaded his fingers through her hair, pushing the rioting mass back over her shoulder. "Aren't you?"

"Nope. There has been research done showing if men don't attain sexual release on a regular basis some chemical builds up that is directly related to testicular cancer."

"No shit?"

"No shit," Claire echoed with a touch of humor. "So you can thank me now."

"Thank you." His lips kicked up in another grin. "So what exactly is regular? Is that once a month, once a week, once a day, once an hour?"

"Shut up, Derek."

"Is that anyway to talk to your mate?"

"I'm trying to get a nap here. Think of what your dad will say if you bring me home too exhausted to enjoy my party?"

"I'll let you have the nap, if you tell me you love me."

"I love you."

"Although I'm a pervert with no sense of decorum?"

"Perhaps because of it," Claire mumbled.

"And I love you for the fact that you're a closet pervert with too much sense of decorum. And you know what?"

"What?"

"I'm going to love you for the rest of my life."

"Me too," Claire murmured as she drifted off to sleep. Life was good, better than good, as long as she had Derek.

MATING CLAIRE

Sea Island Wolves 1

THE END

WWW.JENNYPENN.COM

ABOUT THE AUTHOR

I live near Charleston, SC with my two biggies (my dogs). I have had a slightly unconventional life. Moving almost every three years, I've had a range of day jobs that included everything from working for one of the worlds largest banks as an auditor to turning wrenches as an outboard repair mechanic. I've always regretted that we only get one life and have tried to cram as much as I can into this one.

Throughout it all, I've always read books, feeding my need to dream and fantasize about what could be. An avid reader since childhood, as a latchkey kid I'd spend hours at the library earning those shiny stars the librarian would paste up on the board after my name.

I credit my grandmother's yearly visits as the beginning of my obsession with romances. When she'd come, she'd bring stacks of romance books, the old fashion kind that didn't have sex in them. Imagine my shock when I went to the used bookstore and found out what really could be in a romance novel.

I've working on my own stories for years and have found a particular love of erotic romances. In this genre, women are no longer confined to a stereotype and plots are no longer constrained to the rational. I love the anything goes mentality and letting my imagination run wild.

I hope you enjoyed running with me and will consider picking up another book and coming along for another adventure.

Write to Jenny at:

jenny@jennypenn.com

Siren Publishing, Inc.
www.SirenPublishing.com

Printed in the United States
214631BV00004B/51/P